THE
UNDOING
OF
ALEJANDRO
VELASCO

THE UNDOING OF ALEJANDRO VELASCO

DIEGO BONETA

AMAZON CROSSING

Published by Amazon Crossing, Seattle

www.apub.com

Amazon, the Amazon logo, and Amazon Crossing are trademarks of Amazon.com,
Inc., or its affiliates.

ISBN-13: 9781662527258 (paperback)
ISBN-13: 9781662517563 (digital)

Cover design by Jarrod Taylor
Cover image: © Urs Siedentop & Co / Stocksy

Printed in the United States of America

To my dad, who instilled in me my love for tennis. And to my mom, for always pushing me to follow my dreams. Los quiero mucho!

PART ONE

CHAPTER ONE

June

No one would have recognized the young man who emerged from a black car at the gated entrance to the Velasco estate. Even if they'd been expecting him.

It was not yet evening; the waning sun cast the home in an elegant dance of shadows and light, making it seem larger and more mysterious than the photos he'd studied. He made sure to keep the car waiting by the intercom, for appearance's sake. The man was handsome; his dark hair had recently been cut to fall just so across his brow. His carefully polished shoes gleamed against the cobblestone. He adjusted his suit jacket, set his bag down by his feet, and then buzzed, taking a step back to make sure he stood in full view of the camera.

"Sí, diga," a woman's voice said.

"Mi nombre es Julián Villareal," he said. There was a pause, and the young man knew it was in his best interest not to let it stretch out too long. "Era amigo de Alejandro."

There was a click as the woman took herself off the mic, and a few moments later the gate started whirring open as she said, "Pase, por favor."

This Villareal was a man of impeccable taste. Had been so even when he and Alejandro first met. Still, the man shifted his shoulders, adjusting to the fit of his suit in a brief pang of uncertainty, before waving the driver off. Then he picked up his bag and walked the long driveway to the hacienda-style house. He reached the stone steps, admiring what he could see of the property. Lush palms, fronds of native plants, and little potted citrus trees tastefully surrounded the white stucco walls and adorned an arched passage into what looked like a courtyard. He could hear the whisper of a fountain within, smell the soft scent of the blue and white plumbago flowers. San Miguel de Allende's rolling hills could have been a painting in the background, except for the moving shadows of clouds.

This was paradise. Almost. He felt something dark inside him begin to flutter. He'd been expecting rage, and loss, but not this sensation of . . . desire.

The door opened before he made it to the doorbell; a woman in her fifties or so peered out at him, wearing a mustard-yellow apron over her clothes. The maid, then. "El señor Alejandro . . . no se encuentra," she said, not moving out of the way of the entrance.

It was interesting phrasing, implying Alejandro simply *wasn't there*. Then again, she wasn't the only one versed in coded language. He gave a little nod and clarified that he was here to speak to Alejandro's mother. "De hecho, quería hablar con la señora Velasco."

The woman considered him for a moment, then stepped aside and ushered the young man in, asking him to wait a moment while she fetched the lady of the house. He watched the maid retreat quietly down a hall to the right, and soon he heard the soft patter of her sensible footwear on a staircase somewhere.

From the arched hallway, he could see the large courtyard straight ahead through some glass doors. A mosaic-tiled fountain stood in the middle, lit up against the quickly darkening sky. He imagined the parties hosted in that courtyard, dance partners twirling, laughter tripping off the walls and blending with the splash of the water. Alejandro as a charming sixteen-year-old, mingling with his parents' friends, sipping from a stolen glass of his father's port.

A weight threatened to crush his chest, then—a feeling like rage—and he turned away to examine the rest of the house. Just as he did, he heard footsteps coming down the stairs. He pulled his hands out of his pockets and folded them in front of him to make himself approachable. Then he saw Maria Velasco turning the corner from some unseen room. He knew it was her immediately—Alejandro had shared many photos. An attractive, severe-looking woman in her late fifties, she was dressed in an olive-green pantsuit, as if she'd been conducting business before he arrived. The resemblance to Alejandro was clear as day.

"Julián Villareal? I recognize the name. You were Alejandro's friend," she said in English, the hint of a question in her voice.

"Yes, from grad school at UCLA. We played tennis together." It felt strange to talk about this in the past tense. It had been true just a few weeks ago. "He was a year ahead of me. I took a leave for the summer because . . . well, I'm sure you understand. Ale was a good friend."

Her hand went to the pendant on her silver necklace, a look passing over her eyes that made him wonder if he had overstepped a boundary already or made some other crucial mistake. He held his breath, waiting for her expression to turn hostile. To berate him for showing up with no warning, a stranger intruding on a grieving family.

"I'm sorry," she said finally. "I should know his friends. I used to, even those from boarding school. But in the six years since he went to the States . . . ," she said, trailing off. When a moment passed and she still seemed lost in thought, he decided distraction was the best course of action.

He gestured to the duffel bag. "I actually have some of his things with me. I wanted to make sure they got to you."

That softened her up a bit. "Please, come in. Can we get you anything to drink? Coffee? Beer?" she offered with a smile.

It was exactly Alejandro's smile.

Twenty minutes later, they were both sipping carajillos in the living room as he regaled her with stories from school. He told her about the time Alejandro had been feeling restless and convinced a group of them to drive in the middle of the night to Ensenada in Baja. But no one had thought to book a hotel, and they'd had to sleep on the beach.

"My son? On the beach?" Mrs. Velasco laughed. "When he was little, he hated sand, hated being dirty. He would take a few showers a day. The only eight-year-old who didn't have to be convinced to bathe."

"To be honest, he spent most of the time in the water," he said. "He kept running in. I didn't know why until you said that. I thought he was just trying to lure the girls to join him."

"Both things could be true," Mrs. Velasco said, and they both laughed.

"It's good," he said, swirling the drink in his hand. Made of espresso and Licor 43, the dark brown liquid shimmered in the light, a perfect treat after his day of travels. "To talk about him with someone else. I can't imagine how you are coping."

Mrs. Velasco fingered the leather strap of the watch he had given her—Alejandro's watch—pain flashing in her eyes. She'd barely looked through the duffel bag, which held some books Alejandro had lent him, a pair of nice sunglasses, and Ale's computer, among a few other things he'd grabbed. She was quiet for a moment, then cleared her throat. "Yes, well, we've tried to keep busy. Gabriel, especially, has been occupying himself with work. A merger that was already underway before Alejandro's . . ." She frowned and shook her head, and he got the sense that she was fighting off some intrusive thought, some memory.

She wasn't the only one haunted by memories.

"It's fortunate, really," she said finally, still looking into her glass. "The way life offers these little distractions. Otherwise, I'm not sure how we'd be able to go on." Now she smiled sadly, and he tried to return it but found himself only able to nod, his fingers clenched around the armrest.

They fell silent, and he took a moment to look around the room. The framed tapestry hanging on the wall—handmade Oaxacan was his guess; the golden Don Quixote statuette in the corner, expensive, not tacky. He could hear the tinkle of the fountain in the courtyard, a pleasant susurrus.

"I thought we weren't entertaining guests just yet," a gruff voice said from behind them.

He noticed Maria's face get serious again, and he turned over his shoulder to look. He recognized Gabriel Velasco immediately and rose to his feet. "Señor Velasco, un gusto finalmente conocerlo—"

"English in the house," Maria Velasco said curtly. "Please. And you can call us Maria and Gabriel."

Gabriel held the young man's gaze but smiled.

He recognized the smile—not as Alejandro's, but as the smile of someone practiced in charming a path through the world for himself. He knew exactly what the power of a smile could do.

"My wife's rule," Gabriel conceded with a nod. "As much as I like to show off my Spanish, it's a custom we implemented so the kids would learn both languages perfectly. We've held onto it over the years. Not fanatically, of course, but we do try to stick to it." It was a reminder that he was an American transplant. He'd come to Mexico in his early twenties and had never left. His style and mannerisms felt right in line with the upper crust of Mexican society. Even his Spanish was virtually accentless. He was almost the opposite of Alejandro and Julián, who loved Mexico but had settled into LA with their perfect English, something families like the Velascos viewed as crucial. "But I thought we said no to guests, cariño. Or are you feeling better?"

"It's my mistake," the young man said, reaching out his hand. "I showed up unexpectedly. Just to pay my respects and deliver some of Alejandro's belongings." Still, Gabriel's eyes hadn't moved away from his. He tried not to let his smile falter. His hand was still out between them, an awkward reminder that it had gone unshaken. Finally, he dropped his hand. "I'm so sorry for your loss. Sometimes, I . . ." He took a deep breath. "I feel like he's still here."

He tried to read Gabriel's reaction, to see if his tone had landed in the way he'd intended, but the man was stone-faced. The visitor wasn't terribly surprised, considering some of Alejandro's stories. Considering all of them, actually.

This was the world Alejandro had grown up in. He was finally here, seeing it for himself. And he felt himself divided, half wanting to see it all, to know every detail, and half wanting to light a match and burn it down. He was on edge and tried not to let it show.

"Why are you here?" Gabriel said. The words were harsher than his tone, which was friendly, a hint of a smile appearing now, breaking through the more-salt-than-pepper five-o'clock shadow.

He gave a shrug, acting embarrassed, knowing he needed to soften Gabriel's impression of him. "The truth is, Ale always talked about San Miguel. I was looking for a change from Los Angeles—and I'm on summer break now. All I could hear was Ale's voice telling me about the hills here, the club, the people, the courts. I wanted to pay my respects. Perhaps I may even make myself of use to you in some small way as I search for what comes next for me."

He let his voice trail off, pensive, smiling at Gabriel, looking for a reaction to cross the man's face. But he was inscrutable. A challenge, then.

He felt the part of him that loved to be pushed coming to life. The competitor. Perhaps it was time to play his power card. "You know," he said slowly, "I was the one who—" For a moment, the image of Alejandro's body flooded his mind, made him stutter. "I was the one who found him," he said simply. He had wanted to play the part of someone in shock and pain—the problem was, it was true. The shock had been real—a gut punch.

The Velascos stiffened visibly, and he once again worried that he'd misstepped. Was it too early to have shown that card? *Shit.*

Maria closed her eyes and put her hand to her forehead, as if suddenly experiencing a migraine.

"I'm sorry," he said quietly. "I find myself needing to talk about it when it's no longer appropriate. I can go." He started to button his suit jacket, but Maria's eyes shot open.

"No, stay. It's . . . fine."

"You're sure?"

She nodded. Her husband's body language was a lot less inviting. He leaned over to grab the carajillo that Maria had set on the coffee table, and the visitor could see the veins in Gabriel's hand, the taut tendons as he gripped the glass. "Please sit, Julián," Maria said. "You were saying that it was Ale's talking about San Miguel that made you want to come here?"

He was thankful for Maria's easing the tension, although Gabriel didn't seem too relaxed. He was still hovering a couple of feet away from the young man, who felt compelled to stay standing, despite Maria's request.

"Yes, well, it was actually the tennis club he spoke about most often," he said, sipping his drink. "At UCLA, Alejandro and I hit the courts almost every day, but he was always saying the facilities—and the views—just didn't compare to the club back here in San Miguel. I thought I might check it out while I'm visiting the city."

He made eye contact with Maria and was happy to see her expression warming.

"So you play tennis too," she said. "How wonderful. I remember more now; he told us about you. A business school friend and a tennis rival. That must mean you're quite good, to keep up with our Ale."

Before he could respond to the compliment, Gabriel's hand clapped onto his shoulder.

"A word of advice. People in this town are very private about their personal affairs. If you want to make friends here, you would do well to remember that." Gabriel gave his shoulder a squeeze, then came around to sit next to his wife, taking a long drink from the carajillo he'd filched from her. "We Velascos are no different. More private than most, in fact." Maybe talking about Alejandro *had* been a misstep.

"Your coming here to pay your respects is very kind," Gabriel continued, "but it has been important to us to have our time to grieve Alejandro's accident. Death is a private matter, wouldn't you agree?"

Something had changed in his tone, even if he was being friendly. There was a hint of a growl to his words, like a beast warning its prey. An accident. That was a strange way to describe the cause of Alejandro's death.

It had been ruled a suicide, but he had anticipated that the family might be hiding details about his death from others. Families like the Velascos liked to sweep shameful things under the rug, and, suicide or not, Alejandro's death was shameful. He knew, too, that his being the one to have discovered their son's body made him a liability to them, gave him leverage in their world, especially if they weren't being forthcoming about the details. He was going to need all the leverage he could get.

Maria Velasco seemed to hear Gabriel's tone, too, because she put her hand on her husband's knee and cleared her throat. "Amor, can I talk to you in private for a moment?"

Gabriel shot her a look, then studied the visitor, as if he were trying to suss out secret communication between the two of them. "Of course." They both stood.

"Please, Julián, make yourself at home," Maria said. "We'll be back in a moment."

They smiled politely and left the living room, disappearing through another door at the end of the arched hallway.

He sat quietly for a moment, waiting to see if their voices would carry down the hall. But they were speaking softly, and whatever it was they were going to argue about would remain a secret. Then he noticed a picture frame on a bookshelf. Listening again to make sure they were not yet returning, he got up and took a closer look.

He recognized the UCLA tennis courts in the picture. Ale was in midserve, a modest crowd in the stands behind him, out of focus. He scanned his memory to see if he could recognize what tournament this picture was taken at, whether he'd been there too. He couldn't be spotted in the crowd, could he?

Fighting the urge to place the picture face down, he continued to explore, studying the books on the shelves and the other photos around the room. The Velasco family at a Caribbean beach, back when Alejandro and Sofia were teenagers. The four of them on matching lounge chairs, the turquoise water shimmering in the background. They wore the easy, carefree smiles of all wealthy, beautiful people on vacation. Then again, he knew how appearances could deceive.

The door down the hall creaked open, and he turned to look, expecting them to return. They didn't appear, though. It seemed like they'd just failed to properly shut the door—a breeze moving through the many open-air courtyards must have blown it open—and now he could hear their voices faintly. It was definitely an argument, though hushed. Knowing his window of opportunity was narrow, he stepped into the hall, his new shoes clicking ever so quietly on the Spanish tile floor. There were more pictures on the wall; he could pretend to be looking at these, should he need to.

Snippets came to him. "Says he's Ale's friend, but what the hell do we know about him?"

Gabriel was saying, "I'm not going to trust one of his friends just because he's in my living room!"

Then Maria's voice, much softer, soothing. He cautioned a step closer to the open door. "Came all this way . . . The only one . . ." He took another step, and another. "We may as well keep him close," Maria was saying. "Keep an eye on him. He obviously knows what happened."

There was a pregnant pause, and he froze, about to backtrack. Gabriel gave a resigned sigh.

"He might not even stick around that long," Maria said.

He smiled to himself, slipping seamlessly back into the living room where they'd left him. It had been a risk to bring up having found Ale's body so soon after meeting the Velascos, but maybe it would pay off after all. He hunched over to study a shelf full of various editions of *The Art of War* by Sun Tzu. There were at least thirty copies of the book in a handful of languages.

"Have you ever read it?" Gabriel asked, entering the living room.

He turned around, happy to see a slight smile on the man's face. It immediately called to mind Alejandro's teasing grin. Genuine, now. Not like before. He held one of the editions in his hands, knowing the book was something Ale's father loved to talk about. "Only if you count all the times Alejandro quoted it to me," he said.

This evoked a hearty chuckle from Gabriel, and a slight scoff from Maria, who had entered behind him. She moved back to the couch, clinking the rest of the ice in her glass. "At least I know he was listening sometimes," he added, then clapped his guest on the back and guided him gently away from the shelf. "Tell me, Julián, where are you staying?"

"I came straight here from the airport," he said, though this wasn't strictly true. "If you have a recommendation for a hotel, I'd be happy to take it. One with a good breakfast, preferably. LA has the best Mexican food in the US, but I still haven't found anywhere that makes chilaquiles as tasty as the ones here." He gave a little chuckle; then, deciding to reveal the information sooner than he'd originally planned, he added, "I'm considering staying in San Miguel long term after graduation next year. Maybe the right breakfast can convince me."

"You'll forgive me for being a little short before, but of course you will stay with us," Gabriel said, taking a seat beside his wife, his hand on her knee. "Amalia, who runs our kitchen, makes the best chilaquiles in town. We'd be honored if you stayed with us until you decide to leave." Gabriel cleared his throat. "Or find more permanent accommodations, of course."

"That's very nice of you, but I couldn't impose."

"Not an imposition. My wife reminded me of my manners, and she's right." He patted her knee again for emphasis.

The visitor started protesting again, but then Amalia, the woman who'd answered the door, entered the room, as if sensing she'd be needed. Gabriel asked for a beer for himself and offered him one as well, plus dinner if he was hungry. He politely declined, and then Gabriel asked Amalia to set up the guest room.

"You really don't have to do that. I hear the boutique hotels—"

"For my son's best friend?" Gabriel scoffed, interrupting. "Of course I do."

Had he described himself as that? He had equal urges to deny the comment and to sit with it for a moment. Instead, he just lowered his head, as if embarrassed.

"My husband has made up his mind," Maria said with a smile. "Once that happens, no one in the world can change it." Her words had a subtle edge, like fine-cut glass.

"Except for you, mi amor," Gabriel said, looking at his wife with a cheeky grin.

Again, he picked up on an undertone. It could have been an innocent, flirtatious comment, delivered awkwardly after forty years of marriage. Or it could have been something else.

"All right," he said, trying to hide his pleasure. He had hoped this would happen eventually, but he had expected the invitation to come after weeks of hanging around, putting in legwork, slowly maneuvering his way into the family's good graces. This was much easier . . . though he knew better than to be lulled into complacency by things that came easy. "If you insist, then I'd be honored to stay here with you."

The conversation turned lighter after that, questions about Julián's family, his upbringing, his intentions for his time in San Miguel. He had anticipated this, of course, had imagined having this conversation many times before arriving. Still, it was a thrill to deliver his answers, practiced though they may have been.

"To tell you the truth, I hadn't planned very far ahead," he said vaguely. "I knew I wanted to meet you, pay my respects, and see the city a little." He ran a hand through his hair. "I'm tempted to buy property as I have some money put away. I've arranged for a car I'll be picking up tomorrow, since I prefer not having to rely on taxis, or the kindness of others." He flashed them a smile. "Beyond that, I was hoping to have a tequila or two in Alejandro's honor, perhaps at the club where he spent so much time. If you would have me, of course. Play a little on the clay he loved." Was he laying it on a bit thick? He noticed Maria turning away, trying to surreptitiously wipe away a tear. Strangely, it made him angry. She had a right to grieve, of course. The loss of a child was surely a grief like no other. But as he looked around the house, it seemed the Velascos had not lost much at all. Their futures were untouched. Changed, sure. But not lost, like his was.

As soon as he'd finished that thought, he felt guilt swirling in his stomach, especially when he looked at Maria. He had no idea what it felt like to lose a child, and he was embarrassed he had dismissed her pain, even if just in his head. He was glad they weren't privy to his thoughts. He would have to be careful not to let any sort of resentment show during his time here.

"Good," Gabriel said. "San Miguel de Allende is a great place for those who belong." Another pause as he assessed his visitor once again. "It seems like you will fit right in, Julián." He pronounced Julián's name slowly, with intention.

Later that night, brushing his teeth in the guest bathroom across the hall from his temporary sleeping arrangements, he thought about that line, and how easily Gabriel had delivered it. *It seems like you will fit right in, Julián.* Gabriel was a man used to speaking in layers, and he would have to remember that, maneuver carefully.

As he was closing the door to his room, he thought he heard an intake of breath. He peeked through the sliver between the door and its frame, expecting to see Gabriel there, or maybe Maria, rubbing the pendant on her silver necklace. Perhaps the matronly maid would be making the rounds one last time before she allowed herself to rest.

Instead, he saw a vaguely familiar young woman's face staring back at him.

After a moment, he was able to square the sight of her with the picture from downstairs, and all the times he'd seen her face pop up on Alejandro's phone and on social media. Sofia.

She was visible in the light shining through the crack in the door only for a second, before passing into the shadows, but the moment felt longer than that. It felt like their eyes had locked long enough for her to haunt his dreams, long enough for her to have glimpsed some deep truth about him that he'd rather keep secret.

CHAPTER TWO

If the two boys rallying on the tennis court had noticed Sofia sitting in a lounge chair just beyond the sidelines, they'd probably have been playing even worse. She was waiting for one of the club's private instructors, Javier, to finish giving a lesson. No one else at the club could keep up with her.

She wore a baseball cap, the brim low, obscuring her face, a blessing to be even slightly out of view this way. When a person was a Velasco, the spotlight followed. Granted, it did not follow her in the way it had followed Alejandro, though that difference had always felt more insulting than comforting to Sofia.

One of the boys clipped the ball on a sloppy backhand, and it went sailing toward her. It rolled over the clay, close enough that she could have stood to toss it back. But she pretended not to notice, instead reaching down into her bag to pull out her own racket and a fresh can of tennis balls, which she popped open to take in that distinct smell. If anyone out there bottled up this smell and turned it into a perfume, Sofia would buy whole cases of it.

"Sofia?"

Shit. She looked up, already knowing how the interaction was going to go, even before she saw the vaguely familiar face smiling down at her. "Hey, I'm not sure if you remember me. I went to el americano, too, a year behind you. Nadia Hahn."

Sofia offered a kind smile, squinting her eyes to pretend to search through her memory. She'd graduated from high school six years ago, but Sofia had a feeling that Nadia had been forgettable even back then. "Yeah, of course," she said, making her voice honey-sweet. "I remember. How've you been?"

Nadia let out an embarrassing giggle, which at least she tried to stifle quickly, and straightened out her skirt. "Good! It's great to see you. I'm just back in town for the break. Getting my master's in Boston. No more ballet, though. Kind of hard when you get to be our age, huh?"

"Guess so," Sofia said. She rolled out the first tennis ball from the can and bounced it on the clay by her feet, her gaze going past Nadia to the two boys playing. Both had bad form, though at least the blond showed some hustle.

"That's my brother," Nadia said, noticing Sofia's gaze and mistaking it for appreciation. "On the right. My dad thinks he can be pretty good if he keeps practicing. What do you think?"

Sofia watched for a moment and nodded as if she saw something in both of them. "Sure. With practice, like you said." She pulled the brim of her cap lower, busied herself rooting around in her bag for her water bottle, hoping Nadia would go away.

Nadia instead started prattling on about someone else from high school whom Sofia couldn't remember, and Sofia let her mind wander, surprised that it went straight to the stranger who'd arrived in her home.

It had been unsettling to catch that glimpse of him in the doorway, late at night, his shirt off, his beautifully dark eyes catching the light. Her family often had visitors, but not often the unannounced kind, and almost none in the couple of weeks since Ale had died. And definitely not attractive ones no one had met before. In that moment, she'd been unable to rip her eyes away from him—had let herself get caught spying. This wasn't like her at all. But there was something about him.

In the morning, Julián had been sitting in her spot at the breakfast counter, his shirt half-unbuttoned, abs revealed and gleaming. Her dad had been chatting happily with him, and Julián chanced a glance away, to give Sofia a half grin, before returning his focus to Gabriel who, to her shock, burst into a laugh over something the visitor had said. It was uncanny, as if her father had suddenly transformed into some entirely different human being, one with an easygoing heart.

They had hosted exactly two dinner parties since Alejandro's death, and those were clearly just for keeping appearances. One was "in honor" of Alejandro, though they served grilled octopus, which her brother hated, and didn't talk about him all night (for a change). It had simply been an opportunity for her dad to give a sad little speech, garner sympathy from those in attendance, make sure everyone had heard the official version of the story: that Alejandro had died as a result of a terrible accident.

Sofia hadn't seen her father grieve before then or since, and anytime her mom shed a measly tear, Gabriel forced her to make some excuse to do it in private. Big displays of emotion in public were considered unbecoming for the Velascos, particularly now, while their telecom company, Velcel, was in the midst of a merger with Rapido, the tech conglomerate that happened to be owned by her boyfriend Mateo Hinojosa's dad. The Velascos needed to display some grief in order to show they were human, but they also needed to seem composed, able to handle the merger between the two companies despite the tragedy at hand.

Not that any of that would be acknowledged. Sofia often rolled her eyes at the games her family and the social class they belonged to liked to play, but she played too. Decorum and saving face had their usefulness. She wasn't against ruffling feathers, as long as it served her in some way. And doing anything to upset the merger was not in her interest.

So Sofia had been perfectly pleasant that morning, greeting Julián cheerily, as was expected of her, even though he'd been sitting in her favorite spot at the breakfast counter. She'd had her huevos rancheros beside him and told her dad that she would be *more than happy* to show Julián around the club.

While Julián went on about some business school memory she didn't really care to hear, she'd tried to think about why this guy had been immediately welcomed into their home. They'd heard the name Julián Villareal, sure. But this wasn't one of Ale's friends from boarding school or undergrad, and certainly not someone he'd grown up with, someone whose family the Velascos knew well. Hospitality was one thing, but the only plausible reason her parents would welcome in with open arms some friend of Ale's they'd never met was if he had some dirt on Gabriel.

But from which pile of dirt? Something about Velcel, perhaps? Her father's business tactics weren't always the most aboveboard, Sofia knew very well. And she got the feeling there were also some skeletons in his personal closet. Or did Julián have something on Alejandro himself? That would be an interesting wrinkle, though she figured the first two possibilities were more likely.

Sofia smiled to herself. She liked the thought of a stranger showing up to make her father squirm. She had no expectations that this attractive stranger would be able to outwit her father, but it would be fun to watch him try.

Then she realized Nadia was still talking.

"I was just telling someone the other day that I can't believe he never went pro. Kind of like you and ballet, actually." Nadia giggled again. It was almost sweet, how nervous she seemed to be. What was it about Sofia's family that made people act like this, when they weren't cowering away? At least she didn't have to deal with Nadia's sympathies about Alejandro. The family was keeping the news under wraps as long as possible, though eventually the gossip would surely spread like wildfire. "Me and the girls in class, after you left, we kept checking to see if you'd made it anywhere. Do you still . . . ?" Nadia trailed off, a slight smile on her face like she was thrilled with how friendly the conversation had been so far.

"No," Sofia said, then tried to return a sweet smile. "I always hated dance. Actually preferred tennis. Still do."

Nadia only now seemed to notice the racket in Sofia's hands. "Oh, I bet you're great. You Velascos are like that."

Sofia said nothing, deciding she should probably go before she lost patience and thwacked Nadia in the face with her racket. Anyway, Javier, the instructor, was still in the far court working on some septuagenarian's backhand, one who seemed more interested in being manhandled by him than actually learning anything about tennis.

Besides, her father had sent a text saying she should invite Julián to join her and her friends for lunch. Begrudgingly, she had rung the house and done what he'd asked. Julián was probably already waiting at the clubhouse, eager to talk about Alejandro, eager to snoop, or to share whatever intel he had. She had trouble imagining he was here for anything else.

She packed away her racket, took a long sip of water as if she'd just finished three sets against some imaginary opponent. "I'll see you around," she said, kicking her long, tanned legs over the edge of the lounge chair and rising to her feet. She took the step separating her from Nadia and gave her a quick cheek-kiss goodbye, which seemed to surprise the girl. "It was really nice running into you, though!" she said, matching Nadia's tone as she waved her fingers in the air, not bothering to look back.

Sofia arrived at the clubhouse fifteen minutes later than she'd told Julián, which in her circle of friends was considerably early. She'd expected to find him waiting alone in the restaurant on the top floor of the three-story building, maybe a little annoyed. Making her way to the balcony, where she and her friends always sat, she looked out at the pool, where a handful of kids splashed around, their moms sunning themselves nearby, sipping on margaritas and picking at plates of jicama and cucumber covered in lime and Tajin. In the distance, the town spread out along the hills, with the Parroquia, the gothic church in the center of town, watching over it all. Sofia could picture all those retired American tourists in their khaki shorts, snapping pictures of it with their phones and baking in the June heat.

She was surprised when she spotted Julián at the farthest corner table, joined already by Elizabeth and Lukas. Frowning, she paused and racked her mind: Did they know each other somehow? They were chatting pleasantly enough, their voices lost among the other diners'. Then Elizabeth laughed, and the sound carried over straight to her. It took Sofia a second to remember that she'd texted the group chat a warning about having to babysit one of Ale's friends.

"I see you've all met," she said, sliding into an open seat and taking her sunglasses from where they rested on the low V of the fitted white romper she'd changed into.

She wanted to ignore Julián, show him she wasn't just going to reward him with interest, yet she found her gaze flitting over to him, happy to hide behind the sunglasses. His eyes were mesmerizing, so dark they were almost black, save for the flecks of gold that lightened them. His hair fell past his ears, and his facial hair was somewhere between a five-o'clock shadow and an actual beard over a dimpled chin. To her annoyance, she found herself thinking that he looked like a movie star. Except she couldn't put her finger on which one, a feeling she hated. It was something about his generic attractiveness, his magazine-cover smile. She realized too late she'd been staring at him. A smirk crossed his face, but only briefly. At least he had the good sense to repress it.

"We were just telling Julián here embarrassing stories about when you were little," Elizabeth said, taking a sip from her Clamato. She tossed her long blond curls, stuck her finger in the glass to stir it, then sucked on her finger. Most likely for Julián's benefit.

"Clearly a lie," Sofia answered. "What embarrassing stories are there about me?"

"The time when you complained the girls couldn't keep up with you and they didn't let you on the boys' tennis team, so you stood on the sidelines and whacked every ball over the fence," Elizabeth said with a laugh.

Sofia rolled her eyes. "That's not an embarrassing story. At least, not for me." She was going to mention how Alejandro had been the one to complain to the coach about her being allowed to try out, but a server came by to take Sofia's order just then. Though her friends were drinking alcohol, she asked for a black coffee, wanting to stay sharp.

As she was ordering, Mateo arrived in his usual loud manner, saying hi to at least four surrounding tables on his way in. Sofia braced herself for his approach, knowing before he even leaned in to give her a kiss that he was still wearing too much of that cologne his mother had bought for him. Sofia made a mental note to hide it next time she was at his place.

Mateo tacked on a beer and a tortilla soup to the order, then went over to cheek-kiss Elizabeth hello and slap hands with Lukas. Around Mateo, Lukas was always trying to talk about "macho" subjects, asking him about his trips to the Velascos' hunting lodge, or discussing whatever the most recent notable soccer game was. It seemed to Sofia that Lukas verbally walked on his tiptoes around Mateo, as if to make up for the height difference between them.

Finally, Mateo turned his attention to the newcomer at the table. Sofia had to admit, Mateo knew how to work a room, how to make you feel invisible one moment and then showered in attention the next. It was a skill she admired; she wondered if he'd picked it up from her. "You must be Julián," he said, breaking out his accentless English as he reached his hand across.

Julián shook it and said he was fine speaking Spanish, to which Mateo responded, "No, no, let's make you feel at home. You're American, no? Sofia said you grew up in LA."

It was an innocent enough question, but Sofia picked up on the barbs hidden within his tone and rolled her eyes. "Most of us at this table have multiple passports," she said. "You included." She turned to

Julián and added, "Don't mind us. The country club life will have you boasting about passports one second and then pretending you've never left San Miguel the next. We're all assholes."

Julián smiled and took a sip of his Arnold Palmer. "Nah, Alejandro would have mentioned that."

Despite herself, Sofia cackled at that, knowing her brother would have specifically referred to her and everyone else sitting at that table as an asshole—multiple times—to anyone he'd had more than a passing conversation with. She herself had the thought a few times a week, though mostly she didn't mind her friends' rough edges. Especially since her parents had tried to mold her into a completely smooth surface, a good girl who played her part. For now, she was happy to go along with that. Which meant letting comments like that one slide.

"So, how long are you planning on staying in San Miguel?" Lukas asked. He might as well have spat the question out. Most of her friends could pretend to have tact, save for Lukas.

"Hey now, that's not the Mexican hospitality Julián was expecting or deserves," Mateo said, a subtle tinge of sarcasm in his voice. "You want him gone already?"

Julián just chuckled and said he wasn't sure. "A few weeks, maybe longer. Sofia's family has been kind enough to extend an invitation to their guest room, but I don't want to overstay my welcome."

"Por supuesto que no," Lukas said in that overly enthusiastic tone of his that seemed to both convey friendliness and demean the other person. Sofia wasn't sure what it was all about. She'd say it was probably because Lukas got bullied in school and now needed to make others feel small to make himself feel big. But most of the men she knew employed the same tone from time to time, Mateo included, so who knew. Men tried to lord power over each other in so many unsubtle ways.

"I have to say, I'm surprised Gabriel didn't ask to see a return ticket home," Lukas laughed, meeting Mateo and Sofia's eyes across the table, but neither of them joined in.

Elizabeth smacked Lukas on the arm and snorted. "Lukas here has never even been in the Velasco house—any of them—and here you are getting a sleepover, Julián. How fun!"

She was right of course—but Sofia had only known Lukas a few years. He'd grown up in Guadalajara and had moved to San Miguel to run a hotel that was part of a chain owned by his family, whose name carried a lot of clout. Gabriel had insisted Sofia welcome Lukas to town when he'd moved in, much in the same way he'd now foisted Julián upon her, and Lukas had hooked onto her group of friends with the kind of fervor befitting someone who couldn't find friends on his own. He was the type of boy she wouldn't normally pay much attention to except that despite his annoying attributes—or perhaps because of them—he was actually quite entertaining. He made her laugh and compensated for his lack of height by becoming the life of every party.

"Well, of course, Mateo spends time there," Lukas replied, tossing his slightly too-long hair. "Especially now that he's basically working for Velcel. You, on the other hand," he said to Elizabeth, "have simply made yourself Sofia's little pet."

Elizabeth bristled.

Sofia was glad when the server arrived with her coffee and Mateo's beer, interrupting the opportunity for Lukas to get sensitive or Mateo to pretend he was more involved with her father's company, and the merger negotiations, than Sofia herself was.

Lukas was exaggerating: Mateo didn't work for her father, though that would change once the merger was completed. True, he was usually seated closer to the head of the conference table than Sofia, often seated beside his dad, Sylvio. Mateo had a fancy-sounding title at Rapido— vice president of North American operations—but even he admitted his actual responsibilities were rather laughable. He took clients out for nights on the town and occasionally responded to emails. As far as Sofia could tell, that was the extent of it. Though she had to admit, after looking at Rapido's numbers, the clients Mateo took out often signed lucrative deals.

In contrast, Sofia did not have an impressive title. On the Velcel company website, she was merely listed as *empleada, comunicaciones.* And while she performed all the duties her entry-level job required, there was plenty more she did for the company, and for her father. She had pored over company ledgers late into the night, read through contracts, fired off emails, written press releases, all to make sure that the merger would go through smoothly. In the last couple of years, since graduating from university in Mexico City and officially joining Velcel, she had become her father's de facto right-hand woman.

That wasn't just out of the kindness of her heart. Her father had already acknowledged the work she'd put in, even if he had said it just to her. And even though he tried to avoid accusations of nepotism, it was no secret that such partiality ran rampant in Mexican companies and the families who owned them. Gabriel had even said publicly that, when the companies merged, he would push for a Velasco to be named COO, a position that came with a substantial salary, but also a significant portion of stock in Velcel. And now that Alejandro couldn't accept the position, well . . .

In the merger meetings, all Mateo did was chime in occasionally with MBA lingo, message Sofia surreptitiously from his laptop, and look good in his suit. His few meaningful contributions in the conference room had been her suggestions, voiced to him the night before. Suggestions she would have offered up herself if they weren't, for the time being, more valuable coming from Mateo. Mateo's looking good made Rapido look good ahead of the merger, and what was best for Rapido was best for Velcel and, ultimately, those shares she was gunning for. She'd let Mateo have his moments, for now.

Sofia looked over at Julián to see if he would jump on the subject of the merger. It would prove he was up to no good, sniffing around their business. He was leaning back in his chair, one leg crossed over the other, a position that seemed to Sofia more like an imitation of casualness than casualness itself. He drank again from his Arnold Palmer and ran a hand through his hair, looking around the restaurant.

It had filled up a little more, men returning from their golf games and cigar-laden poker games to meet their families for a late lunch. They would stake their tables for hours on end, the children excused to return to the pool only after the adults had had their postmeal coffees, which would turn into postmeal digestifs.

Sofia remembered running off to the tennis courts with Ale while their parents chatted and sipped drinks for what seemed like hours. The memory wasn't tinged with nostalgia, though, but rather with a bubbling anger. There was no golden-hued montage of siblings killing time together, delighting in each other's company. Instead, Sofia remembered chasing balls for Alejandro, never allowed to hit them back unless it was to help him practice. "Pa dijo," Ale would say. Dad said it, so it was law. Ale hadn't come up with that, just adhered to it, same as her. Mostly.

"What does your company do?" Julián asked Mateo, stirring Sofia from her thoughts.

"What don't we do?" Mateo beamed.

Elizabeth wadded up her napkin and threw it at him. "No business talk. I've had enough of that this week. Julián can Google it if he's so interested."

"Fair enough," Julián laughed. He was watching as Elizabeth stirred her Clamato with her fingers again, the seasoning sauces at the bottom of the glass picking up with the movement, swirling to turn the bright red drink into something more akin to dried blood. "How long have you two been together?" he asked Sofia before unraveling the cutlery from his napkin.

"Two years," Sofia said.

At the same time, Mateo said, "Seven years." When she shot a look at him, he said, "This stint is two years. Seven total." His eyes lowered as he said this, his voice wavering in its steadfastness for the first time. Julián looked between the two of them. "Ah, a break, then. Who broke up with who?" His asking meant one of two things: either Alejandro never talked about her with all his LA friends and Julián didn't really know anything about her, or he knew, and was being polite and trying to make conversation. Or maybe he was trying to dig up dirt on her too?

"Uy, sí, time for chisme!" Elizabeth laughed. She called a passing server, a different one this time, and asked for a paloma. "I never get tired of this story."

"There is no story," Mateo said, touchy as always about the subject. They'd been together in high school when Sofia came back from boarding school in Switzerland, and into the first year of college. Then Sofia had taken a gap year in Europe, and she'd ended things with Mateo, but he'd get pissy if she said so now. That era had been a mess of time-zone-gapped text messages, missed calls, and accusations, culminating in Mateo's flying to Spain to try to surprise her as a grand romantic gesture that had only led to a teary breakup—the tears mostly on Mateo's side, not Sofia's, but he would only admit to that in private. It wasn't that she *hadn't* cried. She'd been nineteen and broken up with her first real boyfriend. Of course, she'd cried. Mateo had just cried significantly more. They'd gotten back together when she'd finished having her fun abroad and returned to Mexico. Not so much a rekindling of the old flame as Sofia's deciding to take a frozen meal out to thaw.

Resentful of Julián's prying, Sofia tried to change the subject to anything else. She asked questions about what Julián planned to do with his MBA once he graduated, and his current life in LA. She tried to find out something—anything—about him. Except Julián kept redirecting the conversation toward Sofia herself. Maybe, she thought, he was doing this because he was secretive. Or maybe he just had the sense to feel a slight bit of shame that he was intruding.

Like Mateo, and most of the people sitting at the table, Julián likely had been floating by throughout his twenties. A trust fund in his name, probably, complemented by jobs at his dad's company, or internships that his family connections had helped secure as a way to land spots at reputable MBA programs. Most of the people in her social circle entered real life in their thirties, usually well after they popped out a kid or two. Sofia was one of the few who had ambitions, as far as she could tell. Real ones beyond hanging onto the freedoms their wealth provided, anyway. At least Julián had the decency to seem embarrassed about it, if that was why he was dodging her questions.

The afternoon carried on that way, lunch, a waterfall of drinks, and Julián getting deeper under her skin with each supposedly innocent question about her and her family. By the time they all started saying goodbyes, Sofia felt like she'd been sitting in a witness stand, getting grilled by the prosecution. Both the restaurant and the clubhouse had emptied out, everyone rounding up their children and their drunk husbands or wives, summoning their chauffeurs to take them back home to the lives they really led, as opposed to the lives they pretended to live in front of everyone else.

Mateo kissed her goodbye as he had to head home and prepare for an early flight to Mexico City in the morning, and Elizabeth had left an hour earlier, probably to meet up with what Sofia had gathered was a secret beau. Elizabeth denied it, but Sofia was sure she was right. She made a note to press Elizabeth on that again soon. She didn't like her friends to have secrets. At least, not from her.

That left Sofia, Julián, and Lukas.

"Can you go get the car from the valet?" Sofia handed Julián the ticket. "I need to chat with Lukas about a friend's birthday party." She would have rather sent him back in an Uber, but that might irk her dad and make things awkward, so she decided she would just have to bear another twenty minutes with him in the car.

Lukas tilted his head, questioning, but recovered before Julián could notice, a hint of a smile tugging at the corner of his mouth. "Right," he said. "That. I have some stellar ideas."

If Julián could tell that Lukas was a terrible liar, he didn't show it. He politely stood and headed toward the lobby.

"'I have some stellar ideas'?" Sofia mocked Lukas once Julián was out of earshot.

"What was I supposed to say? I thought I covered for you pretty nicely." He shifted over to the seat next to Sofia, his knee brushing up against hers. "So, what kind of party are you *actually* trying to plan? I love being in on your devious schemes."

She had to admit, Lukas *was* fun to conspire with. She scooted her chair back and stood, knowing he would follow. "Look, there's something about this guy that seems—"

"Definitely," Lukas interrupted, nodding his head. He was always doing that, assuming he knew the end of a sentence, as if anyone would be impressed by this instead of annoyed.

Sofia took a breath. "Right. Do me a favor—"

"Yeah, anything."

She raised her index finger up, like a teacher warning a student. "Be subtle about it, but keep your ear to the ground. See what you can find out that he's not saying. Dig if you have to, but without making everyone in town know that you're digging, okay?"

"Yeah, no problem." His smile was big. Behind the veneer of pride and humor, he was eager to please. At least with her. She briefly wondered if this was a bad idea, bringing him into this. Eagerness could be clumsy. And Lukas had a tendency to brag.

However, he really did know everyone. Even though he hadn't been in San Miguel his whole life, his family was one of the richest in Mexico, which came with plentiful connections, unlimited resources, and doors that would open for no one else. She could hire a private investigator, sure, but that wouldn't compare with the network of investigators Lukas had access to, all of whom would be a step further removed from Sofia, whose hands could be kept clean.

Lukas also had a surprising ability to worm his way into any conversation, make a few witty jokes, hold eye contact, and end up going home with the prettiest girl at any party (even if they were almost always taller than he was). He was a puppy; that was what people liked about him. People did not put up their defenses for puppies. But puppies wreaked havoc too. Sofia would just have to make sure this one's mess wouldn't be blamed on her.

CHAPTER THREE

Moments before the visitor let the ball sail above his head, after his final bounce, but before he began his serving motion, he thought of Alejandro. It had been like that ever since Alejandro had died, and had only escalated now that he was in Alejandro's childhood home, on the tennis court that his dad had built for him.

Snippets of that night—and the argument they'd had earlier that same week—would sneak up on him in subtle, quiet moments. When he was unable to sleep at night, or tying a shoelace, or when the smell of the tennis courts hit his senses just so.

And every time, there was a fresh pang of confusion, anger—and worry. Who had done this? And what had they known?

Not to mention that Alejandro was really and truly *gone*—and all the plans they'd begun to make were smoke. Were nothing.

He could feel the rage rushing up his spine and powering his arm forward as the racket connected with the ball. He knew he'd hit an ace from the sound alone. Gabriel seemed to have known, too, because he barely made an effort to lunge toward the perfectly placed serve.

"Very nice, Julián," Gabriel called out. "That's how you should have been serving all morning." He took a deep breath and wiped his forehead with the white-and-red sweatband on his forearm. "That's enough for this old man. You take the match, but I want a chance at redemption tomorrow."

He was still catching his breath. Not from their recent rally, or the force of his serve, but from the memory. His knees felt weak, and he was in desperate need of water. The morning had started off cool, but now the heat felt suffocating. He could see hot air rising off the composite court, blurring the air. "Claro que sí," he said, trying to make his walk to the sideline seem casual.

Gabriel was grabbing his own water bottle and towel from the bench beside the court when his cell phone rang. "Good playing. Especially that last serve. But English only in the house," he said, then answered the call.

He waved a goodbye, happy for the chance to recover. He took a long drink of water and stared at the ground between his feet. After a while, he realized his hand was gripping the tennis racket Gabriel had lent him so hard that his knuckles were turning white. He had the brief urge to smash it to bits, but tucked it beneath his arm instead and headed inside to shower.

In the bathroom, he took his time, stepping into the streams of water, luxuriating in the top-notch pressure, appreciating the beautiful mosaic tile even in the guest bathroom. There were dual showerheads, too, so he could stand between them and feel the sting of the hot water completely engulf him. With his eyes closed, a different memory rose up in the steam: Alejandro, naked. The roped muscles of his back. Another body in his arms—a woman. A woman he wasn't supposed to be sleeping with. And yet: Alejandro cupping her breasts, kissing her neck, neither of them noticing they were being watched.

But that was always how it went, wasn't it? Alejandro got what he wanted.

Once he had dressed, he saw Gabriel's racket on the bed and realized he still needed to return it. He was glad he'd been able to control himself before he hit it against something, as it was clearly exquisite quality. Not a Yonex, his favorite brand, but a solid Babolat Pure Drive, possibly customized. Damaging it would have been hard to explain, hard to recover from. He was practiced in self-restraint. He could keep it up awhile longer. He had to.

Had to get answers.

It was a big house, and perhaps because he'd been a surprise visitor, he had never been given an official tour. He still had trouble finding his way around those terra-cotta hallways. Each one seemingly led to another courtyard, another living room furnished with expensive leather couches and regal-looking antiques fitting in with the colonial architecture. It had been less than a week, and he mostly went from the guest bedroom where he slept, to the bathroom across the hall, and down the stairs to the kitchen and dining room. Occasionally, he'd dipped into other areas of the house—stolen moments when he thought he could wander without drawing too much attention. On one such occasion, he'd happened upon what he believed must be Gabriel's study. He hoped Alejandro might have mentioned that his friend Julián had been known to sleepwalk, as this would excuse his presence almost anywhere in the house at night when most were sleeping.

Now, racket in hand, he wound his way up and down the hallways, trying to remember which turns to take to find it again. He assumed he would stumble upon Gabriel sipping an espresso and taking phone calls, maybe looking at stocks on his dual computer monitors.

Instead, he found the study empty. The window was open, letting in a breeze, and the TV was set to the news on mute. He knocked on the doorframe, just in case, then decided he'd take a seat on one of the twin mustard-yellow leather seats facing Gabriel's desk. His intentions had really been to return the racket, but now it was simply a convenient excuse to enter and look around.

He waited for a few minutes, pretending to scroll through his phone and keeping an ear out. Then he decided he'd write a note, an action that would give him a plausible reason to look around the room. He grabbed a pen on the other side of the desk for cover, and immediately set his sights on the first thing that had caught his eye: the top drawer of the desk, cracked open. Through the crack he could see paper clips, more pens, and other office supplies. He stepped back to the doorway to see if Gabriel was coming. Someone's footsteps echoed through the hall, but they were getting farther away, not closer.

He returned to the desk. On top, a blank notepad sat beneath a stack of envelopes. He pulled the drawer open farther. Inside, he saw an unopened pack of gum, a couple of loose two-hundred-peso bills, and the business card for a Manhattan-based real estate lawyer, on the back of which was a handwritten five-digit number that meant nothing to him. There was a folder hidden in the back, chock-full of papers. He opened it and saw the Velcel letterhead on a handful of pages. He wanted to leaf through them, but a door slammed somewhere in the house, startling him. He froze, listening. When he heard footsteps fading away, he pulled his phone out and took pictures of as many of the documents as he could, deciding to look them over later.

He tucked the folder back and slid the drawer shut, moving onto the next one below. More manila folders, these ones empty, a stapler, and even an old Rolodex with faded yellow contact cards. He grabbed it, never having seen one in person before. At first, he was simply impressed any of them had survived the turn of the new millennium. Then he realized something strange about the entries. Some simply listed a city or a country and a phone number without an accompanying name. Others noted only a business type and some slight description. *Laundromat, Spain. No electronics.* He was focused enough on his task to have forgotten to keep an ear out for anyone approaching.

"Pa, ya esta el desayuno," Sofia said as she walked in, before realizing that it wasn't her dad standing behind the desk. "Julián," she said. "What are you doing here?"

He froze for a second, then flashed Sofia an easy smile and gestured at the pen in his hand. "I was just trying to leave your father a note," he said. "He lent me his racket, which I think improved my game considerably. Then I got distracted by this ancient artifact."

A weak lie, now that he heard it out loud. A single second looking at Sofia's golden-brown eyes told him that she knew it too. He held her gaze; turning away would be admitting the lie, even if both of them knew that it was one.

Would she go straight to Gabriel and tell him what she'd seen? If she did, Gabriel's trust in him would be broken, no matter how believable an excuse he gave.

When he saw a mischievous smile start to somehow make her face prettier than it already was, he was sure his time in the Velasco household was coming to an early end. So, he was surprised that she simply said, "Leave it to a dinosaur to have fossils lying around." She chuckled. "That's just hired help my dad likes to use for his dirty work." So dirty the info had to be coded and couldn't be stored online anywhere? He waited for her to explain further, but the only comment she added was, "Time for breakfast," before turning away and leaving him alone in the study again.

◆   ◆   ◆

At breakfast, his nerves were still on edge, but in a different way than they had been upstairs. There was a thrill now, an electric buzz that was not altogether unpleasant. He had to keep himself from glancing over at Sofia, who was seated next to him. His leg wanted to jitter, too, and he had to focus his energy on nodding politely at Maria and Gabriel's conversation.

The food had been delicious the previous mornings. Presumably it was today, too, but right now he couldn't taste it. Not with Sofia tapping him on the forearm to ask him to pass the orange juice, and barely meeting his eyes when he did, giving nothing away.

He could easily read Gabriel's mood: somewhat stressed, impatient, but trying to enjoy himself and be good company. Maria had that edge of nervousness she often did, though this morning she seemed a little more tired than usual, her movements a little slower, the bags under her eyes heavier. Sofia, though, was hard to get a read on. He had to restrain himself from staring at her. What could her motivations possibly be for keeping his secret?

"And so today," Maria was saying, holding her mug of café de olla with both hands, as if needing the warmth it offered, "what's happening in the meetings?"

At the head of the table, Gabriel heaved a deep sigh and reached for the salsa macha jar, drizzling a spoonful onto his eggs. "What else? Paperwork, formalities." He waved a dismissive hand. "The lawyers are just going line by line on every negotiated point and every spreadsheet. And, as Sofia knows, there are so many of them. We should still be on schedule to have it all done by the next board meeting and announce the deal has been finalized."

"That's good," Maria said, still just holding her mug, her eggs mostly untouched on her plate.

"Is there any way to hurry things along?" Sofia asked. She raised her egg-filled tortilla and took a bite. A drop of salsa dripped onto the corner of her mouth, and she used her thumb to clean it up, popping it into her mouth at the exact moment her eyes flitted to Julián. "Maybe we could sneak into their offices and pretend to borrow a pen while we search for something that helps us?"

There it was again, the thrill. In those alluring eyes he saw it all. That she knew what he'd been doing, and that she was enjoying lording it over him, making him squirm. He wasn't entirely surprised by this coming from a Velasco, but he hadn't expected any of this to be, for lack of a better word, fun.

He looked over, sensing Gabriel's eyes on him. As soon as he met his gaze, though, Gabriel's eyes flicked away, and he tapped on the table with a knuckle. "But it's rude to speak of these matters in front of guests. Let's change the subject."

He should tread more carefully.

Sofia looked calmly away, putting a hand on her mom's shoulder. "You feeling okay, Ma? You haven't eaten."

Maria smiled weakly and picked up her fork. "Just a little light-headed. It'll pass," she said, patting Sofia on the hand.

"You should wear sunscreen the days of the audit," he offered. The three Velascos turned to look at him with confused expressions, so he went on, keeping his voice light and airy. "Studies have shown that people associate the smell with vacations and childhood, lowering their stress and leading to less irritability. There's evidence that it can make health inspectors, government officials, even judges, more lenient. And even if you don't need leniency, which I'm sure is the case," he said, giving a little reverent nod, "then it will help ease any nerves you or your employees have."

There was a tense moment of silence; then Gabriel let out a barking laugh. "You know, I was afraid when you came here that eventually you'd start trying to spout some MBA academic garbage that has no use in the real world. But sunscreen? I can get on board with that. I love that smell."

Julián relaxed and started preparing himself a tortilla with eggs. "Who doesn't?"

"It reminds me of when you and your brother were little," Maria said, looking at Sofia, a smile contrasting the sadness in her eyes. It seemed like she was always on the verge of tears. She probably had been since hearing about Ale's death.

"It always kind of made me gag," Sofia said, shaking her head.

"Oh, come on, hija, no seas así." Maria clicked her tongue. "Don't pretend you didn't have a great childhood."

"That's not what I said."

Julián was surprised by the sudden shift in her voice. Then he caught the expression on Gabriel's face. His eyes were locked on Sofia. His fingers tensed as he gripped the cloth napkin. After a moment Gabriel seemed to relax and used the napkin to wipe his mouth.

"It doesn't make you think of our summer on the yacht?" he asked, a hint of a growl in his voice. "Or all those trips to Acapulco and Ixtapa? Tulum and Aruba?" Gabriel shook his head, as if Sofia's preference for smells were a direct challenge to his parenting. "You don't associate sunscreen with the vacations we took you and your brother on? The life we've given you?"

Sofia sighed, and though Julián was still trying not to stare at her, he noticed her fingers tense around her fork. "That's not what I said, Pa," she repeated deferentially. After that, she fell silent for the rest of the meal.

It made him wonder if she might still lash out, change the subject by ratting him out. But other than her heavy silence, the remainder of breakfast was perfectly pleasant. Afterward, Gabriel excused himself to go up to his study, and as soon as he was gone, Sofia went off, too, announcing simply that she was leaving as she stood and grabbed her blazer from the back of the chair, throwing it on over her tight tank top and fitted shorts. He tried not to stare too long as she strutted out of the room.

That left Maria and the visitor alone together. She offered to take him on a stroll around the grounds, which he had still not seen entirely. They exited through the sliding glass door that led from the dining room to the courtyard. There was a large stone fountain in the middle, the water shimmering in the late-morning sun. On one side of the courtyard was a large dining table, and on the other a firepit surrounded by wrought iron chairs adorned with soft pillows and throw blankets.

"Sofia and Alejandro used this a lot when they were younger," Maria said. "This house was always full of their friends. Social butterflies, my children. Social locusts, maybe, if that doesn't sound too harsh. 'Butterflies' doesn't quite describe how many teenagers there were here at any given time." She laughed, and her hand went to that silver necklace. It seemed to be a security blanket for her, or a reflex, anytime Alejandro came up in conversation. Julián would bet that he had given her the necklace.

Past the courtyard was the tennis court, which Julián of course was familiar with. They looped around to the pool, on a cobblestone path lined with bougainvillea, the smell perfuming the air around them.

There was a small pool house with a bench out front. It looked to him like a glorified shack, at least from the outside, and he imagined no one but staff went in there.

"Is what you said about sunscreen true?" Maria stopped and leaned her hand against the side of the pool house.

"I believe so. Don't tell your husband, but I learned about it in business school." He chuckled. "It seems like he disapproves."

Maria heaved another deep sigh. "I think he misses arguing with Alejandro about that. But no, he doesn't disapprove, not exactly." She turned to study her companion. In her gaze, he could see a hint of Sofia. The eyes themselves, sure, but something else too. A hidden intensity, perhaps. Then she closed her eyes and brought her hand up to her forehead, stumbling a little against the wall.

"Are you okay?" he asked, stepping toward her.

She waved him away, smiling weakly and keeping her eyes closed. "It's fine. Just a little stress. Gabriel's been under a lot, and it spreads." She tried to right herself, but he had to step forward and steady her by the arms. "I'm okay; it's nothing." She tried to step away, but he could tell that she didn't have the strength yet, so he kept one hand on her shoulder, propping her against the wall.

"Let me go get your husband," he said.

"No, please. It's nothing." She motioned with her head to the nearby wrought iron bench. "I'll sit for a second, and it will pass. It's the sun, probably. I usually go to the pool house for the shade. I have a little desk there where I do my paperwork. Gabriel would never admit this, but he has no head for numbers. I run all the household finances, and I've been going over Velcel contracts for years. Now Sofia does a lot of that."

He helped guide her to the bench and eased her down. Nearby there was a plant with large leaves, and he stepped over to gently tear one of the leaves from its stem. Then he took a seat next to Maria and fanned her with the leaf, pleased when she sighed happily at the cool air. After a minute or so, she opened her eyes again. "Thank you."

"You want me to go get someone? Perhaps Sofia is still home."

"No, it's okay," she said, giving a quick shake of the head. "I probably don't drink enough water. Ale was always telling me I should drink more." She turned her attention to the pool shimmering in the sunlight and picked up their conversation as if she hadn't almost just fainted. "The business has always had its difficulties, as you might imagine. Yes, stuff they don't teach you in business school: dealing with corrupt officials, balancing a million things at once just to put food on the table for our family, attempts at . . ."

His eyes narrowed at this, and he felt his heart beating fast. He waited for her to elaborate, give him something more to latch onto. He didn't want to seem too eager, but he sensed an opening. Perhaps it was time to gamble a little.

He nodded, sitting back on the bench, keeping his eyes on the pool to match her gaze. "I think I know what you mean," he said, running a hand across the length of his thigh, as if smoothing out some imaginary wrinkles. "My family's dealt with some unsavory situations in our business too."

"Really?"

"The cost of business, my dad always said. When enough money is changing hands, the stakes of almost everything rise. You become a target." He shrugged, and now turned to look at Maria, who was considering him with a bemused expression. He forced a chuckle. "Extortion and blackmail sound like the stuff of movies, but when you're living through them, it's just headaches and too many phone calls."

Maria held his gaze for a few seconds before nodding in understanding. He felt the rush of having played his cards right.

"Lately, though, it's been even worse," Maria went on, turning her attention back to the pool, and Julián was momentarily surprised to see a pair of peacocks strutting through the grassy field beyond it. "Alejandro, of course, made everything harder. He argued with his father on everything." Julián smiled and nodded gently, remembering Ale's having to fly down from LA for board meetings a few times. He had expected that his first time in San Miguel would be accompanying Ale. "Not that he always made things easy on his father. But it complicated things. He's a man who just lost his son." Her hand went to the pendant on her silver necklace again. "And he has to continue running his business, be strong through his grief."

"Then there was this"—she gestured with her hand, as if reaching for the word, trying to pluck it out of the air like a mosquito she wanted to squash—"this thorn in his side. A particular thorn that had been around for a while before . . . the accident." It looked like she wanted to go on, but she stopped herself, this time two tears escaping and rolling down her made-up cheek. She didn't bother brushing them away. "I often wished someone could just reach in and grab that thorn and toss it away. End all of that trouble. And look at us now. I'd give anything to have that trouble again instead of this one."

Julián stuffed his hands in his pockets, a million questions on his tongue, though he didn't want to give voice to any of them. Not yet.

Maria wiped her eyes and took in a shaky breath, then turned to him and smiled as she rose to her feet. "It's all been hard on Sofia, too, though she doesn't like to show it," she said.

"We all grieve differently," he said.

Maria made an approving noise. They kept walking on the cobblestone path around the pool, past more peacocks, arriving back at the courtyard. Maria turned to meet his eyes again. "Will you do me a favor while you're here?"

"Of course."

"Since Gabriel is having Sofia show you around San Miguel, I'd like you to . . ." She paused, thinking maybe about how to phrase what she wanted to say. "I don't know; this sounds strange. But if you could just keep an eye on her for me." Now there was a whole other reason for his heart to beat faster. His gamble was paying off even better than he could have anticipated. "I just worry about her," Maria said. "Sofia doesn't want to talk to me about Alejandro, and that's fine. She takes after her father that way. Like you said, we all grieve differently, and that's her right. But it's my right as a mother to worry."

She sighed, and to his surprise, he felt for this woman. There was something weary about her. She'd lost her son, but, as he knew all too well, the world carried on relentlessly even after death. Even the rich could not pause everything to give themselves time to grieve. Mergers, deals, secrets . . . these could not simply be abandoned. But there was also something else that plagued her, he sensed. The upcoming business deal? Or was it the mysterious "thorn" in Gabriel's side that had her so distressed?

Something stirred inside him, an awareness, like a hound smelling blood—the feeling that he was getting close to a vulnerable point, an opening. In tennis, you could tell how to take advantage of a weakness by the way an opponent shifted their weight, favored a certain stance, the slight squint or grimace they thought no one noticed. Julián had made himself an expert at those tells. Sheer talent, like Alejandro had on the court, was one thing. But people like him had to find other ways to stay one step ahead. No amount of practice ever gave you the upper hand in life—you had to seize it by any means necessary. You had to find the weak spots.

"Maybe your coming here at this time is what we needed," Maria said, patting his hand affectionately. "It will be good for us to have someone who can channel Alejandro during these days. Someone who was close to him in the end. Someone who cares about the family."

"Of course," he said, a smile spreading across his face—perhaps the first genuine smile since he'd come here. "Anything I can do to help."

CHAPTER FOUR

November–May

Back at school, Alejandro used to talk often about the lines of tennis. He would wax poetic about them, how beautiful it was that those white lines on the ground, those ten simple rectangles, coupled with a handful of rules, came together to create an entire world. One where merit and ability were all that mattered.

He would say this while playing tennis, in between sets, whether he was winning or losing (though he mostly won). But he also said it when out at a bar or at a party, or sitting around watching TV. Once, at the beach, Alejandro had been reading one of those ethics books he loved so much, and at some point, he just shouted out, "Yes! Exactly!" And even some girls on the beach trying to flirt couldn't get him to shut up for the rest of the day about how tennis was the utopian world Sir Thomas More had envisioned.

Later that night, even though they'd been drinking in the sun all day and had kept it going well into the night, despite having class the next morning, Alejandro had insisted on sneaking onto the campus courts to play with his friends Julián and Eduardo—they were always a unit, those three, in the early days, anyway. They were too old for this kind of thing, but he had a way of convincing people. Eduardo was eager to go along with anything; Julián was competitive and couldn't say no if the other two were going.

"Won't we get in trouble?" Eduardo had asked. Eduardo hadn't grown up wealthy like the rest of them and worried a lot more about making sure he flew under the radar. He was a scholarship brainiac Alejandro had taken under his wing—a charity case, as Julián sometimes called him. But even Julián had to admit the guy had grit, and clearly Alejandro saw it in him too. Anyone would've assumed that Eduardo was the third wheel in their crew, the hanger-on to the former prep school boys whose fathers had basically paid for them to party throughout their undergrad degrees and then some. But it wasn't like that—if anything, Eduardo and Alejandro were much closer, and Julián, left on the outside, was the one who sometimes resented that. But if Julián's anger was simmering, Alejandro didn't know it yet.

"Look, you all know I have complicated feelings about my privilege. But in this victimless scenario, I am happy to flex it," Alejandro assured Eduardo. "If we get caught, my father will whip out the only thing mightier than both the sword and the pen."

"I swear to God, if you say the tennis racket, I'm going to—" Julián said.

"The checkbook, güey," Alejandro said, drunk and giddy. "But that only proves my point. We live in a desperately imperfect world." He pushed open the door on the chain-link gate and looked out admiringly at the perfectly manicured bright green grass. "Except for on these courts." The way awe resounded in his voice, it was impossible not to at least kind of understand what he was saying.

Alejandro was the first to admit he had been born lucky: into a wealthy family, in a beautiful country where wealth could insulate you from the worst of life. He'd seen more of the world by age twenty-five than most people could even point out on a map. Born into a guaranteed education, at private schools at home and abroad. After he discovered tennis, he attended tennis camps, where the best coaches in the world honed him into an extraordinary player.

That shimmering, glamorous life had hidden plenty of imperfections. Gabriel was a demanding father who believed the only affection children required was to be provided for. In turn, he could ask what he wished of them, and they had to repay him with gratitude. Alejandro said himself that while his father was harsh and distant, he did provide them with good lives.

And that was part of the problem, in a way. The Velascos lived in a world completely devoid of rules and consequences. If they wanted to break a law, they needed simply to know how much it would cost to do so, or whom they would have to speak to. If Alejandro or Sofia messed up at school, a donation would clear it up. Or another prestigious school elsewhere would happily take the check.

This was exactly the point of having power, Gabriel would say. He always had some quote from *The Art of War* to justify that such power was a good thing. Often some strained metaphor about a valley and an enemy's position. And while Maria nodded silently along to Gabriel's idolatry of Sun Tzu, and Sofia kept her own copy, Alejandro had always sought some other philosophy that made more sense.

He'd read Nietzsche for an AP English class in high school, and it had awakened a hunger in him. He started scouring the library for philosophy books and following the philosophy subreddit almost religiously, quoting great thinkers in essays for school and in conversations with friends alike. The only similar urge he'd ever had was for tennis.

Suddenly, Ale wanted to devour books some long-dead men had written. He wanted to think about life and society and the way humans treated each other without right away equating it with war strategy. He found it fascinating that thought was inexhaustible. That for all of human history, thinkers had written about what was right and wrong, and would continue to do so. And the more he read, the more it felt to him like the world of the Velascos was chaotic and immoral, a meaningless game of power and reputation and status.

All this only increased his love of tennis, those perfect white lines, that self-contained world where the only thing that mattered was skill. The game's limited number of rules equally applied to everyone who stepped on the court. And no matter who you were, if you weren't better than the player across from you, you lost. There were inevitable consequences if a person fell short.

After getting his bachelor's degree, he'd tried for a few years to go pro. He'd stopped only when Gabriel had started pressuring him to come back to Mexico, threatening to no longer fund his efforts to keep the pipe dream alive. "You excelled at tennis, and I'm proud of you for that," Gabriel had said. "But a career in sports is not for serious people. You'll work with me and help continue to build Velcel into our family's legacy."

They'd fought about this for a long time. The compromise was an MBA, something that would buy Alejandro a few more years in the States, with at least some time to focus on tennis.

At least, that was how Alejandro always told it. But obviously, he'd left a few parts of the story out, hadn't he? There were some things that haunted him that he clearly couldn't tell anyone.

And it was those secrets that had gotten him killed.

CHAPTER FIVE

June

The guest room the Velascos had put Julián in faced the courtyard, and a gentle breeze now came in through the window. Nevertheless, he was covered in sweat, the sheets tangled around him, when he awoke suddenly in the night. It had been like this for weeks, that terrible night replaying in his head whether he was asleep (on the nights he managed it) or awake. Every time he dreamed it, though, it felt like he was really back there again, instead of just revisiting through the protective sheen of memory. And every time, he woke up feeling even more sure that his friend had not died by suicide at all.

Ale had been murdered. And he wouldn't stop until he'd found out who did it.

The day had been one of those LA scorchers that made the whole city irritable, indignant, as if the weather had no right to treat them that way. He had spent the day in traffic, crossing town from school to work, then back to the tennis courts, which always exacerbated both the heat and the irritability, leading to his evening fight with Alejandro. Later, he would blame the fight on both those factors, the words repeating in his head as if traffic and heat could be blamed not just for the fight but for what came next.

After stewing in his apartment all evening, rehashing the argument they'd had in his head, he had cooled off (figuratively) and decided to make amends. He'd lashed out harder than he'd intended, screaming that Alejandro was a delusional trust fund kid, an asshole who only pretended to step outside of his privilege but never actually had the courage to give it up. He'd said it only because Ale had started to express some misgivings about their plans.

They had been intending to use Ale's father's connections to strike out on their own, start a business together. They'd been dreaming of it, of independence for Alejandro and for him, a sense of purpose. But then Ale had gotten cold feet. Had started saying he needed space. It stung. He had done absolutely nothing wrong.

But he shouldn't have lashed out. This was something he always tried to tame, this rash side of him. He'd gotten so good at tamping it down, sometimes he forgot the damage he could do if the lid wasn't on tight enough. Like the time with the baseball bat, when he was a kid. There were times he'd gone too far, and last night was certainly one of them.

So, he drove over to Alejandro's Silver Lake house with a six-pack and a pound of barbacoa from their favorite food truck. When he arrived, he rang the doorbell. Somewhere nearby, a motorcycle engine kicked into gear and sped away. It almost sounded like it had come from the back of the house, but he dismissed the thought. He knocked on the door, then tried calling. There was still no answer, but the lights were on inside and Ale's Audi was in the driveway, so he assumed Ale must be in the bathroom or something. He sat on the front steps and cracked open a beer to wait, scrolling through his phone.

He lost track of time, and when he was halfway through his beer, he realized how long it had been without hearing any movement going on inside. Once, months before, Julián and Eduardo had arrived at the house early while Ale had been stuck in traffic, and Alejandro had texted his garage code in the group chat. Scrolling through his phone until he found it now, he got up to ring the doorbell one more time and then let himself in.

A hissing noise was coming from somewhere, but the rest of the house felt oddly still. Maybe that was just in hindsight, or due to the uneasiness he had felt because of their fight, wondering if the friendship was damaged. He called out his friend's name, made a joke about how he'd better not be naked or worse.

He stepped through the kitchen, noticing an ice cream carton sitting out, sweating onto the counter. "Ale?" he called out again. The living room was empty, and the soft hissing was coming from the turntable in the corner, next to Ale's typewriter—he'd developed a love of old technology along with his love of philosophy. The record was still spinning, and soft music was coming through the speakers.

That was when he got the sense something was wrong.

His heart started racing as he checked the bathroom downstairs, then took the stairs two at a time. The conversation he'd had with Alejandro just a few days prior replayed in his head. *I'm afraid something bad's gonna happen,* Ale had said—almost casually, over the music playing in the car. They'd been going to some party in the hills, the kind that Alejandro was invited to often. Sitting in the back, he wasn't entirely sure he'd heard correctly, but when he tried to ask Ale to elaborate, the conversation had moved on to the subject of who would be at the party, and he hadn't remembered to bring it up later.

He found Ale in bed, the foam at his mouth already drying, the vomit on the sheets beside him dotted with half-digested white pills. The pill bottle rested on the nightstand like a warning beacon. It took thirty seconds of trying to shake Alejandro awake for the truth to sink in. Alejandro was dead, apparently by his own hand.

Kneeling beside the bed, a cold sweat dripping down his back, he started patting his pockets for his cell phone to call the cops. He looked at his phone's screen, where he saw he'd managed to press 9-1-1 but had not yet dialed.

Then he took a breath to calm himself. He rose to his feet and looked around the room, his mind ticking frantically but steadily, like a clock: noticing, noticing. Alejandro's shoes were still on, which was odd. He was always quick to remind guests not to wear shoes inside the house. There was a chance, of course, that he'd been too distraught to obey his own rule. But surely even the deeply depressed continued deeply held habits. It would be like muscle memory at that point.

There was a glass of water next to the now-empty pill bottle on the nightstand, and while it was only half-full, when he stepped closer to it, he couldn't see any smudges on it, or any sign that it had been drunk from recently.

Had there been some hidden sign of depression he should have picked up on sooner? He looked down at Alejandro again—his body. He tried to read his friend's expression. Was there some sign there of relief that the burden of living was no longer Ale's to bear? Or was there fear in his eyes? Had someone done this to him?

He remembered the ice cream carton on the counter downstairs, the music playing. Something felt not right. He shut his phone off and put it in his pocket, for now.

Was this what Alejandro had been alluding to recently? Had it been a cry for help? Or a premonition? But there'd been no struggle here. No blood anywhere. The sheets on the bed were pristine except for the wrinkles caused by Ale's weight. If there *had been* foul play here, it was no crime of passion.

His gut told him to keep looking. For what, he didn't know. He'd give himself ten minutes and then he'd call the police. Yes, this looked like a suicide. Rather, the scene seemed to want to *tell the story* of a suicide. But none of this seemed like Ale, not the Ale he knew.

Searching through drawers, he had the feeling that as long as he could keep at this task, then Alejandro might somehow not be dead. He knew this was crazy. All of this was crazy. He should have called an ambulance right away. He should not touch anything, especially if he thought there was foul play.

Instead, he opened Alejandro's computer. He needed a password, and it felt silly to even try to guess. He tried "Lomas Lindas," the name of the country club in San Miguel, but that didn't work.

He shut the computer and kept searching, knowing he couldn't keep this up much longer. He pulled his phone out again, tapping it against his leg, wondering if he was crazy for delaying this long. Finally, he dialed, surprised by the tremor of his own voice over the line, how shaky and frightened he sounded.

When he hung up, he felt defeated. He looked at his friend's lifeless form on the bed, not wanting it to be real, almost sure that it wasn't. The operator had said an ambulance and the police were on their way, and thanks to the zip code, that probably meant it was about to get a lot more real in the next five to ten minutes.

Then something caught his eye. On the nightstand on the other side of the bed from where he had entered, there was a book with a slip of paper sticking out. *The Art of War*. He felt a churning in his stomach. Every time Alejandro had mentioned that book, it had been with derision, as if it were some evil stepparent who'd made his childhood hell.

He picked up the little book, opening it to where the paper stuck out. He noted the page number, just in case that mattered. He'd expected the note to be in Alejandro's handwriting, some dig at his dad, some thought about the ethics of the book.

But the note had nothing to do with the book, as far as he could tell, and it was typed, though the words themselves mattered more than any handwriting he could have analyzed.

Enough fucking around. Send the money or the world knows.

The longer he stared, the more he became convinced. This scene had been staged. Not to cover up a crime of passion, but a planned crime. And judging by the ice cream on the counter downstairs, it hadn't happened too long ago.

Suddenly, he remembered the sound of the motorcycle when he'd arrived, how it had seemed to come from the other side of the house.

He raced to the bedroom window, which faced out onto the street. A silly impulse, of course. The motorcycle would have been long gone, especially if the person driving it had anything to do with his best friend lying dead on his bed.

Eventually he heard the sirens, saw the lights dancing toward the house. Before he could think too long about it, he rushed back to the nightstand to replace the book where it had been, and at the same time slide the note into his pocket.

When he did, he saw a flash of gold sticking out against the mahogany table. A cross on a chain, a necklace that Alejandro often wore. It was resting on top of Alejandro's passport, though he would never know why his friend had it out. Without thinking much about it, he slipped the passport into his back pocket, tossed the necklace over his head, tucking it beneath the collar of his shirt as the EMTs downstairs started pounding on the door. Now the grief started to bubble up in his belly. His friend was gone. He was right there on the bed, but Ale was gone.

Before going downstairs, he thought about what the note could mean. A blackmailer, clearly. Maybe someone who'd shown up in person, just a few hours earlier. Someone whom Alejandro hadn't paid off and who was not too pleased about it. Someone who was smart enough to stage the outcome of their anger as a suicide.

Another hurried knock at the door stirred him from his thoughts. He turned to look at Alejandro one more time, and now his dead friend sat up, eyes wide open.

◆ ◆ ◆

That was how he had been waking up for weeks now, whenever he managed to sleep.

He sat up, reaching for the glass of water by his bed only to find it was empty. It was in these quiet, unexpected moments when rage—and an undertone of panic—snuck in. What had Alejandro's blackmailer known?

And would the blackmailer implicate him?

He opened the door and tiptoed down the hall.

Someone in Ale's close circle had to have been responsible for the killing. Ale always said his family kept close tabs on him. Someone had been watching him. He'd been worried about that for some time—Julián had chalked it up to paranoia. But after the murder, he was certain Ale had been right. Someone *had* been following Ale and knew what he'd done.

Knew what *they'd* done. Someone had come to collect.

It was someone close to the family. Maybe the same someone who had also been blackmailing Gabriel—as Maria herself had hinted. Someone close by. Julián would find out who it was.

And he was going to make sure they paid for it. Before his problems got any bigger than they already were.

In the kitchen, he poured himself more water from the filtered jug on the counter, chugging a glass, then refilling it again. It took that long for the dream to fully leave him, for the image of Alejandro's empty eyes to dissipate. Then he heard the sound of a door creaking open, footsteps, the door shutting again. He cocked his ear, thinking he might have been imagining it.

He grabbed a knife from the block on the counter, not understanding why he did it. Maybe the dream was still with him. The certainty that someone knew Alejandro's secrets—and his own.

Peeking through the glass door that led into the dining room, he saw a figure moving through the dark. There was a loud knock as the person stumbled into the entrance table, then muttered a curse. He kept watching quietly, his eyes still adjusting to the lack of light. Then he heard the jingle of keys, another indiscernible noise.

Now he could see more clearly: the long hair, the purse in the crook of her elbow. It was Sofia, coming home from some late-night tryst, judging by her attire, the slight stumble to her gait. He smiled to himself in the dark. He thought about stepping out, then remembered the knife in his hand and quietly walked back to set it down. By the time he did, she was gone, her footsteps silently climbing the stairs.

He waited a minute or two, wondering what she'd been doing. He knew Mateo was out of town and that Elizabeth had had plans. It was a weekday, too, and almost two in the morning. His mind couldn't help but go to something dramatic: an affair, maybe?

As he tiptoed up the stairs, his thoughts were already returning to his dream, to the sound of sirens whirring through the LA night as he slipped out of Alejandro's place, unseen. So he didn't notice Sofia coming out of her room until they almost bumped into each other.

"Jesus!" she whisper-shouted. "What the fuck?"

He caught the faint scent of alcohol, though it was hidden beneath her shampoo, ylang-ylang and rosemary. Ever since he'd arrived, he'd been running into pockets of the smell throughout the house, pleasant clouds that, to his embarrassment, turned him on a little.

"Hey," he said, strangely feeling like he was the one with something to hide. He lifted his water glass, his alibi that he wasn't just sneaking around in the dark. "Did I hear you just get in?"

She shook her head right away. She'd changed out of her party dress and into pajama shorts and a white V-neck T-shirt, and despite the lack of light, his eyes had now adjusted enough that he could see the outline of her nipples through the thin fabric. "No, what makes you think that?"

He opened his mouth to say he'd seen her, then thought better of it. He preferred the game, preferred to tease his lips into a smile. "Must have imagined it."

"I was actually on my way out," Sofia said, and he could have sworn he saw her return a grin. She tossed her hair over her shoulder. "I like practicing at night." It was an obvious lie; he enjoyed the fact that they both knew it.

She momentarily stepped back through the open door of her bedroom, almost brushing against him as she did. He bit his lip to keep his grin from becoming a little too unruly. When Sofia reemerged, she was holding two tennis rackets. "Care to join me?"

CHAPTER SIX

Sofia bounced a ball on the ground, counting to ten in her head, her routine anytime she stepped on a court. It was a satisfying change to the loudness of the nightclub she'd been to earlier. The soft thump of the rubber ball on the court echoed into the stillness. She looked over at Julián, surprised to find herself glad he was there. To her surprise, she'd softened to him when he grabbed the racket and said, "Let me get my shoes," instead of calling her on her obvious bullshit. For fuck's sake, she was braless, a ridiculous choice for tennis, middle of the night or not.

At least the courts were far enough from the bedrooms that no one would hear them, and the garden lights that her mom liked keeping on all night would be bright enough to play by.

Sofia dribbled the ball a few more times, then gently volleyed it to Julián's side of the court. They warmed up with a few minutes of that, not saying much of anything. There was something about the whole charade that felt silly, but Sofia wasn't going to be the one to back off. After a minute or two, the magic of tennis started doing its thing. The circumstances of the game—the late hour, the slight buzz still coursing through her, this near-stranger across from her—it all began to disappear into the ether. All that remained was the game itself.

There was something about practicing that always made Sofia feel like she was in a time machine. She hit the ball toward Julián's left, and then she was ten years old again, picking up a racket for the first time; thirteen years old at a camp in Switzerland, the other girls fawning over

Alejandro and asking her how it felt to have him take all the talent in the family. The thwack of her racket hitting the ball erased the memory and transported her again.

Now she was fourteen, sitting on her bed while her dad held onto her tennis racket and gave a whole speech about how she should pursue more "appropriate activities." That was the year she focused on ballet, at least as far as her father was concerned.

Thwack, she hit another ball, and she knew right away this time that it was too strong. It flew well clear of the baseline. "Carajo!" she screamed out, fighting the urge to bash her racket on the ground. This was how it always was: if she thought of Alejandro when playing, her anger got the best of her. She had to work harder to channel it.

Lately, despite herself, the anger was mixed with guilt, as if her raging thoughts were somehow to blame for Alejandro's death. So often during ballet practices years ago, holding fourth position, her legs sore, she thought the resentment would burn her alive. Sometimes, jumping her way through allegro, she'd kill Alejandro in her mind, thinking she'd be allowed to leave and go play tennis if only he were dead.

And now, he was. And she felt guilty. As if the universe knew that she'd occasionally wished he didn't exist. As if the universe ever granted secret wishes.

She tried to focus on Julián. His movements on the court had an ease to them, though Sofia guessed that he hadn't been born talented at tennis. It was clearly something he'd worked at, trained his body until learned motions were as natural as walking.

Within a few minutes, their rallying turned faster, more intense. It was clear Sofia was a better player and would crush him. But he kept up well enough to make the game interesting. And she was, indeed, interested. There was something about the way he moved that she couldn't keep her eyes off. She missed a few returns that she normally would not have because her gaze had landed on his thighs, on the muscle tensing in his forearm, on the ironically ballet-like fierce grace of his movements.

After twenty minutes or so, they paused for water, Sofia sharing from her water bottle, surprised at the slight, schoolgirl-like thrill this brought her.

"You play well, but you play . . . angry." Julián poured a little water into his palm and splashed it on the back of his neck.

"Yeah, I've heard that before."

He laughed, and maybe it was the booze still in her system, or the unexpected turn the night had taken, but she found herself enjoying the sound.

"And how's it working out for you?"

Sofia pulled out another ball from her pocket and bounced it casually on the ground in front of her. They'd been playing in silence up until then.

"It was the anger that made me a good player," she said. "That's how I got better than Ale. You play angry too; you just try to control it instead of using it."

Julián raised an eyebrow and leaned down to pick up a nearby ball, pocketing it. He turned the racket in his hands, his grip easy and natural. "That's funny; Ale never mentioned you were better than he was."

Sofia scoffed. "That's a shocker." She stopped bouncing the ball to wipe the sweat from her brow. The cool night air felt great now that she took a moment to appreciate it. "I started beating him when I was thirteen," she said, unable to keep the pride from her voice. "It was only when I was *encouraged* to pursue ballet that he caught up a little. But I'd still beat him two out of every three games."

She picked up on Julián trying to repress some thought he had. "What?"

He shrugged. "It's just, Ale was really good. Best I've seen who wasn't a pro, and he was damn close. Maybe he got better since you last played him. When was that?"

She shook her head and bounced the ball between her feet a few times. "Recently enough."

"Why didn't you keep pursuing tennis, then?"

Sofia laughed. "That would not be a serious pursuit for a young woman," she said in a voice that was clearly meant to imitate Gabriel. She kicked at the ground. "I love my family; I love this country. But the sexism runs deeper in both than I'd like it to."

She looked over at Julián. Something about him felt . . . unthreatening. Like he wasn't belittling her, just holding up his friend on a pedestal. She relaxed, and her thoughts must have been clearly written on her face, because he caught her eye and immediately broke out into a grin.

"Okay, I could tell you were taking it easy on me, and I admit that you're probably even better than Ale was."

"Probably, huh?" Sofia shook her head and took the water from him, their fingers grazing. "Should I make you work on the next set, then?"

Julián raised his hands in surrender. "Please, no. I'm out of shape, and your dad already ran me through a few games this morning."

They stood quietly for a moment, listening to the quiet humming of the pool filter nearby, the gurgling of the fountain in the courtyard cutting through the still night.

"You're right. Anger never works for me on the courts," Julián said with that easy smile of his. "I need to be more focused than that, more controlled."

She felt like asking him what he had to be angry about, but then he stood, and she followed him back onto the court, watching Julián's forearms, the muscles shifting as he twirled the racket. Before crossing over to his side, though, Julián stopped by the net and turned to face her. She felt herself blush, and hoped it was too dark for him to spot it.

"Speaking of anger," he said, "did Ale have many"—even in the dim garden lights she could see he made a face, as if he felt it was ridiculous to even use the word—"many enemies? I'm sure, good-looking guy like him, world in the palm of his hand, there had to be people who were jealous, bitter."

Sofia couldn't help but laugh. "I'm sure he must have. But nothing worse than anyone in this family. My father has practically made it his life's mission to surround himself with enemies so that he can squash them. Why do you ask?"

He shook his head. "I just can't shake the feeling that there was something going on I didn't know about. I mean, when someone young dies out of the blue, you question yourself; you question what you were missing."

Sofia considered him for a second, wondering again what Julián was really doing here. "You were right about me not having played Ale in a while," she said truthfully. "We kind of lost touch the last few years." She said it because it felt good to be honest for the moment. And because it sent a clear message to Julián: she wasn't going to entertain lots of these conversations about her brother. But most of all, she'd said it to stall. Because, of course, she hadn't missed the way Julián said Ale had "died out of the blue." As if he knew more about Alejandro's death than he was letting on. He hadn't mentioned depression either. As if he thought it maybe wasn't, as the family had been told, a suicide.

This was an interesting twist. What if her brother had been killed?

For all she knew, Julián had been the one to kill him.

The thought that her brother might have been killed was horrifying. She had, after all, loved him underneath all that anger, in her way. Their mother's sweetness had passed on to him, and for all the times he annoyed her, Sofia never forgot that. But the prospect that he'd been murdered also filled her with a twisted curiosity. Alejandro had always seemed immortal to her. Invisibly protected, not just by privilege and actual security guards but by popularity and good regard. People loved him, treated him as invaluable. It was *Sofia* who'd been treated like the disposable one, the pawn in other people's games.

Julián headed to his side of the court, where he bounced a ball and then made a clean serve that she returned with ease.

For a few moments, she became lost in the rally, too intent and focused to talk.

But thinking of her brother's death sparked more memories. Another thwack, another mental jump in time: She was sixteen years old, riding home from ballet practice, sore but dreaming of the tennis court at home, when a black SUV in front of them abruptly turned to block the road. The SUV's doors thumped open and closed. The Velascos' driver, Ramon, slammed the car into reverse, only to find another car behind them blocking their retreat.

Sofia could remember the sound her phone made as it slipped from her fingers in surprise, bouncing against the car door and falling to the floor. The angry black metal of the guns, the masked man barking orders. Ramon trying to assure her everything was going to be okay, even though she could hear the tremble in his voice, even though it was obvious what was about to happen to her.

Even then, she'd had the thought that her dad was somehow to blame. Even then, she'd thought that they would never let this happen to Alejandro.

In the end, she'd been lucky. Three days in a dark room with enough to eat and access to a toilet. They'd left bruises on her arms when they yanked her out of the car, and they'd bumped her shin against a table as they shuffled her into her temporary prison, but nothing worse than that. Of course, her dad bought her back from them, cut whatever check he had to. But she couldn't feel grateful afterward; she felt only the certainty that she would never have her own power to decide her fate, because she was a thing to be owned and traded.

She'd advanced too close to the net now, and Julián lobbed the ball way past her, stirring Sofia from her thoughts. She caught her breath as she jogged to the ball and prepared to serve.

"Tell me about that MBA life," she asked him. "Was my brother a total loner? It seemed like he got even more serious at UCLA."

Julián returned a backhand her way, enough zip on the ball that Sofia had to slide to get to it. "Not at all. Ale always had a lot of friends, or at least, a ton of people who were desperate to be friends with him—does that count? I guess you could say we had a core group of buddies who were actually close, though. There were four of us for a while, but . . ." He grunted softly as he returned her volley. "After Meryn left, it was just me, Ale, and Eduardo." Sofia hit it back; he let the ball bounce out of bounds, even though he could have easily made the effort to reach it. "Did you ever hear Ale talk about him?"

Sofia shook her head. "Eduardo? No, but again, Ale was in the States for the better part of a decade. In all that time, he only came home a few times."

"Hard to imagine not wanting to come back here," Julián said. "But you know, he was conflicted. About his upbringing."

"What do you mean?"

"He never rejected his wealth, but he wasn't ostentatious at all. He was"—he stuck his fingers through the strings on the racket, testing their tension as he thought—"of a different world." It was clear Julián had thought very highly of her brother.

Or if not, then that was what he wanted her to believe.

"Careful," she said. "If my father hears you saying his house is ostentatious, he might throw you out on the street." She meant it as a joke, but Julián didn't laugh.

He looked away from her, dribbling the ball three times, and just as he was about to serve, he shrugged. "That's part of it, too, I guess. Your dad's imposing presence. Don't get me wrong; I could feel it all the way in LA, and Ale definitely could too. But even with all the stories, Gabriel's . . . not like how I imagined. I suppose it's . . ."

He trailed off, looking up at the night sky for a moment.

"It's what?" she asked, prodding him.

"Oh, nothing. Lost my own father years ago."

She felt the simple pain in his statement. "Ah, I see. I'm sorry."

"Don't be," Julián said. "Relationships are complicated, aren't they?"

She looked at him, wondering what else he might *not* be saying. Everything that came out of his mouth seemed . . . intentional. Sweat glistened on his forehead in the moonlight, and his hair was a little messy from playing. Tucking his racket beneath his arm, he used the hem of his shirt to wipe his face dry. In that second or two, she saw the flash of skin beneath. Not a six-pack like Mateo, but the hint of abs in the shadows, and surrounding the happy trail from his belly button, lines along his hips that pointed downward.

She wondered if that move, too, was intentional.

Julián served, another little grunt. She'd long ago stopped noticing the grunts of opposing players. Often, she was too focused on the game itself to care. But these circumstances were a little different; the stakes were low. She'd already proven her skills, and the way Julián moved on the court had her distracted. So now she couldn't help but equate the grunts with what everyone who never played tennis did: sex.

Or maybe it was just *his* grunts, in particular.

Mateo was out of town, but she'd been bored for a lot longer than he'd been away. Sex with him was obligatory. She'd taught him all the right things to do, and she always finished first, but then couldn't wait to have it all over with so she could go do something she *actually* enjoyed. Plus, his idea of a romantic weekend away was to take her to her own family's hunting lodge two hours outside of town. She loved the place, but it wasn't exactly ripe for intimacy. It was a lazy move he relied on too often, which only served to remind Sofia that her partner had absolutely no imagination, and that life with him could easily fall into boredom.

She tried to focus on the game but found her thoughts returning to Julián's soft groans, the way he moved, the way his muscles looked in the moonlight, and the knowing curve of his grin in the dark.

"I practice here late at night often," she confessed. "But usually, I'm alone. I have to admit, it's nice playing against someone who's a little better than the wall."

Julián barked out a laugh. "You know what, I'll take that as a compliment. You must get tired up against a wall."

Had she misheard, or was he deliberately making it sound sexual?

"You should. Everyone always says tennis is a game where you are your biggest opponent, but that's an oversimplification. You need someone on the other side of the net to push you, keep you on your toes.

Even if they're not quite on the same level as you, skill-wise." She gave him a pointed look, and then served. She was glad to hear him laugh again in response. He almost missed the easy serve.

She gave a little topspin on the next ball, wanting to make him work harder. When she whacked the next one back to him, she felt the old twinge in her shoulder. She'd gotten it a few years ago at a ballet practice, thanks to some idiot partner who hadn't been ready to catch her. Never one to call attention to her injuries, she now just rolled out the shoulder and kept playing.

"And you can't fully test either without someone who knows how to find your weaknesses," he replied, right before he volleyed the next ball over her head. She jumped up and reached, wanting to slam it back down at him, but her shoulder screamed at her. The ball sailed over her head, and when she landed, her free left hand reached instinctively toward the pain. It was so bad, she sat on the ground for a minute, rubbing her shoulder and regaining her breath.

"You okay?" he asked.

She knew—even before he jogged around the net and she got a better look at his face—she knew he'd done it on purpose. Inflicted her pain because he'd seen an opening. Seen, just as he'd said, her weak spot. She'd already suspected he was hiding something, but now she wondered if Julián had a more sinister side, one he, as he'd even admitted earlier, felt the need to keep tight control over. The idea intrigued her, turned her on, even. She loved a good mystery; she liked danger.

Lukas hadn't brought her any dirt on Julián yet—his social media was set to private, which Sofia herself had learned even without Lukas's help. Sofia had tried to go through Ale's social media to learn more about Julián, and though she found a few photos of the two together, her brother's online presence skewed toward minimalism. A picture of the two at some LA food truck with the caption *Buds*. Ale, Julián, and another friend, not tagged, at the beach, unsmiling in a way she was sure was meant to be funny.

She would have expected Lukas to have found a few articles and other mentions online that suggested the twenty-eight-year-old wealthy Mexican American party boy and almost MBA graduate she saw before her. But there was nothing, which meant Julián was either completely uninteresting, or he and his family paid to keep his name off internet search results.

Julián knelt down next to her.

"Just an old injury," she said. She took a deep breath in and out, focusing on her other senses to distract herself until it passed. The court's rich shade of blue. Julián's legs as he crouched beside her, the subtle smell of him, sweat and deodorant. Beyond that, she could smell the chlorine in the air from the pool, the fruity smell of her mother's oleanders.

She came alive as Julián's hand landed gently on her back. "Let me show you a stretch that will help ease the joint pain." His fingers traced her muscles, and he tugged softly at her arm. At first, she yelped—it hurt even more. But then something relaxed, and the movement of his hands on her shoulder blade, finding the tense spot, brought release. She let out a moan.

It was obvious that his attempts at getting close to her, touching her, were driven by other motives. He wanted something, though she couldn't yet say what it was. Nevertheless, the friction she felt between them, the way the air seemed to spark, and his grin reappearing as he watched her eyes flutter in reaction to his massage . . . none of these could be manufactured.

Without realizing it, she'd allowed him to pass some sort of unspoken test. And she'd decided she wanted more of him. More nights like these. She could use someone who wanted an excuse to touch her, someone whom her dad for some reason trusted and had let into their home.

She could find a way to make him useful, like she had done both with Mateo and with Lukas.

She rose to her feet, his hand falling away from her back. Her skin hot where he'd touched it. "I'm sure my mom asked you to babysit me, but I'm a big girl," she said, keeping her tone light. Unable to resist the temptation, she put a hand on his chest and patted him a couple of times, feeling his muscles beneath the shirt, his pounding heart. "And I haven't been bad in a very long time."

She saw his breath hitch in his throat before he responded. "I don't believe that for a second."

She smiled. "My serve."

PART TWO

CHAPTER SEVEN

July

Sofia had said point-blank that she didn't need babysitting, but that hadn't stopped him. Julián had been keeping an eye out for her all week, following at a distance, mostly. Watching from windows. He liked to study her from afar. From a distance, she reminded him less of Alejandro.

Tonight, she walked down San Miguel's narrow sidewalks, ambling, self-assured. In no rush to get wherever she was going, aware of her surroundings, side-stepping white retirees, once even putting her hands on a gray-haired man's shoulders and moving him aside.

Julián watched her maneuver through the tourist throngs. It wasn't like she had a model's catwalk strut, but she was at ease everywhere she went, both on and off the court. He hadn't stopped thinking about their late-night game, how she'd been in such control of her body. He hadn't been able to forget the feeling of her hand on his chest, either, the defiant look in her eye when he'd offered to stretch her shoulder and she'd allowed him to touch her for about a minute before she basically told him to fuck off, with a smile.

Now, a waiter was seating Sofia at the front patio of a restaurant in Plaza Garibaldi. Julián snagged a table at a café across the square where he had a profile view of her; she'd have to crane her neck over her shoulder to spot him. There was plenty of pedestrian traffic to keep him hidden. He only wished he could be closer. What he really wanted was to be within earshot whenever her date arrived.

Her attire suggested it was indeed a date: a dress with a high slit; dangling gold earrings glinting in the sun; her hair done in waves rather than her typical casual topknot. Sofia had mentioned that Mateo was still out of town, so he assumed there was some indiscretion going on. That said, would she really be *this* indiscreet? San Miguel was a small city, and the circles Sofia ran in were even smaller, and prone to gossip. If she were openly cheating, people would know. She ordered a glass of white wine—a sensible choice while it was still light out—and periodically picked up her phone. Julián wished he could see whom and what she was texting.

He wasn't there just because Maria had asked him to keep an eye on her. It was also clear to him that Sofia was hiding more than just her tennis skills. She had the aura of someone with a secret, her demeanor changing when she thought she wasn't being observed, no longer the prim and proper woman she acted like in front of her parents, or at the country club with all those prying eyes. He knew a social chameleon when he saw one.

You're projecting, Alejandro would have been quick to point out.

He breathed. Sipped his own drink—a cappuccino. He wanted to be careful tonight, keep a cool head. Like he'd said during their nighttime tennis game, he needed to maintain control. He hadn't been lying about that.

Sofia sipped her wine and tossed her dark brown mane over one shoulder, exposing her neck. He briefly considered going over and orchestrating a run-in so he could join her. Not a smart move, but a tempting one. She wasn't checking her phone for the time, so maybe whoever she was meeting wasn't going to come for a while. Either that, or it wasn't actually a date. She could be waiting on a friend. Yes, he concluded. That had to be it. She was waiting for another woman.

Fifteen minutes later, she was still alone. He was just about to gesture for his check and walk over when a tall, blond woman with long curls approached. Sofia did that half rise out of her chair to kiss her companion hello on the cheek, and when the woman sat down, he saw that it was Elizabeth, from the club the other day.

He smiled, happy he'd been right, and strangely satisfied that it wasn't an affair. Although, that hadn't been proven yet. They might be lovers too.

He finished his cappuccino and switched to a soda, pulling his phone out of his pocket as a cover, in case Sofia or Elizabeth happened to spot him. Although, rather than scrolling online, he had a few pictures he'd snapped in Gabriel's office the other day when dropping off the tennis racket. Convenient reading material, if not the most riveting.

While keeping an eye on Sofia and Elizabeth, he zoomed in to peruse the documents. A brief about tax implications of the merger, an internal memo about remote work allowances, nothing that held his interest. Nothing to suggest a source of Gabriel's worry, a thorn in his side.

Meanwhile, Sofia and Elizabeth had a long dinner, talking nonstop. He wished he were close enough to eavesdrop. Close enough, at least, to be able to study Sofia. The slope of her neck, the shape of her lips, the exact hue of her eyes. When he thought about her, he felt like a cat pawing at loose threads.

What he saw of Elizabeth from a distance only confirmed what he'd caught onto the day they met. She was not cut from the same cloth as the people around her. Which wasn't to say she wasn't trying very hard to pretend. But, quite literally, her clothes were not of the same designer quality. A scarf was poking out from her purse now, just so happening to cover up the brand's logo. She'd done the same thing at the clubhouse, probably to keep anyone from taking too close a look at the stitching. There'd been other tells too: how she'd stirred her drink with her finger, how she'd stayed quiet when the conversation had turned to travel, hinting that she wasn't nearly as experienced as the others. Certain expressions, as well, pointed at an early life not spent in fancy private schools. As her close friend, Sofia would obviously have already noticed these things, and she'd accepted her company anyway. Which meant either Sofia was like Alejandro in that way—she saw across class divides and they didn't bother her—or she had a specific reason to keep Elizabeth close. Or Elizabeth had her own reasons for making herself necessary.

After a couple of hours of stealing glances, swiping through the photos, and rechecking the internet to make sure the name Julián Villareal had been scrubbed from search results, he noticed a document he'd previously dismissed. What he'd thought was part of the memo was actually, on closer inspection, a medical file. For Maria Velasco. He furrowed his brow and zoomed in, thinking about her near fainting spell the other day, the way she'd offered stress as an excuse. It wouldn't have been strange for them not to say anything about a medical issue to him.

The file didn't give away much—an EKG and a CAT scan that came back with unremarkable results. He swiped through a few more photos in case there was more medical information, then realized he'd been staring at his phone for a while. When he looked up, he noticed the two women standing up from the table. He jolted to his feet, pulling out his wallet, happy that he'd withdrawn a large sum of cash before even entering the country—though until now, nearly all of his expenses had been paid by the Velascos, or put onto their account at the club. Throwing a few bills on the table, he hurried across the plaza, having to avoid a wedding party that was singing and dancing its way through the streets. A girl with a braided crown in her hair tried to stop him and give him a shot of mezcal, but he apologized and flashed her a grin as he passed through the crowd. He could hear Alejandro's voice making fun of him. *There you go again. Hyperfocused on one person, on one goal, and ignoring the opportunity for anything else.*

Past the throng of wedding partyers, he looked around the area, feeling more frantic than he should have. It was getting late, and the girls had probably just hopped into a taxi. The wedding party was moving on down the street, singing along to the mariachi band leading the way. The girl who'd offered the shot was looking at him still, and she smiled a smile he would have been a complete idiot to ignore.

But then he saw a flash of an olive dress and whipped his head around just in time to see Sofia and Elizabeth enter a bar with a doorman and a line out in front. Again, he thought it might be best to forget about Sofia. Go back to the Velascos' house, maybe catch Gabriel in the living room for a nightcap. That might be a faster route to answers.

But a lot less fun.

Instead, he got in line, glad that he'd dressed in a button-up instead of a T-shirt. Most of the other people waiting to be let inside were dressed well, and, based on the music bumping through the door whenever it opened, this was a discoteca. The dark and all those moving bodies would provide good cover. Though it was easy to lose track of someone in a setting like that.

The line advanced slowly, and he could feel himself getting antsy. He kept his eye on the door, in case they left. He wondered if they were meeting Lukas inside, or someone else. People like Sofia rarely went out in small groups. Everything always had to be a big production.

The last time he'd been at a dance club had been in LA, with Alejandro. It had been during those last few months, when Ale had been even more philosophical than usual, bringing up questions of ethics, passages from *The Art of War* just to refute them. If Julián thought Alejandro had actually died by suicide, he might try to connect the dots between those quotes and his death. But there was no such pattern, because it hadn't been Ale's choice at all.

Inside, the club was predictably dark and loud, the sweating, dancing bodies an anonymous mass of exposed limbs, visible only in flashes of strobing red light. He scanned the crowd for Sofia, but from his angle, he couldn't make out a thing. Rolling up his sleeves, already feeling the heat of all those bodies, he pushed his way slowly to a raised bar off to the side.

He wedged his way in between a guy with his shirt unbuttoned way too low, and a trio of white women speaking English who looked like they were barely out of high school. While others jostled for position and sought out the attention of one of the three attractive bartenders, he turned his attention to the crowd, in no hurry to get served.

There were a lot of beautiful people out on the dance floor—a blurred orgy of sweaty bodies, male and female, into which he briefly longed to lose himself—and plenty more crowded into the VIP booths on the other side of the club. Julián assumed Sofia would be seated there, and sure enough, he eventually spotted Elizabeth at a table with a handful of open liquor bottles. There were three guys sitting with her, and Julián couldn't be sure, but it didn't look like any of them were Mateo or Lukas. None of the men were leaning into the girls with the kind of familiarity Mateo and Lukas would have.

He felt a touch at his elbow and turned to see a curly-haired bartender wearing a low-cut top. She didn't bother smiling at him as she nodded her head in a question. "Qué te sirvo?" she asked.

He got himself a sparkling water with a lime, so it would look like a gin and tonic, wanting to blend in with the partying crowd without losing focus. He moved toward the edge of the bar, where he could keep Elizabeth's table in his line of sight. *O divine art of subtlety and secrecy!* Ale would laugh at the fact that a quote from *The Art of War* was going through his mind. But he'd read the little book a few times over on the flight to Mexico, so he wasn't too surprised that some of it had stuck.

Ale was the only other person he knew who could be introspective at nightclubs. He liked to smile and say there was no better place than a nightclub to contemplate what it meant to be alive. "Look at all these people!" he once shouted over the beat of some interminable techno song. "A prime example of hedonism, but just on the surface. They all have a guiding set of beliefs that influence their decisions: What they do here and what they do outside. How they treat the staff, how they treat a stranger who bumps into them and spills a drink on them, what they're willing to do to protect those they love. What they're willing to do *to* the ones they love."

Sofia emerged from the bathroom and joined Elizabeth and the three men. One of them, bearded and wearing a vest, handed her a drink. She waved him off, then reached over to pour her own drink from the fresh tequila bottle at the table, giving him a look that, from Julián's point of view, seemed to say, *Nice fucking try*. He imagined that came just as much from being a young woman as it did from being a Velasco. Their heads always seemed to be turned over one shoulder.

Sofia's group drank a lot, and at one point, he saw Elizabeth pull something out of her purse and place it in Sofia's upturned hand. They smiled at each other, and both brought their hands to their mouths. A party drug, no doubt. So, then—perhaps this was Elizabeth's key role in Sofia's life. Dealer. Or at the very least, enabler.

While he was engaging in some meaningless small talk with an American girl who was *so* impressed with his English, Julián noticed the group get up and go to the dance floor. He chugged down the rest of his drink and asked the blond if she wanted to join him. The excited smile on her face almost made it too easy.

He led her by the hand in that casual way of nightclub touching. The whole reason people came to these places was to touch each other. He brought her along, deep into the middle of the dance floor, trying to reach the spot he'd seen Sofia disappear into.

The music turned to a pop song and the whole room erupted in cheers within the first three notes. Beams of green and purple lights swung around the dance floor, briefly spotlighting Sofia only a few couples away. The blond, who said her name was Lisa, leaned into him and asked him what the song was called. But he pretended to mishear her and said, "I know, right?" Then turned her so he could watch Sofia as they danced.

He could only catch glimpses of her through the crowd. An arm raised over her head as she sang along, her exposed-back dress hanging loose at the top, hinting at the side of her breast. He watched her step close to her dance partner, one of the other guys who'd been at the table with her. She leaned into him, said something in his ear. Julián couldn't catch the reaction, but there was something about their body language that triggered a sting of jealousy. He wondered how Mateo would feel watching her.

Julián pulled Lisa in closer, mimicking Sofia and her partner. He could feel Lisa's eyes on him, could feel her pushing closer into him as they danced. And he didn't mind the fantasy that this created; seeing Sofia, feeling Lisa. He closed his eyes for a moment, relishing the illusion. When he opened them again, he found that he and Lisa had moved even closer to Sofia. They were separated just by a group of four women dancing all together, holding their drinks and whooping loudly.

He stared over Lisa's shoulder for a little while longer, becoming more and more convinced that Sofia's intentions with her dance partner weren't innocent, jealousy moving through his pulse. But if she *was* messing around on Mateo, he might use that to his advantage. He didn't know how or when, but he'd learned in his stint at business school that leverage was always useful.

As they moved closer and closer to Sofia and her partner, the music seemed to fall away, the heat of the room struggling against the air-conditioning, the slight shake in the floor from all those dancing bodies, even Lisa's hands on his back, his neck, her legs straddling his as they danced. There was just Sofia.

Then someone bumped into him, and he heard a man's voice apologize, and he realized he'd gotten *too* close. He turned over his shoulder and saw the man Sofia was dancing with, only now she wasn't with him.

"Everything okay?" Lisa asked, picking up on his sudden lack of attention.

He didn't bother answering, scanning the entire room until he spotted Sofia's slitted dress and brown waves weaving expertly through the crowd. With a quick goodbye to Lisa, who looked appropriately surprised, he took off after Sofia. He got stuck behind a couple who were practically having sex on the dance floor, and by the time he found another route toward the outskirts of the club, he'd lost sight of her.

Did it matter? Would he have learned anything important, or was he getting sucked into the thrill of chasing her?

Before he could keep asking himself silly questions, he thought he saw her leaving through a fire exit in the back. He followed behind, but when he made it to the exit, he found it was locked. He tried again, almost certain he'd seen her leave through this very door, though who knew for sure in the dark amid the strobing lights? He went all the way back through the club so he could leave through the main entrance, then speed-walked through the now-quiet streets to reach the alley outside the exit in question. He found her standing there, smoking a cigarette.

She was alone, leaning against the wall near the door, half-hidden in the shadows. It was only when he was a few steps away that he noticed her hair was lighter; she wasn't in a dress but a shirt. It wasn't Sofia at all. It was Elizabeth.

He thought about just walking past her or turning around, but she pushed off from the wall, tossed her cigarette on the ground in one fluid motion, and called out to him. "Porque carajo nos estas siguiendo, güey?" She stepped directly in front of him, her blond hair swaying forward, and he could smell the cigarette and booze on her breath.

"Whoa," he said, holding his hands up, palms out. "I'm not following anyone."

Elizabeth scoffed and started digging in her purse, coming away with a fresh cigarette. "You just happened to be on the same dance floor as us?" Her pupils were dilated, a sheen of sweat dotting her hairline. There was a wild look to her eyes, like a cornered animal.

"I felt like going out," Julián said evenly.

Elizabeth lit another cigarette and blew the smoke out the side of her mouth, stepping away and seeming to calm down. "Just tell me. Was it Gabriel who sent you?"

Julián's brow furrowed. "Velasco?"

Elizabeth coughed out a laugh. "Whatever. Tell him what you saw; I don't give a shit. But don't insult my intelligence by pretending you weren't here snooping."

With that, she walked past Julián, bumping his shoulder when she passed him, then heading down the alley and turning the corner toward the club's entrance. He was left with a strange feeling in his stomach. It wouldn't shock him to learn that Gabriel had a history of asking people to keep tabs on his daughter—after all, it's why Julián was here right now. Maria had asked him to do exactly that. But what nagged at him was the way Elizabeth had acted almost as if *she* was the one Gabriel might be tracking.

Driving back to the Velascos' estate in the 1968 Porsche Speedster he'd rented (though he wasn't planning on telling people it was merely a rental), he thought again of what Maria had said by the pool earlier in the week. *The thorn in Gabriel's side.* Could Elizabeth have been that thorn? It wasn't impossible that she had something on him, knew one of his secrets, maybe something she'd gleaned through her connection with Sofia. And she was using it to extort him. Needed the money, naturally.

In the alley, his brain had still been swimming in images of Sofia— her body lit by the flashing lights in the club, her smile, the way her hair moved. Now, he reminded himself again why he was here in San Miguel. His friend had been killed in LA, and someone in this town knew it, and knew why. And maybe that someone was Elizabeth.

Had she perhaps been extorting Alejandro for years—maybe even over something he hadn't done, some awful thing about Gabriel that Ale, like a good son, wanted to keep hidden? Or more likely—had she been doing Gabriel's bidding, keeping tabs on Ale? For all Julián knew, that might pay better than dealing party drugs to his daughter. But would she have a motive for blackmailing both father and son?

And going as far as to murder Ale . . . Julián didn't know enough about her to sense whether she had it in her. Still, he knew what it was like when desperation took over every cell in the body. When it felt like the only way to survive the next moment was through violence. That much he understood.

He'd have to keep a closer eye on Elizabeth.

CHAPTER EIGHT

Sofia's shoulder had been acting up the last few days, and the hangover wasn't helping, so after only thirty minutes on the courts, she had to retreat to the locker room for a shower and sauna. She booked herself a massage for later that afternoon, too, since she'd been hunched over her computer, poring over Velcel merger documents, making sure the payroll ledgers and invoice spreadsheets read the way they were supposed to.

Sitting there in the heat, half-heartedly rubbing at her shoulder, she thought about how Julián had stretched it for her the other night. It didn't surprise Sofia that he'd followed her and Elizabeth to the club last night—she'd had a feeling he'd been watching her all week, and this development only cemented her conviction that he was up to something shady.

What exactly did Julián want?

She thought about how his hands might feel on her. Pictured how the night might have gone if she'd shifted away from Elizabeth's friend Iñaki on the dance floor and found Julián in the darkness. If she'd let his fingers linger on her skin, tracing the bared part of her back. The way he moved on the tennis court made her certain he knew how to move in other places too.

"Sofia!" A shrill voice drilled into her very core. She knew who it was right away, just from the level of unnecessary excitement in the woman's voice.

Sofia wished she were wearing earphones. If this were anywhere else in the world, she would just pretend to be asleep. But this was the Lomas Lindas Country Club, her father's domain. Anything Sofia did that could be fodder for gossip—like, say, hissing at Nadia, or taking off her towel and whipping her with it—would certainly make it back to her father, who would go into a whole rant about the Velasco name and acting worthy of it.

She opened her eyes and mustered a facial expression that could maybe be called a smile. "Hi, Nina," she said, enjoying the slight shock on her unwelcome companion's face. "How are you?"

Sofia could tell Nadia was swallowing her hurt and deciding to move on without correcting Sofia, which was exactly what Sofia assumed would happen. It was funny how much people adhered to decorum, even when it caused them pain.

"I hear congratulations are in order!" Nadia said, forcing cheeriness into her voice. "I swear I heard like six different people talking about it just now. You must be so excited, though maybe not surprised. The way Mateo looks at you, I think we all knew it was coming."

Sofia sat up now. "What are you talking about?"

Nadia tilted her head, confused. She had a little smudge of makeup at the corner of her eye, and it was starting to drip in the heat. Sofia waited for her to elaborate. "I'm sorry; I didn't realize it was a secret." She feigned a grimace. "You know how the rumor mill just takes on a life of its own. I won't repeat it until there's a formal—"

"Announcement of what?" Sofia cut in. She knew what was coming, of course. Still, she wanted the confirmation. And she wanted it from this intrusive stranger who was clearly too invested in her life.

"Your . . ." Nadia trailed off. "I'm sorry; maybe it's none of my business."

Through the steam, Sofia could see the hesitation on Nadia's face, second-guessing herself, wondering if she should just shut up. Now she remembered Nadia in high school, tall and pretty, but so desperate to be liked, so desperate to please. "It's okay," Sofia said, softening her tone.

"I didn't know the word was spreading around already." She offered a laugh. "Probably my mom. You know how moms are."

Nadia chuckled nervously, averting her eyes, but her relief was palpable. "Right, yeah, of course. When I got engaged, I swear mine finally learned how to use social media just so she could tell as many people as possible."

And there it was. Sofia wasn't entirely surprised. Mateo had been telling her for months that he'd been looking for rings, teasing her about all the different ways he might propose (each cheesier and gaudier than the last). Wasn't this what *everyone* expected—what they'd been working toward?

But things were, as always, more complicated than they seemed. Sofia had uses for Mateo, obviously. Her dad was going to name her COO soon, something he was less likely to do if she wasn't a huge factor in securing the merger. The merger might never have even happened if she and Mateo weren't together. But marriage was a fate she'd been hoping to avoid. It was a parachute she intended to deploy only if it became necessary.

It was possible that Mateo was the one who'd spread the "news," perhaps while drunk in some club in Polanco in Mexico City, bragging to friends from college that he and Sofia were practically engaged while glossing over the tiny detail that Sofia hadn't actually said yes yet. He probably couldn't even fathom that she might *not* say yes. But while he was confident and a blabbermouth, as well as desperate to marry Sofia, he wasn't insecure enough to try to use social pressure to coerce her into it. Which made the prime suspect her mom, or perhaps both her parents. A manipulative power play to force her hand, to make sure people saw her a certain way.

And there was only one reason she could think of that they wanted to control her image in this moment, with the merger on the horizon.

Someone had blabbed about her partying.

The sauna door opened, and two women in their sixties entered. Sofia smiled at Nadia.

"So good to see you!" She rose to her feet and, without waiting for a response, made her escape.

◆ ◆ ◆

Sofia arrived home fuming but knew better than to show it.

Wanting to slam the door behind her as she entered, she decided instead to toss her tennis bag down on the floor, something she knew both her father and mother hated. She waited for one of them to emerge into the foyer and ask what the noise was all about, but only Amalia appeared, asking if she could get her anything to drink.

"Y mis papás?" she asked, tamping her anger down. She had a lot of practice after all.

She found her dad in the courtyard, drinking champagne. As soon as he saw her, he called to her mom, who was out in the pool house.

A few moments later, her mom came out, beaming a smile and heading straight for the champagne. They didn't have the decency to look ashamed of themselves, or even surprised. Sofia wanted to storm over to them and unleash the tirade that she'd practiced in her head. One of these days she might. But today was not that day.

Her mom approached her, her cheeks flushed, either from the sun or just the joy of getting to tell all her friends that her daughter was engaged. "Felicidades!" she cried, as if the surprise were on Maria's side and not the other way around. Gabriel stood at the table, holding eye contact with Sofia. She could just imagine the *Art of War* quote that was reverberating in his manipulative head. *To subdue the enemy without fighting is the acme of skill.*

"Anyone going to explain to me why people are congratulating me on an engagement that hasn't happened?"

"Yet," Gabriel said immediately. His grin was slight, but that didn't keep it from being any less of the shit-eating variety.

"You could have at least waited until Mateo did it himself," she said. "He was shopping for rings already."

He'd called her a couple of times when she was driving over from the club, but she'd been too furious to answer, practicing rants in her head that she knew she wouldn't deliver. Mateo would pretend to be mad at their parents, but on his voicemails she'd heard the joy in his voice, joy she wasn't ready yet to join in on.

"Come, come," Maria said, leading her to the table. "Have a glass. Who cares how it was announced."

Her mom placed a champagne flute into her hand and then reached up and touched Sofia's cheek with such tenderness that she felt some of that rage start to dissipate. Since Alejandro's death, Sofia couldn't remember seeing her mom this genuinely happy.

Sofia took a sip of the champagne. After kissing each of her cheeks, her father stepped back and looked her in the eye, and she felt sure, suddenly, that all this was his doing. She knew he liked controlling her, liked exerting power whenever he could, but this was egregious even for him. The Velascos did not like to be sloppy. They were either desperate or making a point.

Maybe both.

"We're so happy for you, cariño. And I'm glad you had a chance to work off that hangover at the club; you look very fresh and lovely. Let's focus on that instead of who said what to whom and when."

So there it was. The hangover. He was implying he knew she'd been out partying last night, and he very much didn't like it. He'd wanted to send a message that she needed to behave and not risk her relationship with Mateo. The merger must have him on edge, especially with the final audit fast approaching. But she hadn't seen her father this morning, or the night before. So if he knew she'd been out last night, at a dance club he despised, no less, then there was really only one explanation: Julián had definitely ratted her out.

She clenched and unclenched her fist at her side. Over her father's shoulder, she saw her mom taking a seat again, topping off her glass. "I know it's early and there's no date yet, hija, but I want to know any thoughts you have for the wedding. It's never too early to plan."

Sofia plopped down in a chair opposite her parents and took another long pull from the champagne. It was the expensive champagne that her dad always served guests, making sure to leave bottles around so they could see the labels, but which Sofia thought was too sweet. She'd left the club in a hurry, before eating lunch, and the champagne landed pleasantly in her belly.

Her mom's phone dinged on the table, and she reached for it and immediately started typing in her slow way. "Are you getting as many congratulations as me?" she asked, beaming. "Sylvia Lozano is already trying to get me to use her son's catering company." She sucked her teeth and shook her head.

This was what Sofia was in for, for however many months or years until she and Mateo got married. The chisme, the cattiness, the focus on how things would appear. And for almost every decision that would be made, Sofia's own preferences would be an afterthought. Not that she cared, necessarily. She had never been the kind to fantasize about a wedding.

The anger bubbled up again, mixed with the buzz of the alcohol on her empty stomach. Sofia finished off the rest of her champagne and stood.

"I'm going to see what kind of shit show of notifications is waiting for me on my phone," she said.

Besides, the person she needed to talk to wasn't out here. She'd seen his stupid old car in the driveway, so she knew he was around somewhere.

Her mom congratulated her again and gave her a warm hug, which made her feel sick to her stomach. The competitor in her absolutely hated empty, unearned praise, and she'd done nothing to become engaged. For that matter, neither had Mateo.

She went back into the house, grabbed her tennis bag, and headed toward the bedrooms, thinking not of her own room but of the guest room whose occupant she had to thank for the fact that she was now engaged. Engaged! All because a fucking stranger had tattled to her parents that he'd seen her dancing.

She gave only a single knock of warning before she barged in, half hoping that she'd catch him snooping again, catch him doing anything egregious enough that her dad would toss his ass out, even if he was Gabriel's little spy.

He was on the bed, an open laptop resting beside him on a pile of pillows. Unfortunately, he was shirtless, and her eyes betrayed her by taking in the sight of him before her brain caught them and unleashed the tongue-lashing she needed to deliver.

"Let me guess," she said, entering and crossing her arms over her chest. "You're trying to find someone else to fuck over now?"

"What?"

"Or are you researching other ways to just screw *me*, specifically?"

Her cheeks burning, she realized her phrasing probably could have been better, but decided to move past it. "Have you been here just spying on me the whole time? Did my parents hire you?" She stepped to him, anger bubbling closer to the surface with every question. "Are you even here for that bullshit reason you said, or was that a lie too? Because I knew from the second I laid eyes on you that you were full of shit."

Julián shut his laptop and set it on the nightstand, swinging his legs around. When he stood up, she saw that his soft linen pants were riding low on his hips. She couldn't help but trace the trail of hair leading from his belly button down, right between the two angled lines just below his hip bones.

"Whoa, slow down. What are you talking about?"

"Don't try to play it off like you don't know," Sofia hissed. "You were following us!" She took one step closer to him, trying to ignore the outline of his abs, the way his muscles flexed just slightly in reaction to her movements. In an odd way, it kind of thrilled her, how he'd been watching her, tracing her. Clearly, she had power over him, even if he'd gone and offered up the lowest hanging fruit he could find just to please her father. "So?" She raised her eyebrows.

"I wasn't—"

"Bullshit!" He needed to be put in his place. Needed to know who was *really* in charge here.

Julián looked away for a second before glancing back down at her. He could have been avoiding her gaze, looking for a lie, or gathering his thoughts. She could see the ripple of hesitation across his face, the way he bit his lip—to keep from saying something he shouldn't? Or was it something else? She could feel the heat coming off his body. Anger or desire? Or was it both? This close, she could see the flecks of gold in his eyes. It was annoying how captivating they were.

"Fine," Julián finally said. "I *was* following you."

"Ha. Of course I'm right. So who put you up to it, then? My father? Or you were just being a creep?"

"No, nothing like that." He took a slight step backward, but he was close to the bed and there wasn't anywhere for him to go. She saw his nostrils flare, and something about the fact that he was angry pleased her. Like she'd gotten under his skin. "I was going to that club anyway, and then I heard some guys talking about you and Elizabeth. Looking over at you in a way I didn't like. I was worried about you. After what happened to Alejandro, can you blame me for being protective?"

After what happened to Alejandro. There it was again. The suggestion that his death had neither been an accident nor suicide, but something altogether more sinister.

But she was too riled up to focus on that now. Here was yet another man trying to tell her he knew what was best for her. Even if his intentions had been good, which she doubted, he could go fuck himself. As if she didn't know how to look out for herself. "Right. You're not my boyfriend, and you're not my family." She gave him a little shove. "You can keep your worries to yourself." He stumbled backward at her touch, but caught himself and grabbed her wrists—as if to balance himself. His hands were on hers, and her hands were on his chest, and he was breathing heavily.

She found that she was breathing deep and quick, either from yelling at him, or something else. She wanted to keep telling him off. Rant about how he had no right to follow her, that she could take care of herself. That she didn't care to play whatever game he was here to play.

The words didn't come, though. She stared up at him, feeling her heart pounding in her chest. Or was that his? His skin was warm, his grip on her wrists firm but not hard, not painful. The way he held her—with conviction—was completely unlike the way Mateo did. There was an intensity, an urgency. She leaned just a tiny bit closer and heard his breath catch in his chest. A soft inhale. He was staring at her mouth too. And then, they were kissing.

Some angry, fervent part of her knew she'd been wanting this ever since he arrived. From the way he kissed back, she would have guessed he had been too.

Even though it was hungry kissing, their bodies pressed hard against each other, she could sense the softness of his lips. His tongue darted across hers, and she let out a soft moan. He was still holding her wrists, and though she liked the feel of his hands on her (nothing like Mateo's clammy palms), she freed one hand and reached up, pulling his head toward her to make the kiss deeper.

She knew that this was against all her best interests, but she couldn't stop herself, didn't want to. Now he let go of her other wrist and ran a hand up her side, then along her neck, running his fingers through her hair. He stumbled backward as their momentum pushed him toward the bed, and his lips pulled away for a moment. It could have been the right time to step away, get herself together, maybe go take a cold shower.

But that couldn't be further from what she wanted. She wanted more of Julián, more of this. And so she cut the distance between them, pressing up against his bare chest, and sending them both tumbling to the bed.

CHAPTER NINE

April

Alejandro always got what he wanted, and everyone knew it. But he was so charming, so easygoing, people rarely held this phenomenon against him. His two closest friends in business school, Eduardo and Julián, were both great tennis players, though Julián always struck Alejandro as restrained on the court, whereas Eduardo was studied, fiercely competitive, always driving Alejandro to prove himself. But in any group of three handsome, twenty-eight-year-old men, there were bound to be tensions. They couldn't all win the same prizes and accolades; couldn't all be coveted by the same woman at the same time. The problems had probably been simmering for a long time beneath the surface.

Sometimes two of them would play tennis on the school courts, sometimes all three. Eduardo often practiced alone on the courts after Alejandro and Julián left. On a day when Julián had been in class, Eduardo had stayed for about half an hour after playing against Alejandro and was heading into the locker room when he heard the shower going.

There were some scattered, used towels in the locker room and a forgotten sock beneath one of the benches. Other than the weak pitter-patter of a lone shower running, the only other sound was Eduardo fiddling with his keys to find the one for his padlock. At least, at first. There was the creak of Eduardo's locker opening, and the rattle as he shoved his racket inside for safekeeping while he pulled his towel, flip-flops, and shampoo out of his duffel bag. It was when he shut the locker again that he heard the voices.

A giggle, maybe. He froze, sure he'd heard wrong. Or maybe it had never been quiet enough for the sounds from the women's locker room to carry over. He wrote off the sound and slung the towel over his shoulder, then headed toward the showers, rolling his neck to crack it and ease his tired muscles.

Later, he would argue that he had to pass by the working shower in order to get to the next free stall. That the curtains never quite touched the walls and there was always something visible between the gaps, though common practice was to turn your gaze away as you walked past. But how could Eduardo turn his gaze away when he heard what he heard? The sound of soft laughter, of hitched breath. And then, through the gap, the flash of a woman's body—and Alejandro's. His hands on her skin. Hot water flowing over both of them. Eduardo would have looked away faster, he told them later, if it hadn't been for the fact that he'd recognized the girl.

Meryn. Julián's girlfriend. At the time, anyway. That would soon change.

"I'll tell Julián," Alejandro told Eduardo later, contrite. "I didn't mean for you to see us; I didn't plan for any of it. But I'll do the right thing."

Eduardo raised his hands. "It's none of my business." Though in truth, he liked having something over Julián. A secret just between him and Alejandro. If anyone had asked Julián about it later, he'd have said that Eduardo had been waiting a long time to get just such a power play lined up. That Eduardo had had it out for him anyway, was jealous. Eduardo himself would have said it wasn't jealousy at all, but scorn. Alejandro would simply have said it was all just healthy competition, that it was a person's competitors who made them stronger.

Maybe, now that he was dead, what Alejandro would have said didn't matter anymore.

CHAPTER TEN

The light framing the guest room curtains filtered in weak and gray at first, then pink with the sunrise, into the full brightness of morning. He could tell there was a bright blue sky out there, a beautiful day to go out and enjoy.

Except he remained in bed, exhausted and unable to break the inertia of lying on the mattress replaying what had happened. He hadn't slept all night. The smell of Sofia permeated the room. She had left his room yesterday and snuck away to shower before they all sat for dinner together, where he'd had to sit and not stare at her the entire meal, his pulse pounding in his wrists. It was almost like a fever dream, the flashes that kept replaying in his head. Her face the moment before she kissed him. Her face after she'd pushed him onto the bed and straddled him, sitting up to look down at him, lips swollen and glistening, her hair falling into his eyes. The look she'd given him, inscrutable save for the hunger.

He couldn't forget the feeling of her skin on his, the weight of her against him, rocking her hips into his, the desire he'd had to chase after her when she climbed off him, still fully clothed. She'd paused at the door just to look back and wink before leaving him wondering what the hell had just happened.

And she was officially engaged to someone else. Which made what had happened between them that much more complicated.

He'd had to work hard to avoid her eyes at dinner. The meal had been a Thai beef salad served with sticky rice and fresh spring rolls—a menu that got him thinking about the nights when he would pick up Thai food and bring it over to Alejandro's.

He would force Ale to take a study break, to join him in sipping on a tequila blanco. Sometimes, it'd be all of them: Ale, Julián, Eduardo, and Meryn, giving their friend an hour or two to unwind before he threw himself back in. Sometimes it was just two or three of them. Nights when Ale allowed himself to get philosophical.

"Every case study I have to read carries the double burden of also keeping me off the tennis court," Ale had said one evening to Eduardo and Julián, setting down his spicy basil noodles. "I know studying business is more important for my future. That I'm not going pro at this point, and an MBA will serve me much better, no pun intended. But the truth is . . ." He sighed, staring off in the direction of Dodger Stadium. "Everything other than tennis feels meaningless."

"My friend who's into philosophy would call that nihilism," Eduardo had replied.

Ale hadn't laughed; he'd just taken a swallow of his tequila. "Yeah, that sounds about right," he said. "I'll tell you, it's a lot more interesting to read about it than to live it."

Ale had invited Julián over that night to tell him something important, though he hadn't broached the subject at that point. Maybe because Eduardo had been there too. It had been a chilly night, all three of them wearing hoodies as they sipped on their tequila and passed a joint around, which Ale preferred since it came with no hangover and allowed him to wake up early to hit the courts. Julián usually stayed away from the stuff—he liked to be in control of situations. But that evening, with the Los Angeles lights cutting into the night sky, battling against the stars to provide the light, he had allowed himself to relax and enjoy it. It was the last carefree night before everything went south.

Pushing aside those memories, he dragged himself out of the guest bedroom in San Miguel. He wasn't about to lose the opportunity Gabriel had presented to him.

The offer had come the night before. At dinner, he had asked casual questions he'd hoped would suss out the status of the merger without it seeming like he was prying. After all, his interest was sincere—he and Ale really had wanted to start their own company. In certain moments, he could almost forget that his friend was dead. He could almost imagine he was just here to get some advice from a pro. To get introduced to the right contacts, to build his own Rolodex. And there was one other motive for his questions: getting his mind off Sofia, who was sitting beside him, acting nonchalant.

"I'll admit," Gabriel said, "I had the impression that your schooling didn't have much practical application. I sent Ale to UCLA mostly to pick up on the jargon, impress guys from Wharton who spoke the same language. Maybe meet people who would be useful down the line. But I didn't think he was cut out to run a business, at least not yet." He'd turned his attention to his meal. "But I like you, Julián. You're smart. School obviously taught you something. Maybe I was too quick to judge." Gabriel chewed thoughtfully. After he'd swallowed, he told Julián to ride with him to the office Monday morning so he could sit in on the merger meeting. "Lots of board members. I'm not sure I trust them all."

"Is that a good idea?" Sofia asked.

Maria had cleared her throat before Gabriel could respond. "No more business talk at the table, please," she said with a tight smile. Gabriel nodded and let her change the subject, but when dinner was done and they were making their way to the courtyard for a sherry, he pulled Julián aside.

"My offer stands. Come with me Monday. You can sit in and keep an eye on the board members for me, just like Maria told me you've been keeping an eye on Sofia. I could use an extra set of sharp eyes, if you catch what I mean." He said it so casually, as if he weren't directly implying that his enemies were everywhere, including close at hand.

◆ ◆ ◆

After the meeting, Gabriel insisted that his guest come along with the execs from both companies for drinks.

Perfect, he thought. Nothing like a few shots of tequila to loosen some tongues, spill some secrets. At the very least, stoke some rumors, which he was starting to feel desperate for. He'd been in San Miguel almost two weeks now, and he didn't have much more than a list of names and a series of hunches and suspicions.

The meeting itself hadn't been entirely interesting. No one shot Gabriel dirty looks; no one made little comments that could be taken for hints that someone had murderous intent toward the Velascos. The only thing he learned of any note was that the merger seemed to be hitting a few snags with the audits, but that didn't necessarily mean anything. He knew such processes were complicated, and bumps were to be expected.

The bar was on the rooftop of a boutique hotel, overlooking the Parroquia, its near-pink Gothic towers rising majestically above a couple of palm fronds. The sun was still shining brightly when the first round of drinks arrived, and a few hours later when the sun dipped behind the hills, the drinks were still flowing. The men's ties had long ago been taken off, their jackets hanging over the back of their chairs, their shirts unbuttoned to reveal tufts of chest hair.

By evening, business topics had been abandoned, and they were arguing loudly about La Liga MX, the Mexican soccer league. Not knowing anything about it, he couldn't chime in much. Although that was better than getting caught in conversation with the one board member whose kid had also been an MBA student at UCLA. The overeager board member kept pulling out his phone, insisting on texting his son and putting the two of them in touch. Rather than call attention to himself in this way, he quietly headed inside to the bar to take a breather and ingratiate himself by ordering a round of beers and appetizers for the table—charged to Gabriel's account, of course. He wished Sofia had come, but she'd grabbed a stack of folders at the meeting and said she was going to work with the accounting department to make sure the potential snags got ironed out as soon as possible.

Inside the bar, the atmosphere was almost jarringly different. Just a few tables of people grabbing an after-work drink, a couple scoping out the menu for an aperitif. It was quiet, a far cry from the raucous party that Gabriel's crew had evolved into. Julián had a pleasant buzz from keeping up, but also from the inclusion.

Suddenly a hand was gripping his shoulder and turning him forcefully around.

His fists instinctively clenched, one arm starting to cock back before he recognized the face. It was Sofia's short friend, Lukas. Julián furrowed his brow and relaxed his fists. He was confused for a moment about why Lukas might be there, until he remembered that he was a member of the club.

"Hey," he said, but was at a loss as to what to follow that up with. They'd only met once at the clubhouse, though he had seen Lukas picking up Sofia from the house on a couple of occasions.

"I know what you're doing," Lukas said with a smile that was likely meant to be disarming.

Julián looked around for some clue as to what he was talking about. "What am I doing?" He turned to look at the terrace, wondering if he had offended Gabriel in some way, broken some tacit rule.

But then Lukas's hand came up and landed on Julián's cheek. It wasn't exactly a slap, but it felt like the threat of one, as if Lukas were trying to tell him that he was thinking about it. Julián was momentarily frozen, unsure what was happening.

"Stop sniffing around Sofia," Lukas said.

Julián wanted to laugh. Lukas, he saw now, had that Chihuahua dog energy. Real yappy, eager to fight, as if that would prove how tough he was.

"I'm onto you," Lukas said now. "Whatever it is you say you are, it's a load of crap. I saw that little post you put up on your social media. Is this what you call 'off the grid'? 'Getting back to nature,' are you?" Lukas snorted, and Julián shook his head to disguise the way his stomach dropped.

"You don't know what you're talking about." He laughed dismissively. "I was on a hike in Big Sur when I decided I should come pay my respects, not that it's any of your business. It's no one's business, actually. Which is why I never bothered to update my social media." He looked toward the bartender, who was cracking open beers. He'd been happy with the social media post, but clearly it raised more questions than it answered. It was too late now to do anything differently; he just had to hope that it was only Lukas who was suspicious of anything. He reminded himself that Lukas didn't seem to actually know anything. He was just grasping at straws.

But Sofia's friend apparently wasn't done. He reached out and gripped Julián's shirt, even tugging him forward. "I know your type," Lukas growled. "Alejandro was the same. Guys who think everything you want belongs to you. Stay away from Sofia; stay away from the Velascos."

In one fluid motion, he knocked Lukas's hands off him, then grabbed him by the lapels of his stupid beige blazer. Lukas tried to squirm away, but Julián had two solid fistfuls and wasn't about to let him go anywhere.

He lifted Lukas off the ground and swung him around onto one of the bar stools. Lukas's back hit the bar and nearly knocked over an empty glass that had been sitting there when Julián arrived. The expression on Lukas's face changed drastically, especially as Julián held on and pressed his fists into Lukas's pecs, digging into the top of his rib cage.

"You shut your fucking mouth," he said, leaning in to growl the words into Lukas's ear. "I'd better not hear you accuse me of anything. And if I ever hear you bad-mouth Alejandro again, I'll seriously hurt you. Do you understand me?"

Lukas nodded quietly, fear in his eyes, fear that Julián was frankly happy to see. Then his pupils shifted slightly as he registered someone's approach. Julián let go, and when the bartender reached them, he quickly grabbed the handful of beers the bartender had delivered.

"Lukas!" Gabriel's voice came from behind. "Gusto verte. Todo bien?" He clapped an unaware hand on Lukas's back and then reached to the bar to help Julián with the other beers. Julián kept his eyes locked on Lukas's. When it was clear that the other man was too scared to say anything, Julián turned and smiled at Gabriel.

"I might have to slow down soon," he said. "Can't keep up with you old guys."

"Hey, watch who you're calling old," Gabriel responded, swaying a little. He nodded at Lukas and told him to say hello to his parents for him; then he and Julián turned away and carried the beers back to the table outside.

For the rest of the night, Julián kept looking inside the bar to where Lukas was sitting, sulking at the table with his friends. He was clearly obsessed with Sofia. Going so far as to snoop on Julián's social media? That overprotectiveness was not the kind a mere friend exhibited. Was it the kind a jealous would-be lover exhibited, though, or something darker, more sinister?

Could Lukas's distaste for Alejandro have led him to snoop around the Velasco family, keep tabs on Alejandro, potentially start blackmailing and threatening him? What else did Lukas know, or think he knew? He was clearly sneaky enough to do some digging. And judging by the fact that he was a club member and a longtime friend of the Velascos, and by that very real Patek Phillipe on his wrist, he had the resources and connections to dig very deep. He had been careful so far, but he'd have to make sure not to let his guard down around Lukas, or in general.

Whether Lukas had it in him to be a killer was another question altogether.

Though he thought he'd calmed down, he realized now that his fists were still clenched, his neck still throbbing with elevated blood pressure. He had to get to the bottom of this mess, and soon. Someone had to pay for what had happened to Alejandro.

He wasn't sure he could contain himself much longer.

CHAPTER ELEVEN

July

It had been two weeks since the leaked announcement, and already, they were celebrating her engagement. Sofia stood on the balcony of the clubhouse restaurant, watching the crowd mingle below, all vibrant silk dresses and fitted jackets, photograph-ready. Everyone came to these things to be seen; the free food and open bar were just bonuses. She was not surprised at how quickly her mother had moved to plan an engagement party. Within a few days, she'd already been running a guest list past Sofia.

Maria had taken her aside in the enclosed rose garden by the pool after breakfast the other day. Tears welled in her eyes as she took Sofia's hands and in a rare moment of transparency said, "You know I have only one wedding to look forward to now." The intensity caught Sofia off guard. Usually, her mother tried to hide her grief. Or perhaps her father had simply forced her to hide it for so long that the effort was now second nature. "I just want you to be happy. And of course . . ." The rest, she left unspoken. *And you want* me *to be happy, too, don't you?*

It wasn't that Sofia didn't believe her mother's grief—she did. It was one of the most honest things about her family, and Sofia felt her mother's grief even more deeply than she felt her own. It triggered a protective instinct in her, one that felt particular to the Velascos, for better or worse. They looked after their own. It was just that each person did it in their own particular way.

Gabriel, for example, claimed to want Sofia's happiness, but what he really wanted was gratitude and obedience, a big plastic smile for the sake of appearances. He saw her as a chess piece, not a chess master, despite everything she did for him and the company.

But Maria was truly happy for her. Sofia knew everything her mother did, she did for the family, sometimes to a fault. Still, there was a pressure in her words, an expectation. Even in her most emotionally vulnerable state, her mother still needed to control Sofia too.

The irony was that neither of them saw past the ends of their noses, to the fact that Sofia was always two steps ahead of them. That she, too, was playing a game. She had to. If she didn't, she got played.

Mateo, predictably, was eating up the adoring attention of her parents' friends and relations. From the restaurant balcony, she watched him shove canapés into his mouth, letting crumbs from the mini tostadas de atún fall to the floor. She listened to him show ridiculous enthusiasm for whatever anyone said: "No mames, güey!" *My fiancé, ladies and gentlemen.* Sofia suppressed a sigh, then turned and saw Julián headed toward her.

She couldn't help but smile before she got a hold of herself and suppressed that too. There was a glint in his eye as he sauntered over, a barely hidden shit-eating grin on his face that was frankly endearing. He looked like a teenager who'd just made out for the first time. She preferred this approach to his arriving with a pout, disappointed over her engagement. Jealousy wasn't a good look on anyone who had no claim to her. Not that anyone really did.

Oh, she felt loyalty, of course. To Mateo, absolutely. To her family. All of it, even if Alejandro would have had trouble believing her say that. She felt loyalty to Velcel, too, since it was an extension of the Velascos. Strangely, it was the easiest of all to throw herself into. As if by doing so, she was proving her loyalty to the family. Proving that she would work her ass off to keep the company running, protecting the lives and reputation that it had built for them all in the process.

But that was her choice, and if she ever chose to stop caring for her family, or Velcel, or Mateo, none of them could force her to continue.

Julián raised his champagne glass. "I hear congratulations are in order."

"That's what I hear too." They clinked glasses. She searched his face for some obvious emotion. Amusement or embarrassment or hurt. Did she see all three? Or none?

"Congratulations, then." He turned so he was at her side, facing the party with her, his shoulder brushing hers. His expression now even more inscrutable.

"It's my mother you should be congratulating."

"Ah well, in that case I hope she and Mateo have a beautiful life together."

Sofia laughed. A server came by holding a tray of spoons with a bite of ceviche in each one. Sofia and Julián both grabbed one. The tart citrus lit up her tongue. "Seriously, this party really is for my mother. She's come at this thing with the energy of a spoiled girl who gets to plan her own quinceañera."

"Is that so?" Julián smiled.

"Get this: she not only has a list from her five favorite wedding venues of all the available dates for the next two years, but she also managed to get the names of couples who already put deposits down."

"All right, a little intense. But that's not—"

"And since her favorite venue is taken on her preferred date, she's already digging up dirt on the couple to convince them to change the date. They happen to be family friends."

"Jesus. Sweet Maria? I don't see her having that in her."

"Yeah, well. That's my family for you." She took a sip from her drink, regretting her loose tongue for a moment. Thankfully he didn't keep the conversation going.

She noticed him looking in the direction of Mateo, holding court by the bar, laughing with a handful of his friends, who were no doubt making jokes about Mateo's life being over now. Watching Julián swallow the ceviche, she couldn't help but stare at his lips, at his smirk, at the way his Adam's apple bobbed when he swallowed. She hated that she was this attracted to him—it was a bit of an unanticipated wrinkle in all her plans, not least because she still, more than ever, did not trust him. Not that she needed to. She wasn't going to start dropping her ATM code or anything around him. Just her dress.

She'd been resisting for the past couple of weeks. For one, she'd been busy cleaning up the merger paperwork. There'd been some numbers that hadn't lined up, and so she'd been spending all her free time forcing them to say what she needed them to say, running back and forth between home and the Velcel offices, sometimes tracking down her dad or one of the board members out for a long lunch or "working" from the Lomas Lindas clubhouse. Between burning the midnight oil to make sure the paperwork would pass the final audit, answering her mom's constant, premature phone calls about the wedding, and sneaking in some time on the courts to let off steam, she had barely had a chance to process anything else.

Yet it hadn't escaped her that Mateo had been partying constantly. He kept asking her to join him, sure, but he couldn't seem to get it through his head that she was working hard, not just for her family, but for his too. Julián, on the other hand, had been quietly present, making himself useful in small ways—pouring her a glass of wine when she was working at the dining room table late one night; taking Maria to a doctor's appointment so Sofia wouldn't have to.

Julián had lingered not just in the house but on her mind too: his noises on the tennis courts, the make-out session they'd had. And given that he wasn't stepping away from the contact of their shoulders, she might be lingering on his mind too.

If she'd already been married, she'd have tried to suppress the thoughts, cast him aside. But she wasn't yet. And she had the suspicion that Mateo would approach his last days of official bachelordom in much the same way.

"I guess I have you to thank," she said to him now. "For all this."

"What in the world do you mean? I didn't even have a vote on the passed hors d'oeuvres." He smiled, his eyes squinting slightly in the sun. "Besides," he added in a more serious tone, "regardless of what you may think of me, I hardly think your father would act whimsically in this matter. If he needed to rush the announcement of your wedding, it must be for a good reason, don't you think?"

He was fishing again. He liked to do that. But he was right, of course. She'd been angry about being ratted on by Julián and manipulated by her mother and father, but she was forced to admit her parents' ploy in pushing the engagement had been a shrewd move. If she was in their position, she might have done the same. After all, she was following through with the engagement, wasn't she? If for no other reason than because she worried doing anything else might make her father reconsider giving her the COO position.

That would be, for lack of a better term, a dick move on his part after all the work she'd been putting in on the latest snags in the paperwork. He knew as well as she did that no one else would do everything she had done for Velcel, regardless of her relationship status. But dick moves weren't exactly out of character for her father, and he might interpret anything but a happy engagement as her going against his wishes. As long as he held the power, she felt it best not to challenge him.

"So." Julián took a sip from his champagne as he clearly realized she was not going to offer up any theories about her father's motives. "How's your doubles game?"

Sofia snorted. "I love him, but Matco's a shit partner."

"Let me guess. Always crowds the line? Tries to hit everything?"

She turned to look at him, waiting for his eyes to meet hers. When they did, she hesitated for a moment, drinking them in, their brilliant colors, their intensity. She raised her eyebrows. "You're a quick study." She drank, savoring the bubbles on her tongue. Her mom usually went for the sweet stuff, but the bottle she'd picked out for today was nice and dry, and Sofia considered having a second glass, maybe even a third, something she usually didn't do around a crowd this big, or this nosy. "I've always preferred playing singles, though," she said.

"Late-night singles?" Julián grinned, and their eyes met again. Sofia fought the urge to step in front of him, ignore everything going on around her except for those eyes. Instead, she turned back to the room, let the sight of all those people cool her off a little. It made her feel weary to be surrounded by all of them, buzzing around, sustaining themselves on whatever power they could suckle off each other. Whispering each other's secrets to one another, getting off on their indiscretions and bad luck, as if they, too, weren't being whispered about in a different corner of the room, their whole lives being examined.

"We should play again sometime." Sofia spoke with practiced casualness as Mateo extricated himself from a conversation, then crossed the lower terrace and came up the stairs toward her, that easy grin of his proving him the unassailable, doubt-free center of his own universe. "Another little late-night session would do me good. I think I play better in the dark."

Before Julián could reply, Mateo materialized in front of them, casting a brief and somewhat dismissive nod toward Julián before putting his hand on Sofia's shoulder. Clammy again! How did he manage it when the weather was perfect and there was a cool drink in his hand? "Mi amor, ven a bailar conmigo."

She looked around, momentarily confused. "Are people dancing?"

"Well, no, but it's on us to set the vibe, no? We can show off a little."

"Is that a thing at engagement parties?" Julián asked, tilting his head. "I thought the couple just takes a dance at the wedding."

"It's our party; we get to decide," Mateo said. He brought his arm down toward the crook of Sofia's elbow, just as she was moving to take another sip. Their arms bumped against each other, sending Sofia's champagne flute hurtling toward the ground. Improbably, it bounced once off the terrace's stone tiles, strangely beautiful as it twirled midair. Mateo yelled out, "Ay güey!" in the time it took for the flute to fall back to earth and burst into a dozen razor-sharp shards.

Those nearby reacted with sarcastic cheers and applause, and, of course, Mateo joined in, turning to clap at Sofia as if it had been her fault alone. Three staff members were already on their way, speed-walking toward them with rags, one of them calling for a mop.

"You're cut," Julián said.

She turned and found him squatting at her feet, collecting the larger pieces of glass in his upturned palm. She wondered if it had even crossed Mateo's mind to do the same, squat and help. But then she saw the blood. It appeared along the side of her pinky toe, just a couple of drops like a flower blooming from her skin.

The staff arrived, and Julián stood to let them clean up the rest, depositing the handful of shards he'd collected into a wastebasket one of them had brought. Sofia was transfixed by the blood, which now began pooling and dripping toward the floor.

Julián offered her a paper napkin while Mateo pointed out more glass shards to the staff. The blood was now dripping onto her shoe and in between her toes, the crimson almost an exact match to her toenail polish. She took the napkin but couldn't do anything but stare at her foot, so Julián squatted back down and dabbed at the blood. With his free hand, he held onto her ankle, his fingers warm and strong.

Mateo just then seemed to notice what was going on, and though he wasn't usually the overwhelmingly jealous type, Sofia decided that she didn't want the two of them competing to fondle her foot. She tapped Julián on the shoulder. "Don't worry about it," she said. "I'll go to the bathroom."

"Should I come with you?" Mateo asked.

"No, it's okay," she said. "Blood just makes me a bit queasy. I want to clean it up before that happens."

"What about our dance?"

Sofia rolled her eyes. "I'm doing well, Mateo. Thanks for asking." She took the napkin from Julián and pressed it to her foot for a couple of seconds, meeting Julián's eyes before crossing the floor, offering assurances to a few people who asked if she was all right.

In the bathroom, which had a small couch in the anteroom, she grabbed a few paper towels and held them to her foot, trying to stop the bleeding. After a moment, she checked to see if there was glass in the cut, but the blood came oozing out again.

This time she let it drip, fascinated. What she'd said to Mateo was a lie. Blood didn't make her queasy. She loved to look at it, to imagine the power of life it held in every pulse or gush. Maybe when she was a kid it had made her afraid, but something changed after her first bullfight.

A bullfighting arena was no place for a girl, Gabriel had said the day she'd wanted to go with him and Alejandro. He always said the same thing about trips to the hunting lodge. Sofia had been ten years old, already getting so sick of hearing that she couldn't participate in things she wanted to participate in. So, she had slammed the door to her room but stayed on the outside, sneaking her way into the back of the large Suburban SUV she knew he would take Alejandro in to watch the fight.

She'd hidden until they parked, waited for the driver to go get a soda, then snuck out, got herself a ticket to the cheap seats with cash she'd pilfered from the place her mom used for hiding money. At first, she'd been nervous. All those bloodthirsty men yelling for carnage. She could tell even then that they didn't care much if it was the bull's blood that was spilled or the torero's.

Then there was the beast itself, hulking and angry, frightened, she imagined. Fighting for its survival while thousands of drunkards yelled for its demise. It had been dusty and loud, and the section where she'd bought a ticket was full of men who smelled of sweat and work. She'd thought of them as poor then, though now she knew that they had simply been working class, and she'd been raised in too much of a bubble to know the difference. Although in Mexico at the time, there wasn't a huge distinction.

As the night went on, her focus and her interest had turned fully onto the ring. She didn't care much for the spectacle of it all—the matador's ornate outfit, the cape, the crowd yelling olé. The bullfight showcased some of the worst parts of humanity: rigging a game against an opponent that didn't know the rules, dancing around and puffing your chest out when you won, drunk men yelling for carnage.

Sofia could have done without all of that. Except those thrilling moments when the bull's horns nearly came in contact with the matador or his cuadrilla. She loved the tension in the air, loved the promise of violence, the realization that these men in their gold outfits and swords could easily be torn apart. The bull would fight because it knew that if it didn't, it would be torn apart too.

Then, when the bull was finally stabbed, there was the splatter of dark blood on the yellow sand. The cry from the crowd, which earlier had felt like an affront to nature, now felt like a celebration of life. Not just the matador's, which had been spared, but the bull's, which would be honored now that it was to die. The beast staggered; ten-year-old Sofia couldn't look away when he finally came tumbling down and the blood started pumping out. It was gruesome and cruel, but it was life.

Afterward, not caring about whether she got caught or left behind, she'd gone all the way down to the arena to see the blood on the sand. She'd managed to get the attention of a banderillero and convinced him to give her a bloody flag. She'd kept it for years, transported each time she looked at it to that arena, to watching the blood pumping out of the bull, how one flick of a person's wrists could just . . . end a life.

It had stuck with her, this power living beings had over each other. Anytime she remembered the bullfight or came across that bloody flag among her belongings, she thought about how that was the way of the world. You were either prepared to get torn apart, or you were willing to do the tearing.

◆ ◆ ◆

Finally, her foot's bleeding had stopped. She dabbed some cold water on the shoe but gave up on saving it. As she slipped it back on, she thought about Julián touching her ankle. Despite the flush that caused, even now, it had been careless of her to allow it to happen at the club of all places, with Mateo standing right there. She had to be more careful.

When she reemerged into the party, she clocked Julián standing at the balcony, looking out at the pool. She kept her eye on him as she took a lap around the room and spent a few minutes on Mateo's arm for appearance's sake. He again tried to get her to dance, but she begged off, using her foot as an excuse.

After about thirty minutes, she casually approached Julián, who'd chatted with her parents for a while but was now back on his own on the balcony, scrolling through his phone. He tucked it away when he noticed her. "Foot okay?"

She nodded. "I should live through the day."

"Well, thank God for that." He smiled.

His eyes were still on hers, cementing what she wanted to say. "You can't do that."

"Can't do what?"

"Look at me like you want to devour me."

He raised an eyebrow. "I'm doing that?"

"Yes, you are. Which, you know, I don't actually hate. But not here. Not like this. There are too many eyes here, too many loose tongues." She looked around at the crowd, as if determining the most likely suspects to start running their mouths. "And there's too much at stake."

"Your relationship with Mateo?"

"Sure, that. But there's a lot more to it. Our families are tightly tied together, as I'm sure you've gathered."

"I understand." The way he said those words gave her a shiver; she wondered just how much Julián had learned about her family— once again, that tremor of deep suspicion moved through her as she wondered what he was looking to find. He cleared his throat. What she wanted him to say was, *I can't resist you, but I'll do better.* What he said instead, though, was, "I've been meaning to ask you something. About Alejandro."

It gave her a shock to hear her brother's name—they tried so hard to avoid saying it at home now. Even at the party, it seemed like everyone wanted to keep his name unspoken, lest it curse the newly engaged couple. She was sure they were whispering about him in every corner of the clubhouse restaurant, though. Keeping the details hidden only served to fan people's curiosity.

"I know what you're going to say."

"You do?"

She looked at him. May as well just be blunt. "You have suspicions about how he died, don't you? Go ahead; you've been keeping it all in. Just tell me. Was my brother in some kind of trouble?"

Julián ran a hand through his hair. "That's what I'm trying to figure out."

"But what you *do* know is . . . ," Sofia said, pushing.

"What I do know is Alejandro would not have taken his own life. And . . ."

"And?" There was more; she knew there had to be more.

Julián shook his head. "Do you have any reason to believe that someone would wish Alejandro harm?"

A chuckle escaped Sofia. "I mean, he was part of this family."

"Meaning?"

"You don't get to be as influential a family as we are without pissing some people off. In this country or in any other. A certain ruthlessness is required, and that ruffles some feathers. You know I was kidnapped once, right?"

Julián's head snapped to her, concern furrowing his brow.

"Relax," she said. "It was a long time ago. I'm just saying, yeah, someone somewhere probably wished Alejandro harm. Maybe less than the rest of us, since he was the golden child growing up and then he left probably before he could piss anyone off. Although . . ." She tilted her head, remembering the spats Alejandro and their father had had the last few times he'd been in town.

"What?" Julián asked, leaning closer.

"Oh, nothing," she demurred.

"If I had to guess a reason for someone wishing him harm, it would have to have something to do with the family business," Julián said. "It always is, right? Then again, he never seemed all that personally interested in it."

"Exactly. A waste of a fucking board seat if you ask me," Sofia blurted out.

"He was on the board?" Julián asked. She didn't reply, but infuriatingly, he pushed on. Not that she was surprised. This was what he did—found a little weakness and dug in. "Was he involved much in this whole merger-acquisition thing?"

"Not at all," Sofia insisted, trying to reach a dead end with this conversation. "Ale hated all the Velasco traditions, and his attitude toward the business was no different. He couldn't have been more disdainful of the merger."

"Do you know why?"

Fuck. Again. "Julián, this is my party, not my brother's. If you'll excuse me." Scanning the area quickly, she met eyes with a friend of hers from college who'd just arrived. She turned and said over her shoulder, "Sorry I have to go mingle, but maybe I'll see you on the court tonight. I'm sure we'll have a lot more privacy then." She gave him a wink. Overkill, maybe, but she suspected it would work, and at his blush, she knew it had.

As she wended through the crowd, she thought about their conversation. It had been obvious for some time now that Julián was deeply invested in her brother's death, but how or why was not clear. Did her brother owe him money or something? It seemed too simplistic, and surely Julián had his own funds. Though since he had come here to visit, the Velascos had paid for every meal, had taken him around town as their guest. It occurred to her that Julián had hardly spent a dime of his own in weeks.

Whatever it was he wanted from them, Julián was a pest. But a clever, intriguing one. If he wanted to play games, so be it. She could play games too. And she would not be easily torn apart.

Sofia felt a sense of renewed focus.

This was going to be fun.

CHAPTER TWELVE

Julián turned away from the party, looking out at the pool and the mountains. Sofia was a bonus he hadn't counted on—that buzz between them, the way she seemed to invite danger. He felt lucky . . . and a little wary. He couldn't let his guard down around her. There was always a chance that Lukas had still gone to Sofia with his suspicions, though Julián felt that he'd done enough to silence him. For now.

Still, Sofia seemed to be several steps ahead. Of what, he didn't know. Everyone, everything.

The silver moon started to peek out over the horizon. The club below was quiet, the pool perfectly still. He could see some kid's forgotten water gun hidden beneath the bushes off to the side. In the distance, a cart was driving around on the golf course, collecting balls. He realized with some surprise that he liked the idea of belonging to this little world, liked the way Gabriel had begun to include him. It was how Alejandro had always made him feel, but that was different. Alejandro knew the *real* him. The version of himself that he could never show anyone again. The rest of the Velascos knew only the Julián they had met here in San Miguel.

Still, he could play at it a little longer. He was angry and he wanted answers, but there were moments, like now, when the rage flagged, and, in its place, some daring tingle of hope appeared—something he hadn't felt in some time, since even before Ale's death.

Downing the rest of his beer, he turned around to head back inside and say his goodbyes, get a few moments to himself at the Velasco house. Ale's old room had been mostly devoid of anything interesting, but maybe now that he knew specifically to look for something related to the merger, there might be some other clues to unearth. If he was lucky, Gabriel's office would be unlocked. Sofia's bedroom, too.

No, he couldn't think about Sofia's bedroom, not right now. It was too much. He could feel his pulse flare.

As he turned around, he noticed Elizabeth standing at the threshold to the restaurant. It was a wide opening—a double door that had been propped open to let in the cool night air—and Elizabeth was standing right in the middle of it, making it impossible to go around her. She had her arms crossed over her turquoise jumpsuit, her leg stance wide, her chin up, her watch glinting in the outdoor lights. Among all her knockoff accessories, the watch stood out as particularly expensive.

Julián looked around—there was no one else close by. He smiled. Here, another place he'd wanted to dig, and now she was coming to him.

"Linda noche, no?" he said with a smile, sliding his hands into his pockets and looking up at the night sky as if he'd just noticed how nice it was out.

"Güey, are you ever *not* full of shit?" Elizabeth shook her blond hair. "I know your little secret," she singsonged in Spanish.

Julián's stomach dropped, but he gave nothing away, only tilted his head. "What do you mean?"

Her face lit up, and she started counting off her fingers. "When you first arrived, Sofia said you were going to buy a house, but I've got two close friends working in real estate in town, and neither one has heard your name."

He shrugged, but he clenched his fist in his pocket. "I'm not in a rush. Doing the research myself helps me get a sense of what's out there."

"That's what middle-class people do when they're hunting for apartments." She smirked. "The *rich* hire a real estate agent to do the work for them." She was already raising a second finger. "You also stacked the dishes at the restaurant to make it easier for the server. You used the wrong fork at lunch the other day. And you are constantly thanking the club staff."

"I'm a decent person, and so you think I'm full of shit?" Julián flashed a bemused smile, leaning one elbow on the balcony handrail, even while his heart was beating hard enough that he was afraid it would give him away. "My parents raised me to have manners."

"The Velascos don't do any of that, fellow chameleon. And neither do their friends. Only people who've worked in the service industry or have friends who do. And trust me, no one around here fits that bill."

"You can't know that for sure," Julián said, standing now, feeling his arms cross in front of his chest even as he knew that was the move of someone going on the defensive.

"Ha! Of course, I fucking know that. And if you were who you say you are, you'd know that too." She raised her third finger pointedly, smacking at all three with her opposite palm. Then she took a step closer to him. "Let me ask you this, Julián."

He swallowed hard but only tilted his head slightly to tell her he was listening.

"In all your time knowing Alejandro—he was an enlightened guy, right? Philosophical, ethical, wanted to cast off his privilege?"

Julián could feel his jaw tighten. "Your point?"

"Did you ever see *him* stack plates at a restaurant?"

The answer was clear to him even before he could pretend to take a moment to scour his memories. Still, he looked off into the middle distance above Elizabeth's shoulder, trying to ignore the satisfied twinkle in her eye.

"And anyway, I have a great eye for clothing. Your jackets? Easily could come off as too tight because you've recently bulked up—all that

113

tennis and whatnot. But I can see it. They're off the rack, aren't they? Not a single tailored jacket. What's that about?"

Now he felt his neck going hot. He couldn't lash out—it was far too dangerous to do that here—but good Lord, he needed her to shut the fuck up right now. "You've really had your little eye on me, haven't you, Elizabeth?" he said in what he hoped was a threatening enough tone to get her to back down.

"You're a fraud." She looked unafraid even as he stepped closer to her. "I don't know why or how deep it runs, but don't try to tell me that you're not. I'm not of this world, either, and I'm sure you've noticed signs, if you've got even half a brain. How I'm always just lounging by the pool or with my feet in, but don't ever swim laps because I grew up without swim lessons, so I'm still scared of the water." She took another step closer, bringing her mouth near his ear. "How the purse I brought tonight isn't the real thing, or that I actually glance at the bill to see how much is coming out of my account." He could feel the sweat start to form on his scalp. He kept his hands in his pockets, not wanting to give an inch. "I know you're full of shit, because you're like me. It takes one to know one. But at least I'm not a liar. So just admit it."

He took a step back, a familiar rage rising in him. *No.* He *had* to keep his calm. Especially now, with Sofia and her parents a few feet away. "Since you're feeling like confessing things, then, why don't you tell me about the note?"

"What note?"

Now he felt himself starting to regain some of the power in the conversation. It was always useful having some secret bit of information. He took a quick look at the party inside, making sure no one was following their interaction. Mateo was doing shots at the bar. Lukas was hanging around Sofia. Maria was sitting closest to the terrace, ignoring her glass of red wine while chatting animatedly with some of the other matriarchs Julián had seen around the club.

Julián looked down at Elizabeth, happy to have thrown her off her attack, at least for a second. Now he needed to put her on the defensive, maybe force her to misstep. "The note I found on Alejandro," he whispered. "You were keeping tabs on him in LA, weren't you?" A bluff, and maybe too cocky of him—he didn't have enough on her to make such a big leap. But even if she wasn't the blackmailer, she seemed to see quite a lot about what was going on at the Velascos', and about who was keeping secrets. Maybe he could startle her into saying too much.

"I have absolutely no clue what you're talking about." She retreated a step, her arms dropping to either side of her jumpsuit.

"'*Send money or the world knows*'? I suspected it was you, and now that you've outed yourself as someone in need of money in order to continue blending into this world you don't belong in, I can't help but wonder. So, tell me, what were you blackmailing Ale about? Or was it the whole family? What petty secret were you holding over their heads that could drive you to desperation and even to . . ." He couldn't bring himself to say it. He didn't actually think that Elizabeth was a murderer. A blackmailer, sure. But even with that, he had the feeling she'd be doing it on behalf of someone else.

Before he could decide on how to finish his sentence, though, Elizabeth started laughing. "Oh sure, I could hold some shit over the Velascos' heads," she said. "You Velasco ass-kissers think that family is the center of the universe. But I'm not stupid enough to think holding shit over them will do anything for me. I have plenty of men trying to take me out for dinner. I'm having plenty of fun. Why would I give myself a headache by involving myself in their business? You think Sofia will ever get rewarded for everything she puts up with?" She beamed, then ran a hand through her loose curls, like she was in a goddamn shampoo commercial about adding volume.

He furrowed his brow, looking in at the party and wondering what she meant.

When he looked back at Elizabeth, she'd cut the distance between them again, her confidence renewed. "I have no reason to blackmail the Velascos." She placed a hand on Julián's chest, the gesture somehow both condescending and comforting. Again, he took note of her watch, which seemed to be Cartier, and the real deal. "Don't worry. Just like I have no reason to blackmail Ale, I have no reason to out you for your lies, whatever they may be, *Julián*." The way she said his name like that made his chest go suddenly cold. He'd googled *Julián Villareal* more times than he could count, and there wasn't much there. The service he'd paid to scrub the results was working fine. But that didn't mean there were no weak points, if someone really wanted to dig.

He was playing a dangerous game, and he knew it.

She pulled her hand away, then stepped around him and leaned on the handrail, looking out at the club. After a moment, she turned back and faced the party again. "A word of advice," she said. "Don't fight the Velascos. Get into bed with them. Life is much easier that way." With that, and a wink, she left him alone with his thoughts and returned to the party, which showed no signs of slowing down.

CHAPTER THIRTEEN

May

No matter how tense things got between Julián and Alejandro in the course of their friendship, the tennis courts could usually neutralize things between them. It was basically how Julián knew when Ale was ready to apologize, or to forgive, whichever the case might be. Ale would send a text saying simply, *Courts?* And a time.

Lately, though, Ale hadn't been sending the texts, and Julián didn't know why. Julián would just go to the courts and find Ale there, looking like he'd been playing for hours already. When Julián would approach, Ale would just nod to say he was up for a game, but they wouldn't meet at the net like usual before sets to catch up or make plans. At least, Ale wasn't the one to instigate.

Since Meryn had left him, Julián had felt off-kilter, angry. This was made worse by the fact that, the few times a week that he and Ale saw each other on campus, Eduardo was always there, ubiquitous as a fucking plague in Julián's opinion. Which was partly why, one day after playing against Ale, he had convinced his friend to grab some beers afterward.

They went to one of those divey spots that Ale liked and Julián hated, peanut shells on the floor, almost nothing but hoppy beers on the menu. Still, it was just the two of them, without Clingy Eduardo, as Julián had taken to calling him.

"I've been meaning to ask you about him," he said, when Eduardo's name came up in conversation.

"What about him?" Ale asked. There were some guys nearby playing pool, yelling in that way Americans did. Even after all his time in the US, it still seemed to surprise Alejandro.

Julián paused, swirling the remnants of his beer around, the lightest beer they had on tap. He wasn't a beer guy. Maybe the only thing he and Eduardo had in common. "Do you trust him?"

Ale was quick to respond. "Why wouldn't I?" He drank his IPA and turned at the sound of the door opening, his gaze lingering on the trio of cute girls who walked in.

"I don't know," Julián said, wanting to keep Ale's attention. "There's something about him. You haven't picked up any strange vibes?" When Ale cocked an eyebrow at him, Julián tried to play it more casually. "Don't get me wrong; he's a nice guy, and a damn good tennis player. But there's something off about him."

Alejandro reached for the bowl of peanuts, and Julián had to hold back a sneer, picturing the many, many hands that had done the same thing without so much as a pump of hand sanitizer. Alejandro noticed the repressed sneer but ignored it, eyes flitting to the girls who'd joined the pool players.

"You never get the sense he's hiding something?" Julián maintained, trying to hold Ale's attention, which was more and more difficult these days.

"Like what?" Ale snorted. "Eduardo's the most normal guy I know."

Julián took a long pull from his beer, shooting a look at the pool players. This wasn't going how he had planned. But he'd known that Ale would have to be eased into the conversation. He had a soft spot for Eduardo, who knew why. Just couldn't see what Julián did.

Julián decided to let it go for the moment, and shortly after Ale recommended a change to a different bar, one that was a bit livelier. It felt like a good sign, Ale coming back to himself a little. Maybe another drink elsewhere would loosen him up.

The next bar was having an industry night, and Julián didn't really want anything to do with its accompanying cast of interesting characters, but they helped bring out Ale's gregarious side. Quirky bartenders who talked about their movie-breakdown podcasts, and handsome, boring actors who always worked something about their "reps" into conversations a little too often.

Julián went with it, though, laughing along, all the while gathering his evidence against Eduardo in his mind. Including the fact that Eduardo wasn't on any of the emails that went out from the Anderson email server. Once, the business school had cc'd students instead of automatically bccing everyone, so Julián had proof. Then there was that time when they both were in class when an exam was given, and the professor had been one essay book short. Julián had caught Eduardo avoiding eye contact, which, admittedly wasn't the strongest evidence. But he'd had the sense that Eduardo was to blame somehow.

For now, given Alejandro's reactions when he'd tested the waters tonight, his accusations were a little too circumstantial. Julián could imagine Alejandro rushing to Eduardo's defense. Ale was like that. Always wanting to believe the best in people. So Julián would bide his time, wait for something solid, something Ale couldn't deny.

But the real certainty he felt had nothing at all to do with proof. It was just the way Eduardo *looked*, the way he was always studying others, including Alejandro and Julián, flipping on a smile or practiced frown depending on what the moment required, slipping on his expressions like a smooth, handsome mask. A chameleon, using good looks to charm people—which, fine, they *all* did, but somehow with Eduardo, you could see the calculation in it. The too-big smile, the performative ease. All the while, something amused and rageful danced just behind the mask, in Eduardo's dark eyes. It was, quite frankly, kind of creepy. Even his fierceness on the tennis court sometimes gave Julián a weird feeling like the stakes were higher than he knew.

◆ ◆ ◆

After Ale was feeling good, on the walk to a nightcap at one final bar that night, Julián brought it up again, apparently as casually as he could manage. "I'm gonna say it once more, and then I'll shut up about it," he said. "Don't put too much trust in Eduardo. I swear there's something off about the guy."

As Julián said this, Ale experienced a brief flashback to that regrettable night at the tennis center with Meryn. How he'd seen Eduardo watching through the shower curtain, how Eduardo had pretended not to have seen anything. But that was just a guy who respected social niceties. It wasn't what Julián was talking about, a reason to distrust a friend. Not that Ale could bring this up with Julián now either.

Thankfully, the bar was just a few feet away, and out in front were two women sharing a joint. A perfect distraction from the conversation, from everything else. "All right, Julián," he said, clapping a hand on his back and smiling reassuringly. "Te lo juro, me voy a cuidar." A promise to take care of himself. That much he could offer. As his gaze focused on the tall woman with the braids by the door, whose rich brown eyes met his on the approach, he knew it wasn't a lie either. He was going to take care of himself, in one of the best ways he knew how.

That was Alejandro's way. He saw everyone's petty problems as unworthy of his attention. He tried to fly above it all.

He did not know that soon—too soon—he'd be brought back down to earth. For good.

CHAPTER FOURTEEN

July

For the next three nights, Julián and Sofia met on the courts. They played, at times quietly, just watching each other, commenting on each other's serves or mistakes. Maybe the engagement had put Sofia on edge. She hadn't been acting as recklessly as before, coming into his room like she had. She'd mostly gone from working at home at all hours of the day to working at the Velcel office in the Colonia Independencia, with a stop every other day or so at the country club. The merger was approaching, which she had mentioned on one of those late nights, after a few sets had them both sweating. They'd been drinking water beside each other, their legs touching, skin sticking to skin in a way that made Julián hunger for more. And he could see it in her eyes, too, could feel it in the heat coming off her body, the way she didn't pull away, but rather seemed to lean into him. The desire was mutual.

He was drawn to Sofia, on and off the court. Sometimes he got a sense that she knew what he was up to, and rather than scare him away, it only made him want to keep going. It only added a layer of excitement, the thought that she knew he was watching, knew who he really was.

Their rallies on the court were always intense, rarely truncated by a stupid mistake, by a subpar shot that was caused by a lack of effort. Every set ended in a tiebreaker that felt like the finals at Roland Garros.

If Sofia aced a few shots in a row, his anticipation began to sharpen in response, his reflexes returning to a quickness he hadn't felt in years. If his lob placement threw off her positioning once, then during her next game he couldn't get a single ball past her, forcing him into higher, harder angles.

It was like what she had said during one of their first conversations: a tennis player needed someone on the other side of the net to push them, keep them on their toes. They were either partners who were perfectly in sync, or rivals who kept getting the better of each other. They were, in short, a perfect match.

But there was a saying, wasn't there . . . about what happens when you play with matches?

One morning about a week after the engagement party, fresh from a round of morning tennis with Gabriel, who'd commented recently on his improvements in the past few weeks, Julián stepped into the shower. His thoughts returned to Sofia, hoping that he might be able to get more alone time with her once the merger was done. The audit was due to wrap up in less than a week, and she'd warned him that even their night games might have to be put on hold until the final draft of the contracts had been signed by the CEOs of Velcel and Rapido, Gabriel and Sylvio, respectively.

Once that was done, the family members would be heading on a "restorative trip" to their home in Switzerland, on Lake Brienz. He had managed to get himself invited to join them on this semiannual trip to the house they'd bought while Sofia had been in boarding school.

"It feels like you're our good luck charm," Maria had said, when she'd blurted out the invitation over lunch the day before. "That is, if you're not too busy," she'd added, remembering decorum. "I know you've been looking at houses. How has that been going?"

"Just fine," he had said with a smile, taking a bite of his chile relleno to discourage further questioning.

"I think my mom has a crush on you," Sofia had teased that night on the court. "Honestly, if you come, it'll add some interest to the trip. I love the house in Switzerland, but I get so sick of it after all these years. I'm more in the mood for Spain. Oh well," she sighed, sailing the ball straight over his head.

Still, he'd briefly considered declining the invitation to Switzerland. He wondered if it had been offered just out of politeness, and the right thing would be to refuse. Maybe he could have free range of the Velasco house then, do the kind of digging he'd been dying to.

But the same could be said of Switzerland. Another part of Ale's life that Julián hadn't been exposed to before. At the very least, the thought of being away with Sofia settled the matter. Even if her parents and Mateo would be there. Perhaps especially because Mateo would be there. He could just picture himself stewing in San Miguel, imagining the two of them gallivanting around the Swiss Alps. He'd said yes, hoping he hadn't sounded overwhelmingly eager.

He turned off the shower, dried himself, and dressed. He was going down the stairs, headed toward the kitchen to grab breakfast, when he heard a knock coming from the front door. He was still buttoning up his shirt when he approached the front door and swung it open.

Mateo was standing there, wrapping up a phone call. "We'll touch base later," he said without looking up, almost walking straight into Julián. He noticed at the last second and balked, eyeing Julián up and down.

"Buenos días," Julián said.

Mateo didn't respond, staring through his mirrored sunglasses, mouth slightly agape. "I'm here for Sofia," he finally said. "Why are you answering the door?"

Julián furrowed his brow for a second before realizing: that was a job for the help. He hated that he wasn't on top of his game. He flashed

Mateo a wide grin. "I was just passing by when you knocked. Please, come in."

"Right," Mateo said with a derisive laugh, which Julián took as proof that he had thrown him off balance. Mateo took off his sunglasses and hooked them into the unbuttoned V of his polo shirt. "That's the maid's job, but who am I to keep you from acting like the muchacha."

He could tell Mateo was threatened, rather than insulted, by his shirtlessness. Not much of a misstep, then.

"I believe Sofía's upstairs. I could go get her for you if you like." He toweled off his hair, expecting to see Mateo halfway up the stairs already.

But Mateo had turned around and was facing him by the foot of the stairs. "You know, I've told Sofía this, but I have no problem saying it to you: I don't know what you're doing here, why Gabriel is still letting you hang around. And this proves my point." He gestured at Julián's chest. "Answering the door with your shirt off, like you're living in some American frat house, and not a guest in the Velascos' home."

Mateo had emphasized almost every other word in the sentence, his point getting lost as he punctuated his words with self-important hand gestures. Julián wanted to roll his eyes.

"You know something, Julián," Mateo went on. "This family carries a lot of weight. Not just in San Miguel, or in Mexico. It has the power to move the price of a deal, of a stock price. Its name has far more value than most any other name anywhere."

He couldn't gauge whether Mateo's attitude had shifted or if this hostility had always been there. He wondered if Elizabeth had said something. He folded the towel in half and tossed it over one shoulder.

The smile got to Mateo, Julián could tell, because he stepped away from the staircase and toward him. Mateo had better not try anything physical like Lukas had. One thing Mateo was right about was the importance of acting properly in the Velasco house, and Julián wasn't entirely sure he'd be able to contain himself if he got another chest poke like the other day.

"You're enjoying your time here; I can tell. That's all well and good. But you're out of your depth. You're not worthy of the Velascos' attention, and you're not worthy of mine. The timing of your showing up when this merger is all but done . . ." Mateo scowled and shook his head, looking like he wanted to spit. "I don't like it, and I'm warning you to get out of the way. Gabriel and my father are building something great together, and Sofia and I are going to carry it on. We don't need any interlopers getting in our way."

Without another word, Mateo turned back around and headed up the stairs, leaving Julián standing in the hallway holding his towel. *Interloper?*

What was it with these people? Elizabeth, Lukas, now Mateo. It only made him feel more confident that he was right to be in San Miguel. People only reacted like this when they had something to hide.

And the thing one of them was hiding was that they'd killed Alejandro.

After breakfast, he went back upstairs. He paused by Sofia's door, hearing voices. But he couldn't make out the words, not that he needed to hear them to know it was Mateo complaining about him. Sofia placating him to avoid an argument.

Could Mateo really be the killer? He had the energy of someone who got what he wanted, with or without force.

He wondered about Mateo's potential motives. One came to mind easily: the merger. Mateo was certainly touchy about its going through. If Alejandro had threatened to abstain from his vote, putting the merger at risk, then Mateo had perhaps felt he had something very real to lose.

He pulled up his computer, ready to do some digging on Mateo. The more he thought about it, the more logical it all seemed. Mateo had scoffed at Julián's shirtlessness, perhaps fairly.

But in doing so, maybe he'd also shown his hand.

◆ ◆ ◆

He arrived at the restaurant forty minutes late to meet up with Sofia and her friends. It took everything in him to hold out that long. His father had raised him to believe that showing up on time was a sign of respect, even though that put his father at odds with a lot of his Mexican compatriots. He had always been used to being earlier than everyone in his extended family, and earlier than all his Mexican friends in the States, whose parents preached assimilation, but believed it could come twenty minutes late.

Sofia and her friends, though, stretched Mexican time to the limits of what he could wrap his head around. He couldn't quite stomach such behavior. Forty minutes had been as long as he could stretch it, and that was after taking a few laps around town killing time, reading up as much as he could on his phone about Rapido and Mateo's role in it. It was a midsized tech conglomerate and had gained status after investing in a clean-energy start-up, bringing in investors that helped it grow. It was shortly after that that there were rumblings about Mateo's dad looking to merge with another of the Mexican powerhouses.

He tucked his phone away.

It was a swanky sushi spot with an omakase-only menu. He entered casually, flashing a smile to the hostess as he approached. She led him toward a private room in the back, asking him to remove his shoes before entering. Julián obliged, hearing Sofia's voice coming from behind the thick brown curtain, knowing it was a schoolboy wish that there'd be an empty spot next to her.

Inside, he wasn't surprised to find no evidence that the dinner had begun. There were plenty of small sake bottles, though, and a handful of beer bottles.

"Julián!" Sofia called out on noticing him.

Sofia and Mateo were at the far side of the table. Two of Mateo's buddies who had been at the engagement party were sitting on either side of the couple, and closer to Julián were a guy and a girl that he remembered seeing at the dance club with Sofia and Elizabeth.

Everyone turned to him, and, save for Mateo, they raised their sake glasses in his direction and repeated his name, taking the shot and bursting into giggles after. Even though part of him felt like he was being excluded from an inside joke, it was the warmest welcome this group had shown him. He slipped into the open spot between Lukas and Elizabeth, hiding his disappointment that he was at the opposite end from Sofia, and between two people who'd confronted him already. He tried to get a read on them, as to whether they were going to make a scene.

Elizabeth met his gaze with a little glint in her eye, but she turned her attention toward the man sitting next to her, apparently content to ignore him. Lukas smiled at Julián awkwardly, his body language not indicative of a brewing confrontation. Julián eased into his seat with a quiet sigh. Immediately, Lukas started chatting him up. He couldn't tell if Lukas was trying to get his guard down, or if it was his way of apologizing for the other day.

The first course arrived, a salad with crabmeat, salmon roe, and jellied cactus with a light chile de arbol broth. It was possibly the best thing he had ever tasted, but he contained his reaction.

"Not bad, right?" Lukas said, setting his fork gently on the plate at an angle so the servers would know he was done. Julián nodded his agreement, and Lukas then asked him some questions about his experience traveling, if he'd ever been to Japan. He kept his answers vague, repeating things he remembered Ale saying after he'd gone for cherry blossom season one spring break.

The next course arrived, and everyone paused to listen to the server's explanation. Mateo made some joke that wasn't entirely audible, then snickered with his buddies. Sofia rolled her eyes, and then looked across the table, meeting Julián's eyes and giving him the slightest eyebrow raise.

He returned a smile as brief as a gunshot, knowing everyone's attention would be focused on the server, the food, or Mateo's stupid joke.

As he finished the wagyu tataki course, which was cooked on a large hot rock in the middle of the table, Julián turned toward Elizabeth, who'd been busy chatting with her friend next to her throughout the meal.

Lukas had been needling him with questions, but Julián hadn't stopped being aware of Elizabeth there, the threat she represented. As if to remind him, when he tapped her on the shoulder to ask for room to maneuver out from beneath the table, she shot him a wink, reminding him that she knew something about him, and he still didn't know how much.

After the bathroom, he slipped back into his place, taking a sip of water and avoiding eye contact with Lukas so he could engage with literally anyone else.

Sofia raised her glass, and they all toasted together, though he didn't know to what.

He turned to Elizabeth and asked her.

"Well, my fellow chameleon," she responded, clinking his still-raised glass and not bothering to lower her voice. "We're celebrating our little trip to Switzerland once the merger's done."

"*Our* trip?"

"Yeah," she said, biting her lip and raising her eyebrows at him. "You, the Velascos, Mateo, of course. And me. Looks like we're equally good at getting into bed with them." She winked again, and his blood started to boil. Did she suspect something was going on with him and Sofia? Had she told Mateo as much? What else did she know? He wanted to reach out and smack the glass out of her hand.

Elizabeth was a problem. She was enjoying this so much, and Julián was going to have to figure out a way to get her to stop.

If he couldn't find a way to stop her from coming to Switzerland, maybe he'd have to find a way to make sure she didn't return.

CHAPTER FIFTEEN

Sofia was standing in the back of the conference room when the two journalists who'd come to the merger signing started snapping their pictures. At the head of the conference table, Gabriel and Mateo's dad, Sylvio, took turns signing the contracts to make it official. As soon as their signatures were on the final page, Velcel and Rapido would be officially merged. Determining the new company's structure would be one of the first orders of business, and Sofia fully expected to be named COO within weeks.

The two men were all business for the photos, looking seriously down at the sheets in front of them, as if they were reading the terms carefully, instead of just trying to look like Serious Businessmen for the cameras. Gabriel went first, then slid the papers over to Sylvio, finally allowing himself to smile as he made eye contact with a few of the board members. He skipped over her, as if not even noticing she was in the room. As if they had done this with ease.

Which maybe others believed. But Sofia had been hyperaware during the meeting when it seemed like things wouldn't work out. It had been a minor technicality, forgotten now. But there had been a moment when Sylvio's advisor started expressing his doubts, pointing at some papers and whispering in some ears. A concern about some minor investments, a little bit of financial activity that couldn't be traced. At that exact moment, Maria had come in. Her timing had always been impeccable. A trayful of drinks, a laugh about what a mess the books were until she got her hands on them. And everyone ate it up. Frankly, she admired her mother's skill for distraction.

She would learn it eventually. She would have to, since this was the last time she was going to stand in the background. Her mother was happy to work from there, orchestrate without taking the credit. But Sofia wouldn't settle for that. Not anymore. Her father could avoid her gaze right now, in front of the cameras. But once she was COO, she would be done doing her work behind the curtains.

Beside Sofia, her mother was sitting in a chair after feeling faint again. It was happening more and more. Probably dehydration. Boomers and their revulsion to water. Maria wasn't eating normally, though. That much was real. Sofia couldn't fault her there. Even if grief hadn't wholly enveloped Sofia the way it had her mother, she had felt it. She and her brother hadn't been close even in childhood. Still, there'd been days when her appetite hadn't shown up at all. A couple of weeks when everything she ate felt joyless. Anger at Alejandro coursed through her now. Not unfamiliar territory, of course. But this time she knew he both deserved that anger and didn't deserve it at all.

The anger in her had shifted the moment her parents decided they were going to try to control the narrative, hide the shameful secret. She'd been angry at them, irritable with Mateo, rageful in traffic. She'd never been better on the tennis court.

That was when her plan had started to shift; the chess pieces of her life that she'd so carefully arranged suddenly seemed perfectly placed for an endgame. A fun little *fuck you* to her brother, turning the anger at his death (at his life) into a plan he would have hated.

Well, you could have been around to stop it, she thought.

He would be beside her right now, pouting, no doubt, as the rest of the board members shook hands and congratulated themselves. He would have loudly withheld his vote, straightening his posture as if people would be impressed by the moral stance, instead of annoyed, or enraged. They might not have even reached this stage if Ale were still around. He would have come snooping, would have investigated what she was doing on behalf of their father.

When the merger had been announced at a board meeting Ale flew in for, he had immediately called it into question, pulling Sofia and Gabriel aside. "Mateo's dad's company? Really? How come no one mentioned it to me before?"

"Because this is how you react," their father had said. Sofia couldn't have agreed more. Her brother had the notion that any sort of strategizing stood on immoral grounds.

Gabriel had walked away then, and Ale had turned his attention to her. "You're going to let him manipulate your relationship like this?"

She hadn't said anything then, just let him believe that it had been their father's idea to pitch the merger.

But the idea had been hers all along.

When she had started working for Velcel, she asked her dad for access to the books, saying she just wanted to learn. She did the same with Mateo, who'd been working under his father's wing since graduating high school. That summer they'd broken up when she was in Europe, he'd gone back to Mexico to start learning the family business, a fact she'd filed away until she came back home. By then, Rapido was growing exponentially, and as she ingratiated herself with Mateo's family, she saw a path that would allow her to have more control over Velcel than her father would ever have allowed otherwise.

The plan was simple: if she led the company to a merger of this magnitude, one that could mask all the financial liberties her father took, and that might save him from further scrutiny, he would have no choice but to give her credit. Maybe not publicly, but she hardly cared for that. She wanted the shares, and she wanted the title—and, of course, the power that came with it. Nothing else mattered.

She watched Gabriel and Sylvio Hinojosa shake hands and smile for the cameras, both men grinning like schoolboys in line for an ice cream truck. Behind them, Mateo was clearly trying to catch the attention of the cameras, doing his subtle model face. He noticed her staring, assumed she was gazing lovingly at him, and gave her a wink.

She should tell him not to wink. He looked like a creep when he did. Although right now, she didn't care what he looked like, what he did. All she cared about was that she was one step closer to her goal.

One of the assistants in the office popped a champagne bottle, and the room burst into applause. Sofia grabbed two champagne flutes from one of the assistants going around with a tray, giving one to her mom. "Promise me you'll drink some water with this," she said.

Maria looked up, taking the flute by the stem but making no move to drink from it. She smiled at Sofia, but she looked exhausted. "Water. Maybe the one thing you and your brother had in common," she said, touching that pendant of hers absent-mindedly. "Two, actually. Tennis. And looking after me. In your own ways, of course." Another sad smile, and a thousand-yard stare across the boardroom.

"Estás bien, Ma?" Sofia asked, crouching down to try to get her mom to look at her.

"He should be here," Maria said, her voice fraught, like a guitar string about to snap. Now Sofia could see that her mom's eyes weren't just glazed over with exhaustion. Tears were welling up there.

Briefly, Sofia hated her dad for celebrating so openly, and for dragging his wife along despite her misery. Then her own joy got the better of her. She planted a kiss on her mom's forehead, went to the corner of the conference room where there was a minifridge stocked with drinks for clients, and brought back a bottle of water for her mom.

Her mom would be fine, eventually. Tonight, Sofia was going to celebrate, take her mind off things. All the shit her father had put her through, everything Ale was complicit in, too, just by being born male, by taking a spot on the board that everyone knew he didn't give two shits about, when Sofia was right there.

No more. Her time was beginning. And she was going to celebrate being the rightful COO of the company she had helped save. Of the new company she had helped build.

As if reading her mind, Mateo approached, raising his champagne glass. "Lo hicimos, mi amor!" he said, taking her hand and pumping it up in the air. Yeah, sure, *we* did it. She had screenshots of all their emails and messages throughout the merger negotiations, just in case she ever needed to prove how much work *we* did.

It was a bit of a buzzkill, picturing having to celebrate alongside Mateo all night, his clammy hand in hers.

There was someone else she'd *much* rather celebrate with.

She shrugged away from Mateo's grip so she could congratulate other men who sat in their suits for the past few months and thought only about how to make themselves rich. She was just in the middle of listening to Román Echeverria pat himself on the back for some stupid idea he had about handling logistics when, thankfully, her dad announced that they'd be relocating to celebrate the merger with a taquiza at the country club.

"Everyone is invited! On my personal account, of course," he chuckled. "There's too many journalists around for me not to make that clear," he added with a wink. As he raised his glass to the room, his eyes met Sofia's, and he smiled. She would have liked a little nod as a thank-you, at least. But Gabriel Velasco was a man of secrets, and if he even felt gratitude, he would hide that too.

She'd been careful the last week or so with him. She'd felt her desire creeping up every time they played tennis, every time they passed each other in the hallway leaving the bathroom, one of them wrapped in a towel, Sofia letting hers drop before her door was fully closed, knowing he'd be glancing over his shoulder at her. But there'd been too much at stake to take it beyond that.

Before the papers were signed, all it took was one rumor to make it all fall apart, one bit of gossip that took on a life of its own. If anyone near Mateo got wind of an affair, Sylvio would see the Velascos as

untrustworthy, and he could have pulled the plug on the whole oper-
ation. Or, worse, he would have gone over the paperwork with a fine-
toothed comb.

But that was before.

Glad that she and Mateo had both arrived in their own cars, she
texted Julián on the way to the country club. You'll be at the taquiza
later?

Actually helping secure the taqueros as we speak, he wrote back
right away.

She snorted. Dad really let you move in to become his errand
boy, huh?

Not much I wouldn't do for the Velascos. He added a winking emoji,
and she shook her head at herself. He came across as such a Goody
Two-shoes sometimes, which was never her type. It was those other
glimpses of him that hooked her. A sense of danger that she still didn't
understand. Lukas hadn't found anything solid on Julián yet, though
he'd come tattling to her about his outburst at the bar, the fact that as
far as everyone in LA knew, Julián Villareal was on a hike somewhere
without cell service. Which had only intrigued her more. She knew he
was a fucking liar. But it turned her on, the mystery. That, and the way
he moved. On the tennis court, or when he entered a room, or when
he leaned down to dab at the blood on her foot.

To that point. I might need a break tonight from corporate
schmoozing.

How can I help?

Sofia climbed into her car and sat behind the wheel, biting her
lip. She pictured Julián on his knees in front of her saying that, hands
gripping her thighs. Have you seen the library at the club yet?

Nope. Think I'll like it?

Guess we'll find out.

134

Sofia bided her time as long as she could, waiting for the right moment.

The taquiza was being held at the restaurant by the back nine of the golf course. It was a beautiful spot, allowing guests to really take in San Miguel's rolling hills, and the club's gorgeous grounds. There was a covered courtyard, where most of the guests were gathered, staying away from the direct sunlight, which gave Sofia room to roam when she wanted to get away. She took a minute to bask in this feeling. To be out in the sun on a weekday afternoon, not caring about whether some member of the board might do something that would take hours or days to fix and disrupt her relaxation.

This weight on her shoulders that had been there for years now was gone. She didn't even care how many drunk men talked to her about her dad like he was a genius. Even though it usually irked the shit out of her, Mateo's calling his friends "papa" over and over again just bounced right off her. As he took more and more shots of tequila, the celebration she'd been anticipating became easier and easier.

The only problem now was the little secret Elizabeth had discussed with her. She and Elizabeth had done a shot together at the start of the party, and Elizabeth had given her this weird look, then said, "I know, by the way."

"Know what?"

"How this whole thing happened," she said, moving her finger in the air in a circle, then raising her eyebrows suggestively. "A little birdie told me."

Sofia's blood had run cold. The look in her friend's eyes, the smile on her face.

"Don't worry," Elizabeth had said with a throaty laugh. "Your secret is safe with me. And the little birdie."

Sofia had kept her distance since, wanting some space to just enjoy this day without thinking about everything Elizabeth had just implied.

Wanting some space, too, to find Julián.

Finally, the party reached its peak. Sunset had arrived, setting the clouds hugging the mountains ablaze and making the drinks come a little faster. They'd already been pouring freely. Everyone who'd managed to get invited had eaten and drunk and were getting ready to eat some more. Even outdoors, the roar of chatter threatened to drown out the music playing over the restaurant speakers. Gabriel and three other board members had their arms around each other and were singing along to "Cielito Lindo." Sofia would bet good money that it was not the last time during the taquiza it would happen. The only way a crowd of Mexicans could love the classic mariachi ballad any more than they usually did was if they'd been drinking for a few hours.

Julián had mostly stayed away from Sofia, their eyes occasionally meeting across the courtyard. And she knew it was hot out, but could no one else feel the heat between them? Being married to Mateo was going to be a breeze if he was really this fucking clueless.

As everyone was distracted with all the booze and the elbow rubbing, Sofia sought out Julián again. He was by the taqueros, chatting with the guy in charge of slicing the pork al pastor off its rotisserie spit. Not giving him shit, not just ordering, but looking deep in conversation with him. She got a little closer, enough that they were in earshot of each other. She heard him waxing poetic about tacos de canasta; chicharrón prensado con salsa verde. A good choice, but not exactly a gourmet dish popular among this crowd.

Who the hell was this guy?

She waited for him to feel her gaze on him, and as soon as he looked her way, she turned to the person next to her and announced that she was heading to the clubhouse to meet a friend who didn't know their way around. Loud enough that Julián could hear her.

She could hear Julián's footsteps following behind her on the stone walkway, softly lit by ground lights. But she didn't turn around, liking the thought of his eyes on her, struggling to keep up with her almost frenetic jaunt to the clubhouse.

It was all the more exciting that it was still just early evening. Kids were toweling off from the now-empty pool, or from their after-school tennis lessons. Everyone at the club was getting ready to head back home, or maybe grab a quick dinner at the clubhouse. Women not that much older than Sofia were recharged from their five- (and six-) o'clock cocktail by the pool and were returning to their toddlers, who were waiting for them comfortably in nannies' arms. Already, the line for the valet was building up. In a few minutes, the place would be completely quiet, save for the taquiza-turned-party still raging in the back. And through the quiet domesticity of it all, during just another weekday evening, Sofia marched expertly around the grounds toward the library she knew would be empty, Julián at her heels.

She thought about how to play it once she was in there. A slow burn, perhaps? Pretend to examine the bookshelves, let him get close, build up his anticipation until he couldn't resist any more?

Or would she play coy? Take on the role of the conflicted fiancée. *I mustn't!* she'd cry out, fanning her face as if that little bit of cool air could help her resist temptation. There was something fun about the image, about picturing them both trying to hang onto propriety before lust took over.

In the end, though, there was not a lot of thought involved. Sofia entered the library, leaving the door propped open behind her, knowing it would take Julián about thirty seconds to catch up. She did a quick round of the three-room library, confirming no one was in there. No one was ever in there, save for the rare guest speaker the clubhouse hired to try to appeal to the intellectuals who were members (Ale himself had been a frequent visitor to those talks, the nerd).

By the time Julián entered, shutting the door softly behind him, Sofia was sitting on the big oak desk at the front of the room, one leg propped up on the side table for the nearby couch. She angled her legs and fixed her stare on him so that he would know exactly what she wanted as soon as he entered.

He didn't hesitate at all, heading straight toward her, the slightest shake of his head as if to say, *Are you for real?*

And then they were on each other again, like the first time. Hungry, but not in the way of animals wanting to tear the flesh off each other.

Well, maybe a slight element of that. They were human beings, and they wanted to taste. It was as if Sofia hadn't ever really tasted another person before. Julián was a shock to her system, and she started slipping out of her dress, wanting him everywhere.

Julián's hands were flying to his shirt buttons, while somehow also grabbing at her face, her sides, her exposed thighs, just like she'd pictured.

"How . . . ," Sofia started to ask, but words no longer mattered.

And at that moment, a scream cut through the air.

They stopped right away, breathing heavy, skin on skin, warmth building despite the harsh interruption. For a second, Sofia wanted to ignore anything that was beyond that door. She wanted more, and she didn't care what world she emerged back into, as long as she got to have it now.

Then there was another scream, followed by a burst of voices. Sofia and Julián looked down at each other, pupils still dilated, hair already tousled.

"Should we?" Julián asked, still panting, still looking at her like he wanted to tear into her.

Another scream, footsteps pounding down the hall. "Fuck," she said.

They adjusted themselves in the mirror between the bookcases off to the side of the room, Sofia breathing in the scent of old leather and almost-sex. The scent of Julián and unfortunate timing. It smelled almost like chlorine, though maybe she was just imagining that.

Still, she wasn't surprised that following the commotion—once they'd made sure no one would see them exiting together—led them to the pool. A crowd had gathered as two men splashed frantically into the pool, sloshing through the turquoise water toward a person who floated face down in between lap lanes four and five. A couple of alarmed shouts filled the air, followed by a stillness from everyone else in the vicinity, too shocked to cry out.

Sofia couldn't have been the only one to immediately recognize the curly hair, even though it was darker when wet, lit up by the fluorescent lights within the pool. Her dress, billowing in the water around her body, was easy to identify too: gold, sequined, and low cut, an over-the-top choice for an afternoon taquiza. That was what Elizabeth was like, though, always happy to attract attention.

Now all eyes were on her—on her body, anyway. Lifeless, in the middle of the pool.

PART THREE

CHAPTER SIXTEEN

August

He was officially fucked.

For one thing, his primary suspect was now dead.

For another, this meant the killer was close. And, possibly, onto him. He'd have to tread more carefully than ever; there might be a target on his back.

His initial instinct upon seeing Elizabeth in the pool had been to get away as soon as possible. As if anyone could notice the steady stream of panicked thoughts going through his head. As he'd moved through the chaos of the crowd, he'd tried to keep his expression more in line with someone who hadn't recently fantasized about killing Elizabeth himself. Anyone watching would have simply seen that he was holding Sofia as she dealt with the shock of a dead friend. Once Mateo arrived on the scene and swooped away his now-tearful fiancée, Julián looked like just another speechless bystander gawking at the horror.

But the whole time he was thinking, *Fuck, fuck, fuck.* Because who knew how much Elizabeth had already told others about him. If she'd been saying he was a liar, surely that would come out during police interviews. There was no doubt this was going to bring fresh scrutiny to the Velascos—and to him. It was the last fucking thing he needed.

And he couldn't shake the eerie impression that he was being set up somehow.

They'd sent everyone home and closed the club for the evening as the police continued the investigation. Most of the partygoers seemed more disappointed that the taquiza was ending than disturbed that someone had died. He had tried to get a read on Gabriel's reaction. The elder Velasco had spoken to the police and helped direct people toward the parking lot, looking like a man whose celebration had been shockingly interrupted, nothing more. It all played out that night as if it had been an accident, but Julián knew better. Elizabeth had specifically told him she didn't swim. A savvy girl like her wouldn't simply stumble into the pool—not unless she'd been pushed, with intention. Possibly drugged. But why? The possibility occurred to him that he wasn't the only person she'd been harassing, sauntering around and threatening to out their secrets.

He scanned the area. Killers often returned to the scene of the crime, and if it had just happened, chances were that whoever had done it was still at the club. But his usual ability to read people was turning up nothing. The faces around the pool were blank, portraying nothing but the concern—and shock—that would be expected of anyone witnessing a dead body in the pool.

Later that night, he paced in his room at the Velasco house, the door locked. Had the same person been behind both Elizabeth's and Ale's deaths? Hell, if it *was* Ale's killer, they'd done Julián a favor by killing Elizabeth too. Her loose-cannon gossiping was no longer a worry.

It wasn't too hard to connect the dots between the two bodies. Ale was a Velasco, on the board even, and Elizabeth was probably privy to a lot of information about the Velasco corporation. Especially with the hints she'd dropped the other night. Had she been sleeping with Ale at some point? Or maybe it was just her proximity to the family that had made her a target: her overhearing their conversations, always listening, paying attention. She'd shown she was quite good at that. If she'd discovered something unsavory about Velcel, and if she'd been as cavalier about those secrets as she'd been about confronting him about his, then whoever had killed Ale might have easily turned their attention on her. What could that be, though? Pollution? Bribery? Connections to questionable characters? Whatever she'd learned, maybe she'd tried to blackmail the wrong person, or simply flaunted what she knew.

Lukas and Mateo were still high on his list as suspects; the testy way they'd both behaved around him—barking, territorial, secretive—was a clear indication that they didn't want him snooping around. Either of them could have been keeping tabs on Alejandro in LA, might have connections in that area. What were they hiding? Mateo had more skin in the game—he'd wanted the merger to go through and might've known Alejandro stood in his way.

And now, Julián was about to be in very close quarters with Mateo in Switzerland. Just down the hall from a man who could easily destroy him.

Who might be capable of killing.

Three days later, Julián carefully folded his things into his suitcase, readying for the family getaway. He hadn't brought much with him to Mexico in the first place; he hadn't anticipated staying this long, though he hadn't yet decided where he'd go next either. For a variety of reasons, it didn't seem prudent to return to LA. But he'd been—and still was—single-mindedly focused on the Velascos, and so he hadn't prepared to be away for months, maybe forever.

He'd had some time here to acquire a few nice shirts, of course, and he'd also taken to wearing some of Alejandro's clothes. He hadn't done it consciously, exactly. It had started because he'd simply run out of appropriate attire for Gabriel's various meetings, and Alejandro's wardrobe held a number of pressed shirts and stunningly tailored suits that simply hung there, like ghosts, with unfinished business among the living.

Now, packing for Switzerland, he found he couldn't part with some of these shirts, and he packed them in among his things.

After he'd clicked the suitcase shut, he went down the hall and knocked on Sofia's door. He expected to find her sitting on the bed, crying or staring forlorn at the wall, or whatever people did when they were mourning the death of a dear friend. A death they believed to be a tragic accident.

Instead, dry-eyed, she opened the door, wearing a set of silky pajamas that showed off the outline of her naked body underneath. "Hey," she said. "Is my dad freaking out about being late already?" Behind her, an array of clothes lay scattered on the bed. She checked her wristwatch, a thin gold and platinum band that he was sure cost thousands of dollars.

"No, I just wanted to check on you." They hadn't had a single moment alone since the club library several days ago—his hands on her bare thighs, his breath coming fast in his chest, her head tilted back, baring her throat to his lips. He wanted to see if she was okay, to put his hands on her again, but also . . . to find out what she knew. Sofia claimed she hadn't been in touch with Alejandro in years, but as Elizabeth's close friend, maybe she would have some insights that would push Julián closer to the truth. Especially if that insight had to do with her own fiancé.

Conveniently, Mateo had left town a couple of days ago to schedule some meetings in London before meeting them all in Switzerland. Which made Julián think he'd wanted to get out of Mexico quickly on the heels of Elizabeth's death . . .

It also made him think the reason Sofia hadn't come to his room had less to do with Mateo and propriety than with something else. Grief over her friend's death? Awareness, maybe, of what her fiancé was capable of?

Sofia considered him a long time, tilting her head, like she was trying to understand his angle. Then she stepped aside and gestured at some T-shirts and summer dresses piled on the bed. "You a good folder? See if you can help me fit all this into my little suitcase." He couldn't help but smirk as he picked up her skimpy clothes and rolled them tightly. "Wow, you actually are shockingly good at that," she commented.

"I'm kind of particular about how my clothes are stowed away. While traveling or at home." He shrugged. The truth was folding laundry relaxed him—everything neat and in its proper spot. It suited his hypervigilant nature. Not that he would admit that to Sofia, or anyone in her world. "You're surprised I'm good with my hands?" he added, hoping to distract her with flirting.

She smiled. "Oh, that reminds me. Can you grab something I almost forgot? Top drawer of the dresser," she directed. "The red one."

He went over and opened the drawer, which was full of panties. Near the top of the pile lay a lacy red one-piece. He dangled it on one finger. "This?"

She nodded and turned back to her suitcase. "Mateo got it for me. Engagement present, but I picked it out. He'll be mad if I don't bring it along."

She was facing away, so he couldn't read her expression. "I'd be disappointed too." He came up behind her and reached over her shoulder to drop the negligee into the suitcase. Then, in an effort to steer the conversation, he whispered, "I'm sorry about Elizabeth. It must be difficult." He resisted the urge to rub her shoulders.

"Yeah," was all she said.

"Another loss, so soon after Alejandro's death," he said, pressing. "Did you see her at the party? I mean, you know, before we . . ."

Sofia moved away, to the closet, pretending to be riffling through dresses, though she was clearly avoiding eye contact. "Barely," she answered. "To be honest, she seemed drunker than usual. Maybe the partying just . . . caught up to her. Thought she'd go for a swim, overestimated herself; I don't know. It really is tragic. She was so young." It sounded like there was real emotion in Sofia's voice. "I hate to think about it. I just want it all to go away."

Despite the pain in her voice, it was obvious she was deflecting. She knew Elizabeth didn't swim. And wouldn't have gone into the pool in her party clothes on purpose—or if she had, it would have been in a way intended to stir up the fun at the party, and more people would have noticed.

"I just keep thinking," he said, still pushing. "About what you told me."

She swiveled to him, her eyes wide suddenly. "What exactly did I tell you?"

"Oh, you know, that your family has a lot of enemies. Did Elizabeth have enemies too?"

"Quite the imagination you have," Sofia scoffed, then shrugged. "It was an accident. For someone who says they came here to pay their respects, you sure can't leave the dead alone, can you?"

Julián took in the sight of her. The green-flecked brown eyes, behind which he was sure her mind was constantly churning. Her hair, falling in messy waves over her shoulders. There was an inch of tan skin visible at her midriff, and the desire to push her shirt up, and off her, was excruciating. He wanted to reach out again and pull her to him, undo the buttons on her inexplicably sexy pajama set.

"I guess not," he said. "Come here." He sat on the bed.

"I can't," she said. "Everyone's right downstairs, counting the minutes until our car arrives. Just what would Papa think if he caught you in here, with me still in nothing but these flimsy PJs, not even fully dressed yet?"

"But—"

"Get out," she said. And he knew she liked this, liked torturing him, making him feel just a touch unhinged with desire every time he got close to her, and always a step or two behind her.

But he knew this too: she was hiding something.

Something about Elizabeth's death.

◆ ◆ ◆

After two separate flights—nearly twenty-four hours of travel, all told—they finally arrived in Switzerland. He nearly had a panic attack when he looked through his things and thought he didn't have his passport. Then, he remembered. He relaxed a little, but couldn't breathe easy until he was fully through customs. He knew he'd be on edge going into this trip—it felt like truly entering the lion's den. Sequestering himself with the family. With Mateo, who had arrived on an earlier flight. .

Once they'd collected their luggage, a chauffeur helped them load into an oversized SUV. Julián tried to calm his thoughts, taking in the beauty of the Alps through the tinted windows. Maria asked him if he'd ever been to Switzerland before.

"I've never gotten to see Europe before," he said.

"I thought you said you'd been to Zurich," Gabriel said, gruff.

"Yes, of course, I have," he replied quickly, straightening up, wanting to smack himself. All three of them were looking at him, brows furrowed. Even the driver's blue eyes seemed suspicious through the rearview mirror.

"I just meant that when I was here last—basically every time I have come to Europe—it was for tennis, not pleasure. I never *saw* anything, really. I was usually stuck in hotels, getting ferried to the courts," he chuckled. "It felt like I could have been anywhere in the world. I'm sure Ale had similar experiences."

There was a long pause; then Gabriel turned back to looking at the front. "Tennis *is* pleasure," he said. At the same time, beside him, Sofia mouthed those words mockingly.

"What's your favorite European city, Julián?" she asked after a moment.

"Well, that would be an impossible choice," he replied, regaining himself.

"I agree. It depends on my mood. For romance, it's obviously Paris. But for simple *pleasure*? I say Barcelona." She winked at Julián, and he wondered if anyone else in the car noticed. But when he looked back to her, she was staring out the window.

Julián decided to keep quiet the rest of the ride to the villa.

He didn't know what he'd expected when he heard them call it a villa. A quaint, if slightly over-the-top lakeside cabin. Or maybe something big enough to come with a pool house but that wouldn't really compare to the estate in San Miguel. He hadn't expected a sprawling mansion of stone and marble set halfway up the cliffside, with a staircase leading down to the water, where a sailboat and a speedboat were docked. Inside, everything looked like it was part of an architectural magazine. It even came with a veritable army of waitstaff, all in tailored clothes.

A severe Swiss man with a mustache that belonged in a museum showed him stiffly but amiably through echoing hallways and a staircase up to his room for the stay. He tried to get a sense of where Sofia was staying, but Mateo was already at the villa when they'd arrived, and the two were talking on the terrace and having Aperol spritzes.

He could see them from his room. The view was magnificent, the turquoise lake a dreamy contrast to the snow-capped mountains rising dramatically everywhere he looked. And though he smiled at where he'd ended up, a part of him felt a sense of foreboding.

He was just one mix-up or two from losing control. Of himself, or the situation, he wasn't sure. Maybe both. And then where would he be? At a mansion fit for a Bond villain, surrounded by powerful people who would have every reason to throw him to the dogs. To destroy him.

CHAPTER SEVENTEEN

Sofia was starting to feel a little more at ease after two days of being back in the Alps, breathing in mountain air. That last look Elizabeth had given her at the party no longer replayed in her mind, and she was able to just sit with her lovely, thick, rich European coffee and enjoy herself. She had a blanket over her legs to protect her from the chilly morning air, and a buzzy thriller in her hands, though it couldn't hold her attention as well as the view could.

A few moments later, Mateo came to join her, his own coffee in hand, scrolling through his phone. He had been particularly clingy, following her around wherever she went, appearing at her side when she'd deliberately snuck away to have a moment to herself. He was constantly pawing at her too. Granted, at night, it was nice to get some release from the tension she'd built up with Julián. But his hands were always on her thighs beneath the table, his fingers clutching hers whenever they took walks, his arm tossed over her shoulder as if he were afraid she might at any moment fly away.

Now he gripped her foot through the blanket. "Mi amor, nos echamos un jueguito?" Now she realized that he had a tennis bag slung over his shoulder. Her bag.

"Not now," Sofia said, rejecting his invite to play a game of tennis. "I just want to sit and read and enjoy the view for a little while." She flashed an appeasing smile so he wouldn't make a big deal out of it and then returned to her paperback.

Mateo squeezed her foot harder, digging into a bone. She tried to squirm her foot away, but Mateo held on. "Come on. Just one set. You can read when we're done."

Sofia sighed and lowered the book, but made a point to keep her finger tucked into the page she was at. "Mateo, I don't feel like it right now." Maybe it was too hopeful to assume he would care.

Mateo didn't let go of her foot. He held her gaze, his expression going hard, like it did when he didn't get his way. "Come on. I'm asking nicely. Go get changed and meet me at the court in twenty?"

One last squeeze on her foot, this one painful enough that she jerked it away with a little gasp. Before she could complain, he slipped her tennis bag off his shoulder and tossed it onto her lap, which sent the book tumbling to the ground.

"Carajo," she yelped. She glared at him, then reached down for her book, which had fallen closed on the cobblestone patio.

"You're always playing your dad whenever he asks. Julián too. Least you could do is get up off your ass when I ask nicely." Mateo pulled out the chair adjacent to her without bothering to lift it, so it scraped loudly against the stone floor. He plopped down and grabbed the book out of her hands. "Porfa, mi amor. I'm in the mood to play."

Now his expression had softened again. She hated when he was so transparent about trying to manipulate her. She took a calming breath, quelling the urge to grab the racket out of the bag and swing it at his head.

"Plus, I haven't seen you exercise in the last few days," he chuckled. "I don't want my wife putting on the pounds before the wedding, right? We need you looking your best."

All right, maybe a calming breath wasn't going to help. She gripped the bag in her lap, feeling the racket handle through the leather. The merger was done. She hadn't officially been named COO yet, but if she beat the shit out of her dear fiancé with a tennis racket, would her father really blame her?

"I'm not your wife yet," she growled.

Except Mateo wasn't listening. He grabbed the bag out of her hands now, unzipping it in one fell swoop and pulling out her favorite racket from inside. He tossed the bag back into her lap, then stood and walked over to the terrace railing overlooking the lake. The cliffside gave way right below, and it was a few hundred feet to the ground. Sitting up in her chair, Sofia watched him, the blanket sliding off her, her coffee forgotten on the table. Mateo held her racket over the railing and shot her a smile. "No seas así, cariño. Just one game." He put on some puppy eyes, and his tone made it seem like he was joking. But she could tell he wasn't. Not fully, anyway.

Sofia made a fist, picturing throwing her coffee mug at him. If she did that, the racket might fall over anyway.

It was at that moment that Julián appeared. "Oh, are you up for a game?" He was looking at Mateo and sipping nonchalantly on a cup of coffee. "I woke up with an itch to play."

Sofia watched Mateo's eyes turn to a glare at her; then the mask came back up. He smiled at Julián. At least there was that. He could have easily escalated things, picked a fight with Julián too. Although Mateo liked keeping appearances just as much as her family did.

"All right, sure," he said, eyes flitting back over to Sofia. "I'm glad someone's a good sport." He walked away from the railing, turning the racket handle first to Sofia as if it were a knife. She reached for it, but when she tried to tuck it back into the bag, Mateo kept gripping it.

"Unfortunately, the game will have to wait a few hours." Julián took another sip from his coffee and settled into the empty chair beside Sofia. "Gabriel had the boat taken out and wants everyone to go out for a ride. He sent me out here to ask you two to be ready in thirty to go down to the dock."

"Fine," Mateo said.

If Julián picked up on the tension—and he must have heard at least part of their interaction before interrupting—he made no comment on it. He took a sip of his coffee and gazed out at the landscape the way Sofia had wanted to. He glanced at her and smiled, and even though she was the first to call bullshit on men coming in trying to rescue a damsel in distress, she was glad for his timing.

"All right, amor, I'll see you at the dock." Mateo leaned down and kissed the top of Sofia's head and then walked away. She hoped he felt as thankful toward Julián as she did.

Ale's friend had saved him too.

◆ ◆ ◆

In the den, Sofia found her dad sitting by the fireplace and flipping through a newspaper. He looked up at her as she entered, and smiled. "Guten Tag," he said, taking advantage of Maria's English-only-at-home rule not applying in Switzerland. He loved the chance to show off, even if it was just to her. Maybe because she spoke German too. "How'd you sleep?"

"Okay," she said. "Boat ride so soon?"

"Yeah, the Richardses are in town too. This was the only day that worked, and they wanted to make sure to see us and celebrate. Big things to celebrate! I plan to make that known," he said with a big proud smile.

"Right," Sofia said. "Of course." She hadn't missed the suggestion there: he had something celebration-worthy to announce. The engagement was already public, so that left one thing. The COO position. He wanted to make something special out of the moment. She was surprised not to feel more delighted by this. One possible reason occurred to her: she found it a little strange how quickly everyone was willing to move on from Elizabeth. She hadn't expected that.

But there was another reason for her measured reaction. It was the name, Richards. They were an American family who'd become close to the Velascos because they also had a daughter, Lana, at the boarding school in Basel. Thinking back on those days, Sofia could barely believe that it had only been three years of her life, and more than a decade ago now. That first year in particular had been eternal.

Lana Richards, of course, had been the worst kind of pretentious. One of those girls who was saccharine sweet in class and around adults, but desperate to prove herself among the queen bees.

One afternoon, Sofia had found herself playing tennis against her. Lana had grown up only playing against private school kids wherever she happened to be living at the time, so Sofia should have been able to easily pummel her.

But Gabriel had forced her to switch to ballet a year earlier, and Sofia had been rusty. She missed shots she used to be able to hit in her sleep. She'd felt a step slow. The tendons in her ankles were tense, having forgotten the specific turns and pulls of tennis. Her game was slipping away from her, and the harder she tried to beat Lana, the worse she played.

Of course, Lana had to rub salt in her wounds. "I thought you were supposed to be some sort of big shot," she called out once after Sofia sent a ball sailing over her head. "Maybe you should get a little more practice in before you try to play anyone. I'm happy to help! That's how you get better, anyway, playing against stronger players."

Sofia had felt that rage she was familiar with anytime she heard her dad lauding her brother and belittling her own interest in tennis. But this was coupled with the rage of losing. And she hadn't yet learned to turn that rage to the court itself, so she'd sat there stewing, thinking about what to do with her anger. Thinking about the bullfighter and the bull and how people tore each other apart.

The next morning, there'd been a hike in the mountains for the PE class they were both in. Sofia had played nice, telling Lana how she appreciated playing against her, showering on the compliments. She'd been at the academy for only a few months at that point, but she'd learned that narcissists like Lana were best dealt with the same way her dad was. With flattery and the appearance of obedience.

It had seemed like an unfortunate accident, by design. Just Sofia inadvertently stepping on the back of Lana's shoe during their hike as they were passing through a rocky area, an ensuing stumble that could have felt like a push in the heat of the moment. But Sofia had cried out an "Oh no!" and apologized profusely, even as she gave a little extra nudge with her toe, making sure Lana's foot stuck in the dirt, her ankle exposed to the rocks.

All the girls gathered around Lana on the ground, crowding her and trying to help her through her cries of pain. Eventually, the gym teacher had told everyone to give her room, and had to help carry her back to the school. Sofia had hovered over Lana and asked her how she was going to get her practice time in now.

Sofia hadn't thought of Lana in years.

It was a beautiful day, and despite the earlier unpleasantness with Mateo, Sofia was feeling good. She'd seen the staff pack away a small case of champagne, presumably for a toast to the new COO. Apparently, several other board members who were vacationing in Europe, and two who lived full time in Switzerland, would be joining them on the boat.

It was just like Gabriel always to have his gregarious moments in front of a crowd.

Sofia chatted politely with Lana and her father as they loaded up the sailboat and Gabriel welcomed a handful of board members—mostly older gentlemen and their wives.

They pushed off into the lake, the breeze just right. She was amused to see that Lana, always stunning, was clearly Botoxed and lip-plumped in a way that showed she was just as desperate to impress people as she'd always been. She quickly began to take selfies, making sure to get a few with Gabriel, and Mateo. She even tried to take one with Julián, who comically bolted away, then made a joke about having a bad-hair day. Strange, but she understood the urge to get away from Lana's desperation to be seen. He didn't seem to post much on his social media, though Sofia wasn't too surprised by his apparent inclination to curate what was seen of him.

Gabriel and Jerry Richards had done business in the past two years, and had plenty to catch up on. Mateo was schmoozing it up with a board member who worked in importing. Maria had stayed back at the house, and Julián was stuck next to Lana's absolute dolt of a boyfriend, Alonzo, but he was being a good sport about it.

After forty minutes or so of sailing, they dropped anchor near one of the cliffsides, which made for a good swimming spot. There was a ledge that they could reach and sit on the rocks in the sun, or climb up to throw themselves back into the water, something Sofia and Alejandro used to do a lot of when they were younger.

"Before we jump in . . . ," Gabriel said, walking toward the bow so he could be in everyone's view. He was holding a glass of champagne, and Gustaf, the butler, was going around with a tray, offering flutes to the others. Sofia took one, keeping her smile to herself. God, she knew her asshole of a father well.

A huge weight was about to come off her shoulders as soon as he said the words out loud and made the position officially hers.

He surprised Sofia by first asking for a moment of silence for Elizabeth. "A beautiful life taken too soon," he said, raising his glass at the same time as he lowered his head. Was it a true, rare moment of sentimentality? Or was he just putting on an act? She'd guess the latter, though she wasn't certain whom the display was for.

"Now, on to a happier subject." The boat swayed gently with the waves lapping back from the cliffside, and Gabriel steadied himself on the railing while once again lifting his champagne flute. "As you know, we finally completed a very important merger for our business. And our Sofia here has been a huge asset in doing so."

He turned toward Mateo, who laughed and said, "A huevo, Gabo!" Even Jerry Richards laughed at that, though his Spanish was shit. He'd probably heard that particular expression a hundred times around the Velascos, recognizing it as a term of agreement without knowing exactly what it meant, or why there was an egg involved.

What a jackass, Sofia thought, though she was in too good a mood to let her idiot fiancé ruin it. It was just another reminder to herself and probably to her father that Mateo was a deeply unserious person. She let herself laugh along with everyone else, knowing what was coming.

She'd put good money on its starting with a Sun Tzu quote.

Gabriel cleared his throat and looked over the edge of the boat at the turquoise water. When he glanced back up, he had that look on his face. "Sun Tzu wrote that in the midst of chaos, there is also opportunity." Sofia started to roll her eyes, then caught herself, taking a sip of her champagne to play it off. But out of the corner of her eye, she noticed Julián looking at her with a grin. "And, yes," Gabriel continued. "I'll admit that the last few months have felt more chaotic than I would have liked. Rockier waters than these," he said, gesturing toward the lake. "But now here we are on the other side of things, and I'm extremely excited for the days and years ahead. A new company, new ventures."

Mateo whooped now, probably drunk already, given that Gustaf was refilling his glass again. Whatever. He could have his unearned giddiness today, and tomorrow he'd wake up with a more accomplished fiancée.

"And, though you all know I'm too addicted to work to step away fully, I am excited about new leadership joining me. The new generation rising up the ranks. Another quote from *The Art of War*, if you'll indulge me: 'Those who are victorious plan effectively and change decisively. They are like a great river that maintains its course but adjusts its flow.'" Another self-satisfied smile. *Get on with it,* Sofia thought, eager to just have the words out there.

"If you'll all join me in raising your glasses to the new COO of the Velasco empire, and recipient of the accompanying Velcel shares . . ." He gave a knowing smile here in Sofia's direction. At last.

He waited a beat, milking the drama as if it were a press conference and anyone really cared that much. The Richardses were smiling politely, none of it meaning anything to them. It would be a nice little bonus to gloat about her new position to Lana. How she'd made something of herself instead of just marrying rich like so many of their former schoolmates had.

The board members who'd come along likely knew already. Sofia was just about to stand and thank her dad when he looked at her. But the look was fleeting, just a pause as he searched for someone else's eyes. "Mateo," he said, "it will soon be an honor to call you my son-in-law. But before I'll get to do that, I'll be able to call you my chief operating officer. Welcome to the family!"

Sofia felt like the blood was draining from her body. She was glad that the boat's swaying masked her loss of balance. There was a chorus of cheers, but Sofia just heard a ringing in her ears. What the fuck was this?

She had been so sure. So naively, so wrongly sure, that she understood her father. That the loyalty she had shown—the sacrifices she had made for his company, for the family—would be rewarded. That it would supersede all his outdated machismo. He had promised. Not in so many words, it was true. But how else was she meant to have interpreted what he'd said? That if the merger ever went through, she'd be the one to thank. He'd explicitly said that the COO position would go to a Velasco.

Mateo was downing his champagne again, standing to hug her father. Laughing. Accepting a job that was meant for her. A job that wouldn't even *exist* if not for her. Had he known? Why did it feel distinctly to her that he'd known? The shit probably thought he'd surprise her with the news. It wouldn't even have occurred to him that Sofia had been eyeing the job. Had been working her ass off for the job. One that he, of course, would believe he had somehow worked enough for himself.

She set the champagne flute down on the nearest available surface, afraid that she'd snap it in half otherwise. And then maybe use what was left to . . .

Before she could follow that thought to its conclusion, Mateo whipped his shirt off and threw himself into the lake, whooping like a college girl. A moment later, the board members were flinging off their shirts, too, revealing gray, hairy chests and beer bellies, reddened by booze and whatever sunshine they'd been basking in before coming to the Alps.

Everything went into slow motion around her. It felt like a montage in a film. Sun flares and whitened smiles, playful splashing. Mateo whipped his hair back as he surfaced from his dive. Somehow his sunglasses were still on.

What the fuck was happening?

Swiftly, Sofia cast off her cover-up and dove into the lake. The water was so cold, it felt sharp, and she was surprised that everyone was having such a dandy fucking time when it was this freezing.

She screamed like she needed to in the safety of the murky depths. Mateo couldn't operate his own fucking life without Sofia. How was her dad—who, for all his faults, Sofia thought was a smart man—under the impression that Mateo could be trusted to run a several-hundred-million-dollar company?

When she opened her eyes, the slow motion, beautiful-film effect was still happening. Sunbeams through the turquoise of the lake. Above her, she could see the kicking legs of all the people trying to stay afloat. She noticed Lana's legs, still shapely from years of soccer and tennis in school. And right beside them, Mateo.

She treaded water as her breath ran out, wondering how long it would take to just drag him under.

Finally, she let out some reserves of air, blowing the bubbles out and then following them to the surface. When she came up, she saw that Mateo was yelling something toward the boat.

"Come on, pretty boy! This is a celebratory swim!"

Sofia swam to get a better look and saw that Mateo was yelling at Julián, the only one other than the staff and Gabriel still on the boat.

"Leave him alone," Sofia said, splashing at Mateo.

But Mateo was a dolt and splashed her back. "No! We're celebrating me, and no one gets a pass."

There was so much she could say to him, and somehow, the words that came out of her mouth were, "What about my dad?"

"I can't yell at your dad," Mateo said without the bluster.

"Only if you beg," Julián joked. He stood from the seat on the boat and started unbuttoning his shirt, and despite the frigid waters, Sofia felt herself flush. She was frequently surrounded by handsome men, but even still, Julián's silhouette in front of the bright sun took her breath away. There was just something effortlessly sculpted in his face, the curve of his strong legs, the ripple of his abs.

Julián splashed into the water, and Sofia swam back toward the boat, not wanting to swirl around in more than one fiery emotion.

She might as well deal with it now, ask him why. Ask him what the fuck he was thinking. She should have known that she was not going to find peace on that boat.

After she had toweled off and sat herself next to her father, holding a water bottle this time, one that couldn't shatter beneath the tension in her fingers, she asked him through gritted teeth, "Why'd you change your mind? You didn't think I could do it?"

Gabriel let out a deep belly laugh. He'd lit a cigar during her short time in the lake, and now he coughed out a plume of pungent smoke. "Relax. You'll still be on the board. And you're the wife. I said it would stay within the family. He's family."

"You said it would go to a Velasco," she nearly hissed.

Her father waved his hand dismissively. "Semantics. There's a way these things are done; you know that. It's better if the man is the face of the company. Still." He puffed at his cigar. "Even if everyone knows you're the one behind him, doing all the work, pulling all the strings—you still have to be behind him. Entiendes?"

He smiled. Like this was all a joke. Like this was the only way it could ever go. As if she would ever understand that, instead of rage against it.

So here she was again. Inflamed with rage but having to hide it as her father's guests poured back onto the boat. The worst part was having to look Mateo in the eye. Mateo, whom she'd dragged along for this whole damn ride, this whole fucking roller coaster, knowing she needed to play nice to get this merger done, but certain that once it was all complete, she'd still have an escape. Now, looking at him as he smiled and winked, she could feel herself drowning.

She was going to have to do something.

CHAPTER EIGHTEEN

He had made it through a couple of days in Switzerland without committing another gaffe that could reveal he'd been lying. After misspeaking in the car from the airport, he'd worried someone would bring up his inconsistency again, poke holes in something else he'd said. But it appeared the Velascos and their many guests were enjoying themselves too much to be on the lookout for the little slips that someone like him would have picked up on in an instant.

There were enough people coming in and out of the house that he didn't actually know who was staying at the villa and who was not, let alone who all of them were. Executives and their families, he supposed. Colleagues and friends.

The Velascos really knew how to vacation, though, in the truest sense of the word. Throughout his time in San Miguel, there'd been nonstop chatter about the merger, about the business. Gabriel and Sofia were always glancing at their phones or computers, firing off emails. Now their phones were on Silent, not even a buzzing notification to let them know an urgent email had arrived. There was a constant stream of booze and food in the villa, and someone was always suggesting taking the boat out. Even throughout the night, the house seemed to almost never be completely quiet.

Julián marveled at their ability to sever themselves from their real life back home. From the business, from Elizabeth's barely decomposing body, from anything but the joy of being right where they were. *Perfect hedonists,* he could hear Alejandro saying.

At least their lack of preoccupation and the presence of many guests gave him the freedom to roam around a bit. He'd explored the villa extensively. He didn't expect to find any evidence here in the house itself, but since everyone was too busy with their champagne and caviar, he figured he might as well look around. It was second nature to him, this urge to get the lay of the land, to know where he stood at all times. Call it a defensive strategy.

The day after the boat ride, Julián headed downstairs for breakfast. When he made it to the large dining table, he was thrilled to see that not only were there molletes, one of his favorites, but also that Sofia was sitting there without Mateo.

She flashed him a smile while she listened to the board member sitting across from her droning on about the price of hog futures. Even after all his time in UCLA's MBA program, he was shocked by what some people thought were interesting topics of conversation.

He took a seat next to Sofia and spooned pico de gallo onto his molletes, adding a drizzle of Valentina on top, pleasantly surprised that it was available in Switzerland. He ate quietly, waiting for a good time to jump into the conversation with Sofia, or change the topic and rescue her. Before he could, though, Maria appeared from the kitchen, wearing her fluffy hotel-style robe. Thinking about it now, he realized he hadn't seen her in anything else since they arrived. Somehow, she looked more exhausted than she had back in San Miguel. He wanted to ask if she was okay, but she spoke first, saying that they'd received a voicemail from his parents on the landline.

"Wow, a landline," he said, partially surprised, partially just trying to gather his thoughts at the news.

Maria chuckled. "Yes, even I know it's old fashioned. But it's helpful to have a Swiss phone number to give out for local business." She smiled softly. "I stopped listening to the voicemail when they said who it was from, by the way. I just hope it's not an emergency. Were they unable to reach you on your cell phone?"

His heart started pounding in his chest. This could ruin everything for him. How had they even tracked him to Switzerland, to this house? But he kept his expression light, returning Maria's smile as he pulled his phone out and pretended to scroll through. "Ah, yes, I have a few missed calls, I see now. I'm sure they just forgot about the time zones. They've always been bad at keeping track during my travels." He took a bite from his breakfast, then rose as he chewed and swallowed. "I'll call them back once it's a reasonable hour on their side of the world. I'll check the voicemail now, just in case. My father's health hasn't been very good—maybe something has come up. I think my phone's voicemail has been full for a while." They all nodded in sympathy at that. He wiped his mouth with the cloth napkin, then folded it and set it on the chair. "Where can I . . . ?"

"Gabriel's study," Maria said. "Upstairs and third door on the right. You don't want to finish your breakfast first?"

"I'll be quick." He turned away, trying to keep himself from sprinting toward the staircase.

He had no idea what he expected to find on the voicemail, but a part of him thought that everything was about to come to light, and that this was the end of his time with the Velascos. It had been just over a month since he'd left LA, which perhaps was as long as he could have reasonably expected the truth to stay hidden.

How had the Villareals found him here? He racked his brain as he climbed the stairs, suddenly remembering a social media notification for jvillareal that had popped up on his phone. He had only occasionally been checking the accounts, not posting at all. But yesterday, during the boat ride, a user named lanarichards had followed him. He'd been distracted after the boat ride, trying to get a read on what Sofia had been discussing with her father.

He reached the top of the staircase and started heading toward Gabriel's study, scrolling through his phone to see that Lana had tagged him in a photo from yesterday. It wasn't a full shot of him, at most a quarter-profile pic in the background. He breathed a slight sigh of relief, even though he felt like he could have strangled her for doing it. Julián's parents must have been following his social media closely, and reached out to Lana once they saw the tagged picture. He turned the corner and immediately ran into Mateo leaving his room.

"Just the man I wanted to see!" Mateo exclaimed. "You owe me a tennis match. Don't think I'd forgotten yesterday. We were all a little tipsy after the boat, but I'm still itching to play."

"Yeah, absolutely," Julián said, just wanting him to get out of the way. "I'm just gonna check on something and finish breakfast, and I'll meet you on the court in twenty?"

"Güey, no," Mateo said, a joking whine to his voice. "By then, someone will suggest another boat ride, or a hike, or whatever, and I won't get the chance to beat you like my lovely fiancée has over and over again." He laughed and clapped Julián's shoulder, then turned him back around. "Go get changed. You can have breakfast after. It's always better to build up an appetite anyway."

Julián tried to squirm away from him. "All right, gimme ten minutes, and I'll see you out there. My parents just left a voicemail I should listen to."

"No mames," Mateo said. "Don't give me the Mexican 'ahorita.'"

Julián couldn't help but laugh at that, despite how every second standing there with Mateo made him eager to get away. Everyone in Mexico knew that "ahorita" never meant "right now." It meant in ten minutes, or in two hours, or sometime in the next few years. Alejandro was a notorious "ahorita" sayer, and it almost always meant that what he was talking about would never happen.

Mateo flashed a smile, and despite what Julián had picked up on the other day about Mateo's mean streak, he saw the charm that made everyone believe he was so great. Julián looked in the direction of Gabriel's study, wondering how he could convince Mateo to give him a few minutes alone without drawing attention to how badly he needed those minutes. Mateo might insist on following him to the study, which would be considerably worse than not hearing the message for another hour.

"Come on." Mateo looped his arm across Julián's shoulders and turned him around. "You can call them when we're done. If it was an emergency, they'd still call your cell phone, right?"

Julián sighed, his stomach in knots. But he still couldn't think of a way to beg off. Perhaps playing a game would work out the nerves and clear his mind so he could better see his options.

On their way out, they had to cross the dining room, and the people sitting there wished them luck. One of the board members joked that he'd be out in a bit to start taking bets. Sofia, taking a bite from a mollete, cocked an eyebrow at him. He shrugged, but then had to follow Mateo out to the court, feeling like a prisoner.

While warming up, he tried to get himself in the right mindset for a game, and also try to quiet his worries about the voicemail, and the fear that someone would listen to it while he and Mateo were playing. All of which meant he was terrible once the match actually started. He made silly mistakes, hitting balls that would have been out, running himself out of position. And, of course, Mateo couldn't let a point go by without letting out a primal scream like he'd just won Wimbledon.

But, like every asshole athlete Julián had ever known who just claimed to be "passionate," his celebrations were always followed by gloating trash talk. "I thought Sofia said you were good at this shit. Come on, pretty boy; do better than that!"

Julián wasn't even bothered by that. He knew some guys back in LA whose whole approach to sport was to be an asshole to throw off their opponents. If he let people like that get to him, he never would have won a match.

What started getting him really angry was Mateo's wanting to chat between points. It always took Julián out of his game, out of the moment. Mateo bounced a ball three, four, five times. Julián wished he would just serve, the voicemail lingering in his mind, though it had been pushed to the back of his mind by the game, and his shitty performance. If he wasn't going to be able to focus, he figured he'd try to throw Mateo off his game too.

"So, how're the wedding plans coming along?"

Mateo stopped the bouncing and finally went into his serving motion, but then stopped with a chuckle. "To be honest, I can't believe I'm getting married." He rolled the ball around in his hand.

"No? I thought you and Sofia being together this long meant it's been planned for a while."

"Don't get me wrong. Sofia's the best. But getting pinned down to just one person, no matter how hot she is?" Mateo laughed and shook his head, bouncing the ball again. "This stays between us, but locking myself down feels kinda crazy, you know? I can get plenty of play." He winked at Julián, who was staring across the court, trying to resist the urge to whip his tennis racket at Mateo.

"Yeah?" he said instead, only a little surprised that Mateo was enough of an asshole to be saying these things out loud.

"I guess I'll just need some excuses to get away every now and then. Good thing the new gig will come with plenty of opportunities for work travel, if you catch my drift. Those shares in the company are gonna fund a lot of good times." Again, another wink. "If you're still around when we get back, I might turn to you every now and then. Take you out for some drinks on the company credit card, you know? You're a single guy. We can go have some fun together."

He couldn't believe what he was hearing. He'd assumed Mateo was shitty, but this was another level. He was almost flattered by the implication that he was trustworthy, and that Mateo thought Julián held enough influence over the Velascos to cover for him, or be his fall boy when he got caught out with the wrong crowds.

Just as he was wrapping his mind around everything Mateo had said, the jerk decided to serve. The ball went sailing past him. A fault, but of course Mateo wouldn't admit to that. "Forty-love!" he called out.

Rather than argue the call, Julián leaned into his anger the way Sofia would, by going for the kill. He turned it on the way he hadn't in weeks—months, even, not since Ale's death. His rage clicked in and, though he'd told Sofia weeks ago that playing in anger meant he didn't have complete control of himself, he proceeded to kick Mateo's ass mercilessly.

When they wrapped up, Julián winning the set six to three, Mateo almost looked impressed. Not humbled, by any means. That was probably beyond him. But he did congratulate him as they headed back inside the house. "I didn't think you had it in you. Kinda thought you were the roll-over-and-take-it type."

"First impressions can be deceiving," he responded, matching Mateo's tone. "There's a lot you don't know I have in me."

He assumed that would be the end of it. They opened the double doors and headed into the house through the living room. A few were gathered around the fireplace and asked how the game went, Mateo choosing then to be humble, of course.

He excused himself to go shower, thinking he'd have time to sneak into Gabriel's study before. But Mateo followed, saying he was going to shower too.

His mind had by now left tennis and was back on the pressing matter of dear Mama and Papa Villareal calling after him, on the message they had left that anyone might hear. Seriously, who still had a landline? But then Mateo said the name Elizabeth, bringing him back to the conversation.

"I don't even know who she was boning, but she was full of herself. You didn't hear it from me, but a gold digger, clear as day." He smacked Julián across the chest and snorted. "She tried coming after me once or twice. Led me on until I smartened up and started ignoring her, figuring that would get her to stop hanging around. But I think I wasn't the only one nearby she had her eyes on."

They'd reached the top of the stairs and should have been headed off to different bathrooms. But Julián couldn't pull himself away, despite it all. "What do you mean?"

"Oh, come on, Julián. You and I know that no one really hangs around the Velascos unless they want to be in bed with one of them. Or already are."

Mateo clapped him on the shoulder and barked a laugh. Julián was too shocked to know how to respond. There were thousands of questions shooting through his mind he wanted to ask. But by then, Mateo had turned and headed down the hall to his room, leaving him standing alone on the landing.

He looked in the direction of Gabriel's study, and the voicemail message, but there was a sick, twisted feeling deep in his gut, and he decided that he could use a shower first, in case the voicemail was about to change everything. He rinsed off quickly, then went back to his room to dress, the sense of urgency returning.

However, when he opened the door to his room, he was surprised to see Sofia's face looking back at him. "Hey," she said. She was sitting at the desk by the window, looking like she'd just been staring out at the lake and waiting for him. "How was the match with Mateo?"

Julián ran a hand through his wet hair while holding the towel wrapped around his waist with the other. "Truth be told, your fiancé is a bit of a prick on the courts. It felt good to beat him down."

Sofia snorted and stood up from the desk. "I wish I'd seen that." She stepped around the room, studying it as if she hadn't been sitting there when he arrived. "Hmm. I kinda had you pegged for an immediate unpacker," she said, looking at his suitcase in the corner, which was covered up in a mix of discarded worn clothes and another pile of clean, folded ones.

"I wasn't expecting any company," Julián said, after what felt like too long.

"Well, you have it," Sofia said, now taking a seat on the corner of his bed. She took another look around the room, but there wasn't much to see. "So?" she asked after a moment.

170

"So, what?"

"I feel like I haven't gotten to hang out much. How's Switzerland treating you?"

"No complaints."

"Really? I have some complaints," Sofia said, running her hand along the comforter and sighing. "There's just so many people around. I wish my dad knew how to get away without inviting half the company along." She tossed herself back onto the bed, her hair splayed out around her. He'd seen her in a skimpy, bright orange bikini all day yesterday and still managed to maintain a feeling of control. But for some reason when she lay back now, her loose button-down shirt revealing nothing except a bit of collarbone, her bare legs curled over the edge of the bed, Julián felt a tug in his belly.

"Yeah, I get that. Any big plans today?" Julián took a step toward the door, feeling the primal urge to shut it, make the whole world just him and Sofia again, if only for the next few minutes.

"Not really. Mateo and Alonzo went into town for ice cream," she said. "I don't blame him; the ice cream spot is great. But he insisted on going right away, fuck what anyone else had planned. Sometimes he's such a child. As I'm sure you've noticed on the tennis courts. And other times." She laughed, her eyes on the ceiling, which made it easy for Julián to keep looking at her. She was just so pleasant to look at. "God, you should hear him try to sound smart in the boardroom. Pena ajena, right?"

Julián laughed. It was one of his dad's favorite phrases, for which, as he'd told Julián for years, there was no English translation. Though Julián later pieced together that it meant having second-hand embarrassment.

"There were so many times that I had to jump in and save him from himself. Save the whole merger, actually." She popped up onto her elbows, her eyes meeting Julián's. She bit her lip, and he wasn't sure if it was because she was trying to stop herself from saying these things about her fiancé, or for some other reason. He knew how involved she was in the business, and he wondered just how much she knew about Velcel.

"I've been wondering," he said, trying to act casual, but not even believing it himself. "How exactly did this merger come to be?"

"What do you mean?"

"I mean . . . your families have known each other for a while. You and Mateo have been together, at least on and off, since high school. When did the idea that the two companies should merge come about?"

Sofia laughed. "Is that really what you're asking?" She tilted her head down and raised her eyebrows at him.

Even as her grin started to form, he could sense that he was onto something. He could see a twenty-year-old Sofia, living her party life in Europe and having Mateo show up at her door, begging to get back together with her. There was something always whirring behind Sofia's eyes, and he was sure that, even as a young woman, she'd look at a situation like that and try to find how to make it work for her.

Julián didn't have to ask to confirm. Maybe the details he imagined were off, but he was sure that the merger had been her idea.

"You know, sometimes I wish I weren't stuck with him," Sofia said. She brought her legs up onto the bed and lay sideways, resting on one arm. He saw a flash of red beneath her shirt. She wasn't wearing any shorts either. "But I'm such a rule follower that there's no way out for me."

"Is that so?" Julián rested an arm on the dresser next to the door. "I didn't really have you pegged as a rule follower." He paused, biting his lip. "Actually, almost everything I've learned about you makes me think you're not a rule follower at all."

"Guess we're both making wrong assumptions about the other," she said. Then she laughed. "No, you're right. I'm not. Except with my family. No matter what happens, I'm a Velasco, and I do what I'm told. Always eager to please."

Their eyes met, an electricity still crackling between them.

Then she stood up, walking slowly toward him. He thought for a moment she was going to reach out and pull his towel away, but she stepped past him—and shut the door, enclosing them both in his room. She locked the door, then turned to him and began to unbutton her shirt.

Underneath it she was wearing the red negligee. The engagement present from Mateo. It looked even better on her than it had dangling from his fingertips just days ago—sheer red lace across her breasts, then veering down into a satiny V between her legs.

It would look even better on his floor.

Afterward, Sofia lay naked against him. He'd taken her up against the dresser, first—still in the little lace number—before flinging it off her and going another time on the bed, her hands gripping the headboard as she cried out softly. Just thinking about her trying to contain her moans, breathing into his neck, made him want to start all over again.

"I didn't peg you for a cuddler," he said, one hand behind his head.

"Like you said, not a rule follower," Sofia said, trailing her lips against his bare chest.

"Are you trying to make the argument that cuddling is somehow rebellious?"

"It is when people assume you're the frigid get-away-from-me-as-soon-as-I've-cum type."

Julián laughed, slipped his legs farther between hers, feeling the heat and dampness of her. And for some reason, he felt the urge to ruin it. He didn't want to. He wanted to stay in this moment. But as the silence lingered on, his mind couldn't help but flit back to real life, and this did not seem like a part of real life. He licked his lips, preparing for this moment to be over.

"I think I asked this before, but for some reason he's on my mind. Did Ale ever mention our friend Eduardo to you? I've been trying to remember what happened to him."

Sofia sighed, moved her head onto Julián's chest, her fingers running circles around his navel, little tickles that once again made him want to lean into her and start it all over again.

"Doesn't ring a bell, no," Sofia said absently.

"You're sure?" Julián asked, surprised. How could Ale never once have mentioned Eduardo's name to his sister? Even in passing conversation with his parents, who might have repeated it to her.

It made him aware again of the outside world. Of who he was and what he was here to do. As fun as this was with Sofia, he had other plans to tend to. He had to go listen to that damn voicemail, and maybe reach out to Lana to see what, exactly, she'd told the Villareals.

"Hey," Sofia whispered. "I know you lied to me before."

He froze, wrapping his hand around hers. "What do you mean?"

"You said your dad died years ago, but this morning you said his health was bad. Which is it, Julián?"

He let out a breath. "My dad and I used to be close. He's sick now, but we haven't talked in a long time." It felt strangely good to share something true with Sofia. "I misspoke. He's just been dead to me for a while, in a sense."

She gazed up at him. "I understand," she said.

Julián pulled himself away from Sofia, kicking his legs over the side of the bed. He stood and reached for the glass of water he'd brought in with him earlier, which he'd set on the dresser.

"Everything all right?"

"Yeah, couldn't be better." He turned and flashed her what he hoped was a confident grin. "I could use another shower, though. You made me sweat more than playing Mateo did," he smirked.

Sofia sat up and reached out to him, pulled him back to the bed. "You sure you're done? A tournament match takes at least two sets."

His hands came to her waist, and he wanted to say no, because he had shit to take care of, and it was urgent . . . but he wanted to say yes more.

By the time they were finished, he was out of breath all over again—triumphant. Convinced he'd won this round, even if he no longer knew exactly what game he was playing. He almost didn't want to shower—didn't want to wash the smell of her away.

After a long hot shower this time, his mind swirling, he went back to his room, half hoping to find Sofia still there. She wasn't, but the bed was still tousled, the smell of sex lingering. He opened a window, keeping an ear out. But the house seemed mostly empty. Perhaps another boat ride, or some other outing. He was happy to have been left out this time. Now that she was gone, he kept thinking about her obliviousness when he'd asked about Eduardo. He should be relieved by her response, but strangely it had the opposite effect. A reminder of how far away she was from his old life, the life that seemed to want to tether him, pulling him backward into the past . . .

In Gabriel's study, he found the landline next to a fax machine, strange relics that were ridiculous, but fit Gabriel's vibe well enough. He took a breath, steeling himself, then lifted the receiver and tried to figure out how to play the damn messages. There was some robocall in Italian that got cut off. After that he heard the click and fuzz of a real call, and then a woman's voice.

"Hi, this is Elena Villareal, calling for Julián." There was a beat, and he thought he heard her voice choke, though it came out like a laugh. "We were so glad to hear that you're with your friend's family. We'd heard you left UCLA, but no one could tell us anything for certain and . . . well, you know how we don't like it when you jet off around the world without telling us. On social media, it said you were on a hike? We hope you give us a call back and just say how you're doing. And maybe when we'll get to see you again. I know, I know, I can picture you rolling your eyes. But . . . please. We are worried."

There was another beat, and the cackle of background noise, as if she were dialing them from a public place. Then the click that marked the end of the message, and the machine saying there were no more messages. He breathed a sigh of relief. If someone had heard that, it wouldn't have given him away.

The good news was that no one in LA knew for sure where Julián had gone. The bad news was that they'd find out soon enough, especially if Julián's parents were asking questions.

He hung up the phone, still gripping it in his hand so hard his knuckles were going white. He didn't like this one bit. And he might even have been at risk of smashing the phone so hard into the receiver that it would have broken, or of punching a hole through the ornately wallpapered wall, if he hadn't been distracted by what he saw next.

CHAPTER NINETEEN

It had taken Julián a few weeks of sniffing around the admissions office, the bursar's office, and basically anyone who might have access to official records. Unfortunately, the university bureaucrats weren't very willing to part with information, and no amount of schmoozing seemed to work. In Mexico, there was almost nothing that couldn't be accomplished with a little sweet-talking, but it appeared things worked differently in the US.

Eventually, Julián had come up with a convincing enough story to tell the department head about Eduardo being sick in the hospital and needing to see what classes he was enrolled in in order to notify his professors. He'd talked to an administrative assistant at the end of the day to make sure they were ready to get out of the door, and more likely to just give him the information so they could go home.

She looked like an international undergrad student, probably forced to work on campus for peanuts so she could help pay the exorbitant tuition and board. He wished she were Latina. Spanish always helped grease the wheels, even in this country with all its rules. But he decided to be patient, let her clack away at her computer. Her eyes kept flitting to the bottom corner of the screen, checking the time. She must have had an essay to write, or plans to meet up with her roommate and friends for a champagne night at a local dive bar.

"And you're sure that's the right spelling?" Anya said in her eastern European lilt.

"Yup. Not finding anything?"

"No. Strange," she said, frowning.

"Any idea why that would happen?" Julián asked, the corner of his mouth already pulling up. He knew what it meant, but he wanted to hear her say it. Wanted his suspicions confirmed.

"It's either some mistake in the system, or he's not currently enrolled. How long has he been sick? Maybe he didn't finish registering for this semester?"

Julián tapped the counter. "Yeah, maybe. I'll go talk to him right now about it. Thank you so much. You've been very helpful." He turned away and went down the hall, pulling out his phone to text Eduardo and see if he wanted to meet for lunch.

The two met at a spot Julián had picked out. Eduardo arrived looking smooth as always, but his pulse was visible against the skin of his wrist. Despite their closeness to Alejandro, Eduardo and Julián almost never hung out without Ale there as a mediating force. Eduardo, in fact, had made it clear that he hated the insouciant way Julián played tennis, and the way he conducted himself in general.

Both men despised the way the other was always watching, wary.

"Hey," Eduardo said, pulling out the chair across from Julián. It was an outdoor table, shielded by an awning and looking out at the Americana. Julián had wanted a fairly public setting. Eduardo would later suspect it was because Julián wanted Eduardo's humiliation to be out in the open. He would not be wrong.

"Hey, you just get out of class?" Julián said. He'd thought about toying with him as long as possible, but this conversation had been a long time coming. Even though he didn't like beer, he'd already ordered them a couple just because he knew Eduardo liked those stupid Arnold Palmers.

"Yeah." Eduardo grabbed the menu and looked through it, scanning, maybe to see if there was some new item he could afford.

"How was it?"

"I dunno. It was class. You know how Robinson gets. Too into the sound of his own voice."

Julián nodded. "Sure, sure. What's your grade in that class, by the way?"

Eduardo kept his eyes on the menu, but Julián sensed the apprehension. "Hovering around a high B, I think. Why?"

"See, I'm kind of surprised by that." On Eduardo's confused look, Julián smiled. "You know, since you're not technically in that class. I mean, you literally attend all the time. But you're not enrolled, are you?"

Eduardo kept up his confused expression, but Julián could see a moment of panic flash across his eyes. "Yeah, right. I'm going to MBA classes every day without actually being enrolled in school." He forced a laugh and looked down at the menu. "What are you getting? Wanna share fries?"

"It's been bugging me for weeks now," Julián continued, ignoring Eduardo. "How you always wait until there's a group of people entering a classroom to go in. How you claimed you dropped LaFevre's class, and she's the only one who takes attendance all the time. There's something off about you, I've been telling Ale. And now I know what it is. At least, part of it. You're not a student here at all, are you?"

Now Eduardo looked up from his menu. Julián couldn't read his expression—he would have expected panic, guilt, embarrassment.

Still, his lack of response said enough for both of them.

Julián couldn't contain his giddiness. He'd been right, all this time, that Eduardo was full of shit, but Alejandro had refused to believe it. "I fucking *knew* it," he said, slamming his hand down on the table. "I don't know why you're trying to leech onto us. What you're playing at." Julián barked out a laugh and then moved the second pint glass closer to Eduardo. "Go on; enjoy this beer, on me. It'll be your last before I start spreading the word. Get you banned from campus so you stop using the tennis courts, you freeloader. Fucking stalker."

After a while—long enough that even Julián was starting to get uncomfortable—Eduardo reached for his beer and took a sip. Then he returned his gaze to the menu. "I'd advise you not to do that."

Julián opened his mouth to say something back, but Eduardo interrupted him by standing up so suddenly, his chair went toppling to the ground. People around them stared, particularly when Eduardo made no move to pick it up. Instead, he pointed a finger at Julián.

"Want to know why Meryn left you?" Eduardo asked, throwing Julián off. He furrowed his brow. "Well, do you? 'Cause I know."

"What the fuck are you talking about, man?"

Eduardo shrugged. "Ask Alejandro."

Julián's stomach tensed. If anyone had asked him, he would have said he'd actually been enjoying this encounter up to this point, but that this was the moment when he started wondering if this had been a bad idea after all.

No one got a chance to ask Julián that, though.

Eduardo simply turned around, then, and left, stomping away through the crowd, which left Julián to pick up the chair and apologize to those around him.

"He just got some bad news," he said, watching as Eduardo turned a corner and disappeared from sight.

CHAPTER TWENTY

After listening to the voicemail from the Villareals—expressing understandable anxieties about their son's whereabouts—he took a moment to compose himself in Gabriel's study, trying to decide if he should let off steam somewhere else or investigate what had caught his eye. A strap poked through from the lowest drawer of the desk, which had been left open a few inches. He looked toward the door, then leaned over to pull the drawer open all the way. The strap was part of a duffel bag, and something about it made him want to inspect it.

He shot another look toward the door, then zipped open the bag. At first glance, it seemed empty, but then in a side pocket he found a gold wristwatch with a thin band. Something about it felt familiar. He held it up and saw that it had stopped ticking.

Just then, he heard steps approaching outside, and he stood up quickly, slipping the watch into his pocket out of instinct and sliding the drawer shut in one motion, right as Maria opened the door to the study.

"Gabo, eres tú?"

Fortunately, his hand had landed on the phone receiver, which he now picked up with a smile.

"No, Señora Velasco, soy yo, Julián. Finally got around to listening to the voicemail. They were just checking in. I'd been having so much fun here, I forgot to give them a call."

Maria smiled back, blissfully unaware. "You're a good son," she said. "Makes me miss mine."

He stepped around the desk, feeling the watch still in his pocket as he walked toward her. She was leaning against the doorframe, looking like she might fall over at any moment. "Is it okay if I turn the light on?" he asked. "I didn't realize how dark it has gotten."

"No, don't," she said. "No lights." She shook her head and made a little moaning noise. "This medicine . . ." She made as if to walk away but didn't quite have the strength, and Julián had to swoop in to catch her by the arms. "Plus, this house is so unnecessarily big," she went on, patting Julián's hand and gesturing toward the door. "I was trying to get to bed."

"You want me to get you some tea?"

"Oh, that would be lovely, thank you," she said. She leaned into him, and together they stepped into the hallway. Julián was struck by how light she was. As they shuffled along together, he felt a surge of affection and care for this poor woman. Everyone was still out, gallivanting around the countryside no doubt, and here she was alone with just the staff—and Julián.

She'd lost a son, and not only was her husband forbidding her from telling the world how he'd died, but she was going through some medical issue, also in the dark.

When he eased her into bed and set the cup of tea beside her, she surprised him by grasping his hand in hers. In the setting sun streaming into the room, he saw that her eyes were wet with tears. "You remind me so much of him," she said, her voice breaking.

Julián felt his emotions rise up in his throat, and he did what he could to contain them.

"You're a gentle soul, Julián," she said, smiling. Then she groaned as she sank into the pillow, closing her eyes. "Ale was too. A beautiful, gentle soul, and this world is worse off without him."

"It is," Julián said softly. Maria was still gripping his hand, and he found himself squeezing back.

"I couldn't save him," she said now, letting out a long, controlled breath, like she was fighting off nausea. "It was my job to protect him, and I failed. I would do anything for this family. For Gabriel, for my children. But sometimes when doing things for others, a person makes mistakes. Terrible mistakes."

A weak sob escaped her throat, and she turned her head away as the sound of laughter from downstairs carried through into the room. He could hear Mateo's obnoxious cackling, louder than it needed to be, as if he were trying to prove he was having a better time than anyone else. Gabriel's growl of a voice carried through, too, then more laughter. Everyone must have just gotten home.

He squeezed Maria's hand and pulled the covers up for her.

"I didn't protect him," she said again, drowsier this time, her body finally relaxing.

Within a few moments she was snoring, and he was left to listen to the sound of her breathing while downstairs someone turned on music. He waited a few minutes, until Maria's grip naturally loosened; then he got up and shut the door quietly behind him. He stood in the darkened hallway, gathering himself. The poor woman was blaming herself. But even a perfect mother would not have been able to save Alejandro from the convoluted web of lies surrounding her family.

He went back to his room, his hand in his pocket before he opened the door, ready to examine the watch, glad his instinct had been to keep it and not put it back in the duffel bag. As he'd been talking to Maria, it had come back to him where he'd seen it before. And now, taking a closer look at it in the light, he could tell his hunch was right. Cartier. He'd seen it on Elizabeth that day at the clubhouse when she'd confronted him and had hinted about being closer to more of the Velascos than just Sofia.

The suspicion over what it was doing in Gabriel's study, shoved into a duffel bag in a drawer, was already sinking in before he flipped the watch around and saw the engraving on the back. *Love your enemy.* From *The Art of War.*

Julián went to the window and cracked it open, needing the cool mountain air as his thoughts swirled around. Could Gabriel and Elizabeth really have been sleeping together? It seemed unlikely that there was any other explanation for the engraving.

But why would Gabriel still have it, then? Did it mean that Gabriel was there when Elizabeth died?

Suddenly, her death came into clear focus. It was so simple. Powerful men found ways to silence their mistresses all the time, didn't they? Especially when those mistresses demanded—or knew—too much. Elizabeth may have gained knowledge to some of Gabriel's shady business dealings and ran her mouth about it, or simply threatened to go public with their affair. Jesus, their affair. Poor Maria.

He climbed into bed, where he tossed and turned for a while. Laughter echoed throughout the massive house, along with the faint thumping of music as the others continued their partying.

Julián pulled a pillow over his head, wanting to gather his thoughts. One other thing made him think Gabriel was likely the killer. Ruthlessness was one of his main qualities. Ale used to say it; Sofia had said it recently, too, and that was even before Gabriel had handed the COO title to that leech Mateo after Sofia had been the one to save the merger.

Above it all, Julián couldn't believe the gall, to have evidence of his crime just sitting right there, easily discoverable by anyone poking their head into his study. If this theory was true, Gabriel had no fear of getting caught. Probably because he'd viewed Elizabeth as disposable and felt the rest of the world would agree.

Julián thought about Elizabeth, her body floating in that pool. His little problem taken care of.

When his thoughts had exhausted him fully without bringing sleep, he pulled himself out of bed and walked through the finally quiet villa. There were no signs of the dinner that had stretched well into the night, other than an ashy firepit with one charred log still emitting a thin tendril of white smoke. Everything else had been cleaned up by Gustaf and the rest of the villa's staff. Hours and hours of eating and drinking, and none of them had to lift a finger for themselves. He wondered what that did to the psyche, never having to clean up after yourself.

He grabbed a blanket from a pile that had been folded and stacked into a basket near the terrace's lounging furniture and settled into a love seat with the blanket over him, looking at the moon's reflection shimmering on the water, the gentle lapping of waves against the dock below, audible only because there was absolute silence otherwise.

Watching the first hints of sunrise appear in the slivers of sky visible between the mountain peaks, he remembered all the stories Ale told him about his dad. How he'd forced Alejandro to go hunting with him and some Montana businessmen a few times. They'd gone out to the Velascos' hunting lodge, about an hour from San Miguel, deep in the woods. In front of everyone, his father had pressured him into shooting a wounded deer between the eyes. Alejandro had hated the sickening feel of pulling the trigger on the helpless animal, despite Gabriel insisting he would be putting the doe out of her misery. That it would "make him a man," to do what was right. In fact, Ale later told Julián, he knew it was his father who'd purposefully shot the doe from afar, knowing he'd have the opportunity to make his son finish the job. "Sometimes you have to do what you have to do, son," he'd said.

Had it been like that with Elizabeth too? All this time, he had been looking at her as a suspect but missed the tragic truth. True to the role people like her often played in such stories, she was just another victim of the Velascos.

He clenched his fists around the watch. Gabriel was a killer. He had no doubt about this.

The question now was whether he'd also been the one to kill Alejandro.

CHAPTER TWENTY-ONE

Sofia loved being up so high. The world far below her, almost like no one at all existed, save for the few others in the helicopter with her. Today, that meant just her parents, Mateo, Julián, and the pilot. Looking at the sight of the Alps around her, the lake below, the sun reflecting off the turquoise expanse and the snow on the mountaintops, she actually felt perfectly content. Especially with the whir of the blades overhead, the constant droning drowned out everything except her own thoughts.

"A huevo!" Mateo's voice crackled through the headphones. She took a deep breath at his childish excitement, trying to resist the not entirely serious urge to shove him out the helicopter door. "Mi amor, estás viendo esto?"

Where the hell else would she be looking? She patted his leg, allowing him his little burst of eagerness, under the circumstances, then focusing on the whir and the landscape and how close she felt again, as she once had, to everything she'd wanted. Out on the boat two days ago, her father's little announcement had set her back, undoubtedly. She'd been blindsided, furious. But Sofia was not one to stay down when she was kicked. No matter how hard it had been to swallow. Yesterday, she'd revenge-fucked her way into some semblance of calm, and after she'd left Julián's room, she had come up with a plan. Another one.

If her father wasn't going to hand her the job and the shares that she'd earned, then she was going to simply have to take them in her own way.

As of this morning, that was exactly what she'd done, and now everything was going to work out just as she wanted. One step closer after this morning, and she felt like celebrating.

But first, the waterfalls.

The helicopter landed at a ski resort, closed for the offseason. Sofia jumped out first, instinctively ducking down to avoid the blades. This was her ideal way to celebrate. Go somewhere beautiful and then just slowly run away from Mateo and her parents on the hike, speedwalking ahead of them so she could have a little time to herself to appreciate her plan.

She'd done this hike a few times before, the first when she was at school. Back then, the villa visible from the waterfall wasn't the Velascos'. Gabriel had brought them back here, right before she graduated, in order to point it out and announce that it was theirs now. They could come back here whenever they wanted.

It was hard to remember her mom back then, a fit woman who liked going on morning runs, who socialized most nights of the week, instead of only when her husband requested her presence. That day, she'd practically jumped into Gabriel's arms, to the embarrassment of both Ale and Sofia, who weren't used to the sight of their parents being affectionate.

Maria agreed to come on the helicopter but had already said she wasn't sure if she'd join for the hike this time, which Sofia thought was probably for the best. It looked like just getting out of bed had exhausted her. When they'd taken this helicopter ride in the past, Sofia remembered her mom leaning to look out the window like a little girl, her eyes bright with glee. This time her expression had been peaceful at best, though distracted was probably more accurate.

But it turned out that the resort had been able to secure an extra large ATV that could make the trip on the rugged trail. The hike was short, anyway, since they'd taken the chopper most of the way up. Sofia led the way, not bothering to pace herself, happy for a little alone time. She thought Julián might be able to keep up with her, but when she turned to look over her shoulder, she found him walking alongside the ATV, chatting with her mom. Mateo and her dad were walking together, laughing it up too. Had Mateo already spilled the beans? Should she go make sure he didn't get ahead of himself? Unlike Julián, who seemed to get along with her dad out of his own self-interest, Mateo seemed to actually enjoy his company. She wasn't sure she preferred that. But the truth was it didn't much matter if Mateo spilled the beans now.

Fifteen minutes later, she heard the roar of the waterfalls getting closer. She picked up the pace. It was probably her favorite sight in the world. The trail kept going ahead to the pool at the bottom of the falls, but this overlook was the true gem of the hike. She could take in the full sight of the water gushing down. At certain times of the year, it was more of a stream, and sometimes the falls were frozen solid. But now, in late summer, they were in full force. There was something about the sun glinting off the wet rocks, the turquoise lake far below, the various towns dotting the shore like an afterthought. The blues and greens so vivid, it was as if this were the place where those colors originated, where they were sourced for the rest of the world.

She had about thirty seconds to take in the views before everyone arrived, and she was thankful for the waterfalls drowning out everything else, a continuation of the sound of the helicopter blades. She wasn't so desperate as to equate the sound to applause, but fuck it, a little self-congratulation was in order. And it was all the more satisfying that no one knew what she'd accomplished yet. Everything else she was going to achieve.

Men liked to announce every little thing they did. They wanted claps on the back, press conferences, champagne in their honor. As for Sofia, she was happy to climb a mountain and take in the sights without anyone knowing about it.

Yes, there was still a tiny bit of rage that it had come to this. That her dad hadn't just given her the position she'd earned, that she had to play along with his plans for a little longer. It was enough to make her want to throw herself off the ledge. Not that she ever would. She wouldn't give them that satisfaction, that confirmation of their underestimation of her.

She was pleasantly surprised when it took a few minutes for anyone to join her, and even more so to see that it was Julián. He was sweating slightly, and she could smell his pleasant musk wafting over, reminding her of their secret romp the other day. Her fingers twitched with the urge to grab his shirt and pull him close as she remembered his hands on her hips, his lips on her skin.

"Stunning, isn't it?" she said, cocking an eyebrow at him.

"Yeah," he said quickly, though he was looking at her, not the falls. "I overheard Mateo saying something about how this hike is a celebration of something. What I want to know is, What are we celebrating? I thought you and I already had a pretty good private celebration yesterday . . ."

"We did, didn't we?" She beamed at him, then turned to take in the sights one more time. She almost couldn't find it in her to be upset at Mateo's big mouth. When she noticed that Julián was studying her, confused, she pulled her hand out from the pocket where she'd been keeping it strategically throughout the morning. The diamond band was far less ostentatious than her engagement ring, so there was a chance Julián might not have noticed it. Her mom was the likeliest to, but not in her current state.

She flashed it now at Julián, studying his face for his reaction. She knew there was a chance that it was a cruel move, that their little fling had resulted in some feelings on his part. But she had the sense that he might understand her plan with just a look. That he would see what she was doing by pushing the marriage up. She was taking back control of her own life. If she wasn't going to be COO, she would at least have the shares the position came with. She waited for a knowing look, an understanding grin. But he kept his expression neutral.

"What's this?" he asked, his voice even, giving as little away as his face did.

"Mateo and I made it official this morning," she said, pulling her hand back and admiring the ring herself. They'd driven early to Bern, where the uncle of one of her former boarding school classmates worked as a judge. He'd signed the paperwork, and they'd gone straight to the Mexican consulate to show them the marriage license and ensure it would be recognized back home. The clerk had pushed back a little, saying the process would be much longer. But all it had taken was a phone call to Lukas, who had connections in the Registro Civil in Mexico City. They'd have a few hoops to go through back home to make it official, after which they would be husband and wife, with all the privileges that bond came with. Including shared possessions.

She'd been the one to pick the ring out after all the bureaucracy. Mateo couldn't be trusted to choose something not visible from space. She'd also been the one to convince him that they should just elope that morning. They'd still have the big wedding her mom wanted to throw back in Mexico, but she wanted the marriage official as soon as possible.

Julián opened his mouth to say something, but then closed it again. He was surprised by the news; that much was clear. Hurt? Maybe. A part of her was happy to see the power she had over him. Though in truth, she had been enjoying his company more than she'd care to admit. She had even hesitated to go to the courthouse with Mateo because she'd been thinking of Julián. But she had told herself that he was just a fun romp. A kindred spirit of a sort, sure. But soon they'd each move on with their lives.

As he was about to speak again, they heard the crunch of the ATV's tires announcing the others had arrived. Sofia ignored the distraction and looked back at Julián, wanting to hear what he had to say. But he kept his eyes on the rest of the party and gave them a little smile and a wave. He went over and helped Maria off the ATV, while Gabriel and Mateo walked unaware toward Sofia, talking about European football.

They stood and watched the view for a while, still chatting obliviously while Julián took two steps at a time with her mom, who seemed to be struggling with the short walk to the lookout point. Eventually, Sofia had to say, "Pa, ve a ayudarle a mamá, no?"

He looked annoyed for a moment, then finally remembered to be a decent person and went over to his wife. Julián stayed with Sofia's mother, too, both men easing her back into the ATV to have a seat. Mateo cast a brief glance in that direction, then slung an arm around Sofia, spinning her around so he could take a selfie with her with the view in the background.

She could push *him* off this ledge—the thought came to her with an eerie calmness. Convince him to walk back with her and have the others take the ATV down, then say he had fallen over the edge while taking one of those selfies. Maybe they'd suspect her for a fraction of a second, but she'd be able to sell it: the heartbroken new bride.

She could see it so clearly in her mind's eye. The heaving sobs she would deliver to her parents first, then to the Swiss police. Playing catatonic for a while, wearing the ring in homage to her dead husband, but mostly because she really fucking liked the ring, and it would be a shame to have to stop wearing it.

She gripped Mateo's arm, perhaps a little too hard, fighting the powerful rising urge inside her.

"Is your mom drunk or what?" Mateo said with a laugh.

Confused, she turned back to her parents and Julián, and saw her mom wobbling as she tried to get back into the ATV, looking like she was about to faint.

Forgetting the murderous thoughts from moments before, Sofia dropped Mateo's arm and ran to her mom's side. Julián was helping Gabriel catch her and ease her down to the ground. Mateo was on his phone immediately, trying to dial the resort below to get a doctor. "No signal," he muttered, trying again.

Julián put his head to Maria's chest. "She's breathing, heart's beating. She just fainted."

Sofia held her mom's head, trying to lightly slap her awake. Her eyes fluttered, but nothing more, so she turned toward the ATV driver, who was already speaking German into his walkie-talkie. "A doctor!" she said.

The man nodded at her. Maria was coming to already, a soft moan escaping her lips. "Estoy bien," she said. She spoke so softly that Sofia could practically see her breath fall to the ground before it could even reach her. All thoughts of announcing her elopement flitted away, replaced by guilt that she'd done it at all, knowing how it would hurt her mom. Her mom, who clearly was not okay.

"Deep breaths," Julián said. "Don't get up; we're here. We're here for you."

Sofia watched him, his eyes on her mother. It was amazing that a man so reserved just a second ago was now displaying such open tenderness.

Once they'd gotten her mom some water and she'd gathered sufficient strength, they returned to the resort, Gabriel riding with Maria in the ATV, and Sofia, Mateo, and Julián walking down in hurried, uncomfortable silence.

Well, except for all the oblivious blabbering Mateo was doing about the wedding celebration he still wanted to have. "I can't just marry the woman of my dreams and not show her off to the world, you know?" he said to Julián, giving him a little nudge in the ribs. "We're thinking we'll have a little early honeymoon to properly celebrate," he added, now nudging Sofia. "Your family's hunting lodge." He turned back to Julián. "Sofia's always liked that place. Not as a real honeymoon, of course. We'll go somewhere even nicer for that. Just the warmup."

She had suggested the hunting lodge as a diversion, knowing they were heading back to Mexico tomorrow and that Mateo was getting restless. She wasn't stupid; she'd seen the way he looked at her last night, when he came home and she had barely washed the sex out of her hair.

But if he overtly suspected anything was going on between her and Julián, he hadn't let on.

And now, he seemed content as a pig in shit with the fact that she was wearing a ring and officially "belonged" to him.

At the resort, a car was waiting to take them back down to the villa, where a doctor would meet them to check in on Maria. Before they loaded into the car, Sofia pulled Julián aside. "Thanks for helping. I appreciate it."

Julián nodded sternly, but he held her eyes, which gave away a little more longing than he'd allowed himself to show earlier. At least, Sofia thought it was longing.

"Of course," he said. "Ale was like a brother to me. He was family."

Mateo came up from behind Sofia and wrapped his arms around her possessively. "Yes, and now they're *actually* my family. And this little Velasco's all mine."

◆ ◆ ◆

Sofia's phone had been buzzing since they'd regained reception, not far from the villa. But she didn't care to check it until the doctor had assured her that her mom would be okay. Her pulse had steadied, and the doctor seemed to think the dizziness had been brought on by altitude.

He suggested that she see her regular doctor when they got home, and recommended drinking plenty of water and resting until then. *Yeah, no shit,* Sofia wanted to say. Instead, she said, "Danke," and saw him out.

In the meantime, her dad had taken Maria upstairs to bed. Mateo was out on the terrace, scrolling through his phone, and apparently Julián had gone to the villa's courts alone. She thought about joining him—she could use a little rally to let off some steam before they all flew back to Mexico—but her phone buzzed again, and this time it caught her attention.

The notification had come from Lukas. And when she took a minute to actually look at her phone, she saw a huge scroll of missed calls, most of them with a voicemail attached—*all* from Lukas and a few texts saying simply Call me and Urgent.

When she dialed him back, he answered before the second ring, because of course he did. She could picture him just staring at his phone, desperately waiting for her to call back. What a needy little man.

"Thank God," he said right away. "I've been trying to reach you."

"Yeah, Lukas, I know. I have my phone in my hand, and I see the thirty-seven thousand notifications of your doing that. What's so important?"

"I'm going to the police," Lukas said, all of a sudden sounding out of breath.

She paused. Her first thought was *Elizabeth.*

"Lukas, slow down. What is this about?" She glanced around and stepped toward the terrace where she wouldn't be overheard.

"Sofia, it's serious."

"Jesus, Lukas, just spit it out," she said, her voice dry in her throat.

"Since you asked me to keep an eye on Julián, I've had my contacts in San Miguel and in LA looking into him, and your brother."

"Okay. And?" She wanted to strangle him through the phone. What was this melodrama for?

"The police have suspicions about your brother. How he died."

"Okay . . ." She let out a breath.

"And also . . ." She could hear him panting, like he couldn't wait to get this part out. "About Julián. His parents have just filed a missing person report. His car was just found at the bottom of a cliff." He paused as if to maximize his words' effect. "And there was a body inside."

CHAPTER TWENTY-TWO

"Julián Villareal?" the immigration officers had each asked, looking quizzically between him and his passport when he and the Velascos returned. He'd nodded and held his breath going through immigration both in Europe and in Mexico, but they stamped his passport, and he was waved through without incident.

Before leaving Switzerland, he hadn't found a single moment to talk to Sofia alone about her actually having married Mateo. Not that there'd been much time. As soon as the Swiss doctor had cleared Maria for travel, they'd all packed their bags to go back to Mexico.

And almost as soon as they landed, Sofia and Mateo had left to drive out to the Velasco hunting lodge for a miniature honeymoon. Sofia's hastiness—after rolling around in bed with him just days prior—didn't sit right. And he'd seen the wariness with which she'd been eyeing him ever since they came down the mountainside after that ill-fated hike. Something was up; he just didn't know what.

On top of that, he was now alone in the house with an almost entirely bedridden Maria, and Gabriel, who in all probability had killed Elizabeth.

In comparison to Switzerland, the house was already quiet. But now that Sofia and Mateo were gone, it felt nearly abandoned. Almost haunted. Portraits on the walls all seemed to stare at Julián, as if to say, *We know who you really are.* It gave him the chills, and he wondered if he'd caught some kind of bug or altitude sickness from the travel.

Gabriel stayed in his study all day, and Julián had explored the house so much that there was little snooping left to do. He drove his rented Porsche around to clear his thoughts, then went to the courts to hit some balls against the wall. All the while, there was this terrible hopeless spinning in his gut. This fear that his time was running out.

On the second evening, he went back to the Velascos' and was reading various LA newspapers on his phone, looking for any headlines that might be of particular interest to him. Perhaps Julián's parents had made enough noise to trigger an investigation, for example. He was in the living room when he heard the intercom ring and Amalia answer. Julián had learned his lesson with Mateo and didn't rise to go to the front door. A few moments later, Amalia passed by to let whoever it was in.

It turned out to be Lukas. Julián assumed that he was here for Sofia and hadn't heard about the mini honeymoon either. Instead, Lukas came straight to the living room toward Julián, who was having a cup of coffee to try and beat jet lag, or whatever this gnawing feeling was.

"Julián, I have something I'd like to discuss with you." Lukas's tone was a little gruffer than he cared for.

"Wonderful." He crossed his legs and kept his coffee mug in his hands so he'd at least have something to do while Lukas started yipping at him.

"Let's go outside." Lukas crossed the living room and headed toward the courtyard. "You'll need the fresh air."

Julián sighed. He wanted to stay right where he was, especially because he didn't want Lukas to feel like authoritatively crossing the room meant he had any authority at all. But sometimes it was easier to just go along with things than fight someone who'd make a big deal over every detail. And being outside made it less likely that Amalia would overhear whatever Lukas had to say.

He rose from the couch and followed outside, where the day's lingering heat made him instantly sweat. Lukas, too, was already sweating, though maybe that had been the case even before he arrived at the Velascos'. He seemed fired up, standing in the courtyard with his hands on his hips, his chest all puffed out. He was gripping a manila folder so hard that it was bent.

"What can I do for you, Lukas?"

"Enough of the fucking pleasantries," Lukas barked. "Did you do it?"

Julián took a long sip from his coffee, keeping his eyes locked on Lukas's. If Lukas thought Julián was going to confess something with such a weak attempt, they were both going to stand there sweating for a long time.

Lukas scoffed, and then approached Julián, his body language indicating he was gearing up for a fight. But he stopped a few paces away, maybe having learned his lesson the last time. "You did. I fucking know you did, and I'll find the proof for it. So you should confess or get ready for me to bring the hammer down on you."

He resisted the urge to snort. Laughing at little angry guys never really helped anything. But if Lukas thought Julián was a killer, this was a strange approach. His wealth probably made him feel completely insulated from harm. "Why don't you tell me what it is I supposedly did."

"You killed her!" Lukas growled, taking a step closer, his hands off his hips to protect himself in case Julián decided to put him in his place again. Inside the folder, Julián could see a few loose sheets of paper, though he couldn't make out what they were.

He furrowed his brow. "Killed who? What are you talking about?"

"Elizabeth!" Lukas shouted, a bit of spittle flying off his lip and landing at his feet. This was interesting. Lukas had arrived at the same conclusion that Elizabeth had been killed. Lukas had been suspicious of him from the start. Even without any evidence, it made sense that Lukas thought he was guilty.

"The police ruled it an accident, didn't they?"

Lukas scoffed at this and was about to start going off again, but it was too late and still too hot for him to listen to Lukas say any more than he had to.

"Even if she was killed, it's ridiculous to think I'd kill her. Why would I do that? I barely knew her."

"Well, maybe she knew what I know about you," Lukas said, opening up the manila folder and pulling out a piece of paper.

He reached out to see why Lukas was showing him this, but before he could get a grip on the folder, and as a creeping suspicion went up his spine, Lukas turned the page to show a picture of a crime scene. A car, smashed to bits among some trees at the bottom of a cliff.

"Where did you get this?" He tried to keep his voice steady as he saw that it was a police report from the LA County coroner's office. "What even is this?"

"I've been having interesting conversations with the police, both here and in LA. You see that dark stuff in the driver's seat? It isn't just blood; it's a body that's begun to liquify. This poor person was found in the car at the bottom of a cliff not too far from the UCLA campus. They believe it's been there since May, not long before you arrived here." Lukas paused and studied his face. Before he could say anything, Lukas continued, "The car, it seems, was leased under the name of an MBA student at UCLA. One of Alejandro's classmates and closest friends. When they went to ask him about it, he wasn't available for questioning. They haven't been able to find him at all. They haven't even been able to reach him by phone, so of course they already suspected that was him at the bottom of the cliff."

He felt all the muscles in his body growing tense as he looked at the picture of the destroyed car, the viscera staining the driver's seat.

"My contact at the LAPD just called to tell me the lab results came in on the body, which matches DNA they took from the missing car owner's apartment. Do you want to know who was driving that car?"

Remain calm, he told himself. If he failed to remain calm, it was all over. This was just Lukas in front of him. Not the police.

He swallowed, all the spit drying up and going hard in his throat.

"Don't you want to know his name?" Lukas demanded.

He shook his head.

Lukas stared at him, eyes lit up with indignation. With—triumph. "This man in the photo was Julián Villareal."

He tried not to flinch.

Lukas shut the folder and tucked it back under his armpit. "So, tell me then, my friend. Who the fuck are *you?*"

PART FOUR

CHAPTER TWENTY-THREE

May

Eduardo and Alejandro both believed the same thing about tennis—
that the courts were equalizing. That out there, it was only the rhythm
of the rally and the pure skill of the player that mattered.

The thing was it had never been hard for Eduardo to blend in
with the likes of Julián and Alejandro. All three were light-skinned and
white-passing. Eduardo, with his natural good looks, would so effortlessly watch and mimic the casual, crooked grin girls loved. He would
shove his hands in his pockets to seem strong but unassuming and hold
eye contact but never for too long. He was a consummate studier of
other people, and drew his affable persona over himself like a cloak.

Sometimes even Eduardo didn't know who the real Eduardo was.
But that didn't matter. Because the real Eduardo had been nothing; he'd
learned how to turn himself into something. Into whatever he needed
to be.

Eduardo had been drawn to Alejandro like everyone else was. He
loved magnetic, brilliant people. There was so much to learn from them,
so much to absorb. That was what had led him to spend his time on the
UCLA campus in the first place. He worked nearby and one day had
found someone's student ID, which he found he could use to access the
tennis courts. And that was where he met Alejandro.

It had been a pleasant surprise to find Alejandro equally drawn to him. He'd learned throughout his life that his quiet demeanor, his tendency not to give much about himself away, only added to his own mystery and appeal. Alejandro, especially, seemed intrigued by Eduardo's reluctance to divulge much about himself.

And this seemed to piss off Julián, which was a bonus. Eduardo and Julián were friendly, too, at first, but over time, Julián had revealed himself to be arrogant, drawn to Ale for his wealth and status more than for the man himself. At least, that was what Eduardo had come to learn. Alejandro, rare soul that he was, either forgave this quality in Julián, or was blind to it entirely.

Then Meryn and Julián broke up, and the group went from four to three, a shift in dynamic that further heightened the tension between Julián and Eduardo. But Ale was good glue, and for a long time, he kept things smooth between them, despite having been—as Eduardo knew, but Julián did not—the reason for Julián and Meryn's breakup.

It had driven Julián—the real Julián—crazy that Ale, philosopher of privilege, someone who, though he examined that privilege, still had been born with a silver spoon in his mouth, deemed a friendship with the son of a janitor from Aguascalientes worthy of his time. Eduardo's father had been an immigrant who'd moved to Los Angeles with no papers, no money, and no English skills at all. Honorable, sure, but from a different world entirely than the one Julián and Alejandro belonged to. Eduardo had lucked into knowing Alejandro at all and, in Julián's opinion, didn't deserve his company.

That was because Julián—the actual Julián—had always belonged in Ale's world. He had gone to an international school in Mexico City, where his classmates had been the children of diplomats and business tycoons. He'd traveled extensively, had a trust fund in his name. The Villareals didn't actually know the Velascos, but they'd known *of* each other, had friends in common. Eduardo, on the other hand, had only lucked into this world. And he'd remained in that world because of Ale's graciousness. Because Ale had been a rare soul.

When Eduardo was growing up, his dad, Beto, had spoken a lot about rare souls. Those people who moved through the world with a glow about them, who had the almost magical ability to touch the lives of those around them in a meaningful way.

Beto worked at a country club in LA where the vast majority of people were decidedly not rare souls. They were rich people who moved through the world as if it belonged to them and only them. They left behind messes after they ate, tossed their wet towels on the floor instead of the nearby hampers. Most said "please" and "thank you," sure. But they talked down to Beto, or were dismissive of him in general. Few looked him in the eyes, something Eduardo himself witnessed on the occasions when he was allowed to come to work with his dad.

A manager at the club, another one of those rare gentle souls, would let Eduardo run around, pretending to be one of the members, as his father worked. Eduardo's mom had died when he was young, and this manager took pity on him. Eduardo even swam, ready with lies about who his parents were in case anyone asked. One day he'd wandered onto the tennis courts, empty because it'd been too hot for all the country club people spoiled by AC.

He'd watched people playing before, strangely enrapt by the game, the rhythmic thwacking of the ball against the rackets, those people always wearing white. But until that day, he'd never held a racket himself, never felt what it was like to hit the ball over the net.

So that was what he did, enamored by the first clumsy attempt, which had missed the ball entirely. The next swing sent the ball sailing well over the net and out of bounds (the beauty of the game: so simple that he knew more or less how to play by just looking at the lines on the ground). The one after that went straight into the net. But it didn't matter to Eduardo. He already knew his goal was to get better. From then on, he skipped the pool whenever his dad was allowed to bring him in.

Eventually, he learned the ins and outs of the club enough to know which locked gate was loose enough to squeeze through, and which night shift security guards were cool about letting him in, as long as he brought them a two-liter Coke and cleaned up after himself.

One of those nights, when Eduardo was thirteen, Jonas Schmitt, a tennis coach on the country club's staff, spotted him practicing with a racket he'd found in the lost and found box. Instead of asking what he thought he was doing after hours, or who he was, Jonas had asked for a game.

After fifteen minutes, the former German pro had approached the net. "You've never actually played against anyone, have you?"

Eduardo had merely shrugged. Either it had been such a pitiful response that it made Coach Schmitt feel bad for the kid, or he'd been looking for a passion project, someone to coach who wanted to be coached, rather than rich kids forced into the sport by their parents.

Eduardo started feeling like someone when he stepped onto a court. First, against Coach Schmitt, then in tournaments around the city. There, he lied about how long he'd been playing, lied about being a member of the country club, lied about what his dad did for a living.

On the court, however, nothing was a lie.

That was the whole truth, and Eduardo told it all exactly that way to Alejandro when Julián ratted him out.

But whoever said the truth would set you free must've been a good liar. Alejandro understood Eduardo's story—pitied him, maybe, which Eduardo hated, but took his side, nonetheless. Julián, on the other hand, didn't.

And that was why Julián had ended up dead.

CHAPTER TWENTY-FOUR

Lukas stood in front of him now, looking at him with a mix of indignation and fear. Eduardo had seen that look before. It had been in the moment just before someone fully recognized that the man standing in front of them wasn't the man he thought. It was the look he'd seen in the real Julián's eyes, before he died.

In many ways, he had been playing this game a long time. Longer, even, than he'd been playing tennis.

"You'd better start explaining yourself. You're going to have to talk with the police eventually, so might as well start with me," Lukas said, crossing his arms over his chest.

Even now, Eduardo could feel his mind whirring to keep up the lie. It was amazing, the instinct for self-preservation. His eyes darted around, searching for an exit. A weapon, maybe? But no. Every step of what he'd done up until now was rational. No one would have opened a single fucking door for him as Eduardo, the janitor's son. But Julián Villareal, with his pedigree and loaded coffers, had been given an easy pass straight into their world. Could anyone really blame Eduardo for having taken what Julián no longer needed? A name, a passport, an identity that was effortless to slip into, an image everyone liked and wanted and approved of. Even coveted.

None of that would last; he'd known that. But he'd thought he had a little more time. Then the heat had started to build. Elizabeth's death, then the trip to Switzerland, the unexpected call from the real Julián's parents. That damn Lana and her selfies. A flush of anger filled Eduardo on remembering that, but he tamped it down. Now was not the time for anger. He knew too well where anger could lead.

When he was sixteen, there'd been an incident at the country club. Some kids had caught onto Eduardo being the janitor's son. He'd flown under the radar because he physically looked the part, but they'd started to notice his threadbare clothes, his dirty sneakers, the way he spoke to the staff like he knew them. They turned it into a game to harass him, had thrown racist jabs at him, had threatened to call ICE. Eduardo was a citizen, but his father was not, and he didn't take kindly to those threats. When one of the kids—a tall white kid named Brandon who was getting recruited to play college baseball—came to the courts one day and started batting tennis balls at Beto, who was cleaning the stands, Eduardo lost it. He rushed at Brandon, ripping the bat from his hands. Brandon was still laughing when Eduardo swung the bat at his knees.

His dad had been fired; Eduardo had dropped out of school to find work to help sustain them both. His father hadn't looked at him the same way after that. At least until the dementia started to set in, and it was like it had all been erased. Eduardo saw how he changed again in his father's eyes, this time back into the innocent, tennis-loving boy Beto had once known.

Now Eduardo held his hands out, palms toward Lukas. "I can explain. But I need to know if I can trust you with the truth, Lukas." He kept his expression soft, repentant. He thought about smiling to disarm, but that would only put Lukas further on edge. Was Lukas really here without the police? The arrogance.

"First of all, I didn't kill Elizabeth, okay?" he said. "I wouldn't do that. I didn't kill anyone. But"—he lowered his voice—"I think you're right to suspect foul play."

Lukas snorted. His jaw was tensed, his hands gripping the sides of his shirt, which had come somewhat untucked—unusual for dapper Lukas. "You're a liar," he spit. "Why would I believe a word you say? The cops definitely won't when they come talk to you."

208

So, he hadn't already contacted them. Interesting. Lukas had come here to play hero, apparently believing himself on such moral high ground that he didn't think Eduardo would do anything to him. He believed Eduardo would just hold his hands out in surrender.

That attitude reminded Eduardo, in fact, of the real Julián. The way he'd discovered that Eduardo wasn't formally enrolled in the business school, and lorded it over him, when in fact he should have been impressed at what Eduardo had pulled off. It wasn't easy to fake your way into a prestigious program like that. It took brilliance and skill. A lifetime of studying not just books but people—of becoming an expert chameleon. Someone like the real Julián had nothing more than money and influence. Nothing of real internal value.

Now it was Eduardo's turn to squeeze his fists at his side. He didn't want the anger to show up, not now. Not again.

He stepped closer, so that he could speak softly to Lukas instead of having to raise his voice and risk attracting the attention of Amalia—or worse, Gabriel. But Lukas stepped backward, bumping into the decorative trellis at the edge of the courtyard. The trellis had several spots meant to hold potted plants, and the pot closest to Lukas wobbled. It was a heavy stone pot containing a succulent with a pretty orange flower. Lukas reached out to steady it, then held out a hand to warn Eduardo against getting closer.

Eduardo froze midstep, again raising his hands. But his patience was starting to thin. "Look; you're right. My name isn't Julián Villareal. I came here—"

"To what? Worm your way into the Velascos' good graces? Use their son's death to try to get close to their daughter? I bet you killed them both. I bet you killed Alejandro; you killed Julián; you killed Elizabeth, you sick fuck. Who are you?" He began to turn away even before Eduardo could answer.

The rage was surging now, causing Eduardo's pulse to spike. He was trying to explain something to this asshole, who was now walking away from him. Before he could really consider what he was doing, Eduardo cut the distance between them, gripping Lukas by the shoulder with his left hand and whipping him back to face him.

He didn't mean to do it this way, but now his right hand was flying up, the frustration boiling over. He gripped Lukas by the throat, squeezing hard enough to keep him from shouting out, hard enough to make him see what a fool he was being.

"Just listen to me, goddamn it," Eduardo said in a low voice, shooting a look over Lukas's shoulder to make sure no one had heard the momentary scuffle. Except he didn't know anymore if he wanted Lukas to listen. He already knew more than he should. Way more. "Alejandro was. My. Best. Fucking. Friend. You prick. You know nothing of friendship."

Lukas looked shocked—and more than a little scared as he reached up to grab Eduardo's arms and try to shake the larger man off him. "You're a fucking murderer!"

"Shut up, Lukas. I've warned you. You don't know what you're stepping in."

Lukas thrashed. "Whatever you've done, you're going down for it," he said, squirming. Scared. Like an animal. Like the doe Alejandro had been made to shoot right between the eyes. Eduardo had the irrational thought, then, that Gabriel had perhaps been right. Maybe to become a man, you had to be willing to do whatever it took. In the name of what was honorable and right. In the name of the Velascos. He squeezed harder, his fists narrowing around Lukas's neck, causing his face to redden.

He got close to Lukas's face, desperation snarling out of him. "You can't tell anyone about this, okay? You're gonna get back in your car. You're gonna tell the cops you know nothing. You're gonna pretend you never even saw me tonight. I'll go, okay? I'm not going to hurt anyone. But you have to shut your fucking mouth."

"What—did—you—do?" Lukas squealed out, still trying to get his arms around Eduardo and turn the altercation around in his favor. But

Eduardo was strong. Much stronger than Lukas. He kept himself lean, so people couldn't always tell just how powerful he really was.

"Relax," he said quietly. "I didn't kill anyone."

"You killed Alejandro," Lukas gasped out. "I know you did. Just wait until Gabriel finds out. You're a dead man."

There was spittle forming at the sides of Lukas's mouth. Eduardo had to loosen his grip. He had to calm the fuck down, but how could he? What stung most was the idea that he could be seen as the bully here and not the victim. It was wrong. It was backward. Julián had been the bully. The real Julián. Alejandro—he'd only been trying to help Eduardo . . .

"I warned you. Stop saying that."

"You killed Alejandro. Just like you killed Julián." Lukas's eyes were starting to turn red. A burst blood vessel, maybe.

Still, Eduardo couldn't pull himself away. "I did not." His jaw was clenched tight enough that it hurt.

"You did. You killed them both."

Eduardo's arms were shaking from the effort of restraining Lukas against the trellis, which rattled against the weight of the altercation. "I didn't kill Julián fucking Villareal, though he deserved to die. I didn't kill him—Alejandro did."

That got Lukas's attention. "You're fucking crazy." In his shock, he managed to somehow thrash out and scratch Eduardo's face. Eduardo, taken off guard, reeled back, loosening his hold on Lukas. Lukas stumbled to the side, trying to get away. Bumping again into the succulent plant in the in-laid stone pot on the trellis, which wobbled out of its holder and started tumbling toward the ground. Lukas took advantage of the distraction to turn away.

In an instant, Eduardo's tennis reflexes acted—he reached out and caught the swaying stone pot, about the size of a lamp, or a racket, and swung it.

The pot made contact with the back of Lukas's head.

A sickening crack filled the air.

Lukas fell to the stones.

Eduardo saw the blood starting to pool. Far too much of it for the short period of time since Lukas's body collapsed. And now, the heat in his own veins ran ice cold.

Fuck, fuck, fuck. Not again.

Eduardo was as still as Lukas for a moment. He shot a panicked look toward the arched doorway, sure that Amalia was going to come ask if everyone was okay. Maybe Gabriel would come down from the study, ready to yell at the commotion.

But nothing happened. Eduardo breathed in, thinking. "Lukas, get up," he said, but the whisper barely left his lips, and he knew that when he reached down to take his pulse, he wasn't going to find a heartbeat.

Just like last time.

◆　◆　◆

Last time it had been Alejandro swinging the unexpected object. A bowl where he kept his keys. And the victim hadn't been attacking Alejandro, but Eduardo.

After Julián had threatened to out Eduardo, he tried to make good on that promise, heading straight to Ale's. Eduardo had followed him there, begging him to just let him be. Then, like Julián should have known that Ale would, Ale jumped to Eduardo's defense. Said that Eduardo's lying about his admission status didn't mean he deserved to have his life turned upside down, have it taken away. Ale had shrugged and said he didn't believe education was only for the rich.

Julián had been livid, spittle at his lips as he shouted that he had had enough of Ale's philosophizing. That Ale had his head too far up his own ass to see that Eduardo was a leech. Eduardo had then tried to defend himself, calling out Julián's jealousy, his pettiness. He threw in a barb about Meryn, which in retrospect was in poor taste. That had incensed Julián, who'd lunged at him.

And it was as the two got into it, rolling around Ale's living room, that a loud crash had rung out, and Julián had fallen to the floor, leaving Alejandro Velasco standing over him, holding the shattered remains of a ceramic bowl, the rest of it scattered next to the blood that was already pooling on the ground.

CHAPTER TWENTY-FIVE

August

Alejandro had always hated the family hunting lodge and its adjacence to violence, but Sofia had loved it since she was a kid. The lodge was located a couple of hours west of San Miguel, in the Sierra de Pénjamo, and something about the quiet and the landscape resonated with her. It was both desertlike and forested, the mountain peaks rising dramatically every morning out of the fog. Walking in the woods there, she sometimes felt like she was the last person left alive, a feeling that thrilled her.

Except right now she wasn't the last person alive. Her husband, a man who'd suggested a hunting lodge as a goddamn honeymoon spot, was with her everywhere she went. He was with her when she woke up. He was at the stove pretending he knew how to make them breakfast, his scrambled eggs watery because he'd salted them way too early. After their typical and, in a way, obligatory morning sex, he stayed in bed instead of going off to the office like he normally would have, and his continued presence almost felt like an invasion of privacy.

When Mateo had cracked open a beer that afternoon, she jumped at the chance to be alone and casually said she'd go on a hike for a little bit, adding she was sure that he was craving some distance too. Instead, he popped right off the seat and brought his beer with him, packing another two for the road, one of which he might offer her.

On the drive to the trailhead, he started talking about their future kids, even though she'd told him the morning they got married in Switzerland that it wasn't on the table for at least two more years. That had been a lie to placate him and change the subject; she had no intention of having children with him, but she hoped he wouldn't bring it up again. "You were serious about that?" He laughed, and drank from his beer, then continued the conversation about his ideal timing for kids, what part of San Miguel they would live in, or if they wanted to maybe move to Mexico City for the private schools.

He kept it up on the hike itself, despite Sofia's silence, as if conversation were whacking a tennis ball against a wall and you didn't really need another party to keep up the game. From the baby conversation, he went on to what they should have for dinner. Sofia kind of enjoyed thinking about food while building up hunger on a hike. It was like dangling a carrot in front of yourself, and at the end you got the reward. Not that this was a normal hike where she was thinking about normal things.

It soon became clear that Mateo was under the assumption that Sofia was going to be cooking the meals he was suggesting.

"What about our relationship makes you think I'm going to go to the store after this hike to buy groceries and then put together a meal for us?"

Mateo slurped his beer and crushed his can, tossing it into the woods.

"Don't do that," she sighed, and went off the trail to pick up the can. This was going to be her life, cleaning up after this idiot. For a little while, anyway.

"Claro que vas a cocinar, mi amor. I've made you an honest woman. My understanding is that means you cook for me." He laughed to himself and smacked her ass, then pulled out another beer from his backpack, cracking it open and guzzling down half in a matter of minutes.

She let him drink and laugh it up, not wanting to pick a fight until they were back at the lodge, where she could more easily deal with him. At least, that was her mindset until they were in the car headed back and Mateo decided he couldn't let it go. "So, what are you cooking for me?"

She reached across the center console to smack him. "Shut the fuck up already."

"I'm not kidding. We brought groceries for us, right? I want you to be able to cook. For our kids one day." He burped. "But for friends too. What will people think of me if I have a wife at home who can't even make enchiladas?"

"We'll obviously hire a chef, Mateo," she said, trying not to growl.

"She'd better not be cuter than you," he said. A direct threat, no doubt. Loyalty wasn't implicit; it had to be earned. And even then . . .

They were speeding along the curving roads headed back to the lodge. If there weren't a chance that she'd get seriously hurt or killed, she might just swerve the car into a ditch. It was Mateo's car, and though he was wearing his seat belt, he had his legs up on the dashboard, the seat belt strap against his neck instead of his chest. She had a much better chance of walking away unharmed than he did. She squeezed the steering wheel until her knuckles turned white. There were other ways to hurt him and walk away unscathed.

"All right, you can drop this regressive machista persona you think you need to adopt because we're married now," she said instead. She sped up, in a rush to be at the lodge already, where she could at least get a few steps away from him if she wanted to.

"No seas así," Mateo scoffed. "Getting defensive when I'm mostly joking." He pulled his phone out, scrolling through social media, his eyes glazing over with all the beers he'd had. "But in the end, we both know the maids are going to cook anyway. No need to get your panties in a bunch, querida."

Sofia didn't bother responding to that. Let him keep drinking until he passed out and gave her some peace. When they got home, he'd switch to tequila, which would make things easier for her. But it seemed Mateo wasn't done with his tirade yet. "You don't see me getting all pissy about your running around behind my back, do you?"

Even though she didn't want to give him the benefit of a reaction, she did glance away from the road, shooting him a look.

"You're smart, Sofia. Probably smarter than me; I'll admit it. But don't take that to mean I'm an idiot." He slid his feet off the dashboard and reached behind the driver's seat for the backpack they'd brought with them. A few seconds later, he cracked open the third beer.

"Switzerland," he continued. "If you're wondering when you messed up. I went looking for you the day before we came back home, to see if you wanted to grab dinner in town." She doubted that part was true. He probably just wanted to make her feel guiltier. She gripped the steering wheel and kept her eyes on the road. "When I couldn't find you, I had a feeling that maybe you'd be in that creep Julián's room, since you two had become buddy-buddy. Thank God for me I didn't catch you in the act or anything. But I did discover the little red lace number. The one I fucking bought you. You fucking whore."

He slurped at his beer and unbuckled his seat belt as Sofia pulled up to the gate and rolled her window down to punch in the security code. She thought about the cameras that would watch the car roll in and eventually back out. She thought about driving away and making an escape as soon as he got out of the car . . . but it was too late for that, wasn't it?

She was too far in.

Inside the lodge, Mateo went straight to the fridge, chugging the rest of his beer so he could start working on the next. "Don't get me wrong; I'm still happy to be your husband. Happy to be a part of that wonderful fucking Velasco world." Mateo burped and wiped at his mouth with the back of his hand. He tossed the empty can toward the bin in the corner, but missed. The beer rattled back toward them, a few drops spilling onto the tile. The fresh can didn't seem to be enough for him, though. He left the kitchen and went into the adjacent dining room, where a bar cart stood in the corner. He grabbed at the tequila añejo that her father kept in a glass decanter, just as she'd expected. There were no glasses in the bar cart, as she'd planned. She'd moved them all when they'd arrived and Mateo had gone to use the bathroom.

She grabbed a low-ball glass from the kitchen and brought it to him.

"See, not so hard to do things for your husband, is it?" He practically snatched it from her, barely looking at the glass as he poured in three fingers' worth. "I think that's a good entry point, actually, to mention that I'm not going to punish you for what you've done to me." He brought the tequila up to his lips and sipped, a surprising amount of self-control for the drunken mania he was exhibiting. "Carajo, qué rico," he said, more to himself than to her. Now he took a bigger swallow, and Sofia tried not to breathe a sigh of relief.

Except Mateo was smiling in a way she'd never seen before. His eyes looked crazed, and it wasn't just the booze. Sofia had seen her now husband turn into an occasional asshole before. But the look he was shooting her now felt unhinged. "I'm not even going to punish you," he said again, his voice softer than before. He took a step toward her, and she instinctively stepped back.

Mateo only laughed, drinking more tequila, then grabbed her wrist. He was trying to make it seem like a normal tender touch, but it was firmer than needed to be. "No, wait; I misspoke. I'm not going to *hurt* you. And I don't even see it as a punishment, but I think you might. Which is okay. You're allowed to feel things however you're going to feel them." Another drink of tequila. Sofia kept her eyes on his, trying to keep track of how much he'd drunk. How quickly would he be out? Maybe not quickly enough.

"See? I'm a modern man. Privy to all the lingo." Another drink. Except now he put the glass down on the cart and tightened his grip on her wrist. "But from now on, I am going to demand a little more respect. I'm going to demand obedience." He squeezed harder and pulled Sofia closer. "That's not too much to ask, is it?"

Sofia shook her head, knowing better than to push back now. "No, of course not."

He took hold of both wrists. Sofia had felt more or less in control until that moment. But suddenly she was wondering if she had misread the situation from the beginning. Misread Mateo from the beginning. He leaned in close, the tequila practically fuming off him. Maybe he had drunk enough. "And if you don't obey me, I will ruin you. I love you, Sofia. I really do." As if to prove it, he let go of one of her wrists and grabbed the hair at the back of her head, tilting her as he approached for a kiss. It was a move that under the right circumstances turned her on. Right now, it made her feel like a chicken with its neck exposed to the farmer's ax. Mateo kissed her, hard and long. She resisted the urge to pull away.

"Understood," she said. "Let me get a glass and join you. We can go get more comfortable by the fireplace."

Mateo still had her by the wrist, though, letting go of only her hair to reach for his tequila, downing it quickly and pouring himself more. Sofia kept her eye on the glass, now going from nervous to frightened. She tried gently tugging herself away from him, but Mateo only hardened his grip.

"No," he barked. "We're gonna do a little trial run; how about that? You'll sit with me while I drink, and you'll do what I say for once."

"Mateo, you're hurting me," Sofia said, trying to sound playful instead of scared.

"Well, you hurt me!" Mateo shouted. He slammed his glass down on the bar cart and yanked Sofia back toward him, his free hand going back to her hair, but this time not even attempting to make it a seductive move. His pupils were dilated, his nostrils flaring as he wrapped her hair farther around his fist. "You humiliated me, and I'm not gonna let you take control of our lives like that; you hear me? This shit ends now!"

Mateo pushed her toward the wall, causing a framed painting of agave fields to clatter to the ground, barely missing her head. His forearm was against her chest, just below her throat. And now fear took over her system entirely. Out of the corner of her eye, she looked for anything that she could use. The tequila glass was the closest option, but she wasn't sure if she could reach it without alerting Mateo to what she was doing.

Thankfully, finally, she saw the drugs start to take effect. She watched as Mateo's expression changed, and he blinked back what she guessed was a sudden bout of nausea. His grip on her loosened ever so slightly as he took a deep breath and shut his eyes against whatever was happening inside him.

Sofia took the advantage to sidestep away from him, smacking his forearm the way she'd learned in a self-defense class in order to get his grip on her wrist to slip. He swung frantically to try to get her back, but that only threw his balance off. He reached out one more time for her, but with too many sedatives in his system, what he should have done instead was take hold of the wall to steady himself.

Sofia had grabbed one of her mom's prescriptions before leaving San Miguel, then slipped the pills into his beers on the hike after preparing the glass for tequila earlier that day. She had emptied three capsules worth of powder, knowing Mateo would ask for the amber-colored añejo that would disguise her little addition. Sofia was well-acquainted with how easy it was to hide spiking a beverage.

Elizabeth herself should have been more watchful. She should have known better than to drink from an open glass if she hadn't seen where the glass had come from. Even if Sofia had handed her that glass.

Still, they were only meant to knock you out for a little while, make you loose enough not to notice you were getting robbed, or being guided laughingly toward someone else's car.

You had to know about appropriate doses.

Now Mateo was on the floor, face-first, still conscious, but losing the ability to do anything but breathe. He managed to flip himself over, and Sofia saw that he was covered in a cold sweat, his face pale. Good. She was glad he would see her face before closing his eyes for the last time. She wanted him to know that she had done this to him.

CHAPTER TWENTY-SIX

This time, Eduardo was going to have to act much quicker.

With Julián, he and Alejandro had been alone, able to wrap the body up in the rug Julián had fallen on. After Alejandro's initial panic subsided a little—begging Eduardo to understand he hadn't meant to hurt Julián, apologizing, crying, all the normal responses—Eduardo had managed to get him under control, and they started making a plan. Eduardo had noticed the way Alejandro's eyes went dark, watching as Eduardo began to lay out what they had to do . . . as if he were seeing the true Eduardo for the first time. Eduardo had wanted to explain how it was that he knew what to do. He'd spent his whole life trying not to get caught, trying to blend in, trying to go unnoticed. It wasn't that he knew how to get rid of a body. He just knew what grabbed people's attention, and how to avoid it.

They had taken their time cleaning up the blood, then used the privacy of Ale's garage, where Julián always parked, in order to twist and jam his body into the trunk of his own car.

Of course, Ale had been freaking out the entire time, on the verge of shock. Eduardo had talked him down, convinced him that the most important thing was to keep calm. No reason to fuck up their lives by going to the cops over it either. This wasn't Mexico, where bribes were straightforward. Yes, the rich got away with crimes in the US too. But did Ale want this following him around the rest of his life? And Eduardo had been there as well. He could get pinned for the murder. He didn't have access to the kind of lawyers the Velascos did. Ale could get away with this, but Eduardo would not.

Now, Eduardo looked down at Lukas's body, no luxury of time or solitude this time around. And since there was no narrative he could provide to explain how Lukas had *accidentally* cracked his head on the stone pot, and since the blood was starting to run even quicker, he had to act fast.

He ran inside to the chair where, just minutes ago, he'd been sipping on a coffee, which had now gone cold. He reached for a throw blanket nearby and ran back outside. He wet the blanket in the fountain and wiped what had accumulated on the cobblestones. The pot had remained intact, with just a streak of blood on it. He wiped it and replaced it in the trellis, then wrapped the blanket tight around Lukas's head to absorb any more blood still there. He'd have to come back later with cleaning products, once the body was gone, of course. But for now, at least, the area wouldn't attract attention.

He hooked his arms under Lukas's armpits and lifted, keeping quiet as he strained against the deadweight. Thankfully, Lukas was smaller than Julián had been, and Eduardo was able to lift him off the ground and support his weight. The side exit to the private driveway was nearby. Eduardo poked his head around the corner to make sure no one was coming, then shuffled through the archways as fast as he could. Lukas's car was just off to the right, a lucky turn of events, since the Suburban parked beside him would provide some cover.

Eduardo rummaged through Lukas's pockets for his keys. Even leaning on the railing, he almost broke an ankle a couple of times on the way down the steps. After catching his breath at the bottom, he shuffled to the side of the driveway less visible to the distant security cameras. He unlocked the back door, then slid Lukas in, out of sight.

Sweating, Eduardo walked calmly back into the house, considering everything that might give him away. Amalia had opened the door for Lukas, so she had to be made aware Lukas was leaving. Eduardo also needed to clean the spot in the courtyard near the trellises, but getting actual cleaning supplies meant explaining to Amalia why he needed them. He'd have to settle for a superficial scrub and assume that he would do a good enough job with the rest that no one would test the Velascos' tiles for blood or bleach.

There was a linen closet downstairs in the guest bathroom, so Eduardo hurried quietly to it, soaked one of the dozens of washcloths, and grabbed a second for drying. In the courtyard, he got on his hands and knees to clean, ready with a story about searching for a lost contact lens.

He'd acted quickly enough not to have too much of a mess left, though, and he hoped there were too many throw blankets and washcloths and napkins for anyone at the house to miss the handful he'd used. It'd be best to burn them, or at least get rid of them in different locations, so that Lukas's body, if it was ever found, would not be connected to the Velasco house.

Content enough with the courtyard cleanup, Eduardo grabbed the coffee cup and brought it into the kitchen as he usually did. He set it next to the sink with a smile toward Amalia, who was washing the blender, the smell of roasted salsa in the air.

"Voy a salir con el señor Lukas," he said, announcing their exit so Amalia would know Lukas had left and that she shouldn't expect Eduardo back soon.

"Going so soon? It's nearly dinner!" said a booming voice. Gabriel had come down from his office, and Eduardo froze, paralyzed to the spot, holding up a stiff smile like a mask. "You can't let me eat alone, my friend! You'll catch up with that shrimp later." He slapped Eduardo on the back and then guided him toward the table. "Amalia has made her pollo en mole negro. It could earn a Michelin star if I ever let her walk away from here."

The table was already set for two people, and the assumption would have annoyed Eduardo if he didn't have much bigger fish to fry. Fish that were dead and bleeding in the back seat of their own car.

"Maria's still not feeling well, and with the lovebirds enjoying themselves at the lodge, I need a little company." Gabriel laughed and pulled out the chair at the head of the table for himself, motioning for Eduardo to take the seat next to him.

"I'm sorry, Gabriel, but I made plans with—"

"You'll break them," Gabriel said firmly, though his tone was still light. "Lukas is a big boy. He can entertain himself while you have dinner with the man who's been hosting you this summer."

Eduardo smiled thinly, his mind flashing again to Lukas—was the skull leaking blood onto the floor of the car? With Sofia gone and Maria bedridden, no one at the house would leave and see Lukas's car. But would anyone new arrive and see it parked there? Eduardo couldn't rule that out, but the Velascos hadn't had that many visitors since he'd arrived, and he could see Gabriel asking people to give Maria some space.

He took a seat, reaching immediately for the glass of water already waiting for him, swallowing in big, rapid gulps. Amalia came by moments later with the food, and now Eduardo was going to have to pretend to have an appetite as images of Lukas flickered through his mind—those surprised eyes, that grimace, the stunned look as life flew out of him on contact.

"Joder, qué rico se ve," Gabriel said, unfurling a napkin and thanking Amalia as she retreated back to the kitchen.

Eduardo smiled and agreed, reaching for his silverware, feeling like a puppet, his movements jerky and automatic. He couldn't help but wonder if this was a trap. Had Gabriel heard or seen something? The courtyard wasn't entirely out of sight of the house.

What would Gabriel do to Eduardo if he knew the truth?

What had he already done to Elizabeth?

"You seem to be in a good mood," Eduardo said calmly. Getting Gabriel talking about himself was his best bet to make it through this dinner.

Gabriel had a good laugh at that, already on his second mouthful. "Is it that obvious?" He shook his fork a little in the air. "Now that the merger is done, the cherry on top is that a thorn in my side was removed. A low-life blackmailer."

Eduardo's head shot up at that. "Who?"

Again, Gabriel used his fork to wave the question away. "I'm not told the details. It's better that way. But everything is finally coming together now. My daughter is on her honeymoon with a decent man. It feels like for the first time in months, I can breathe." He laughed and scooped some rice through the thick black sauce.

Eduardo looked down at his own plate. The tines of his fork had dipped into the mole, revealing a reddish tint to the liquid. His mind flashed with images of Lukas on the floor, so similar to Julián lying on the ground with his head bashed in and Alejandro standing over him. Alejandro on his bed, blank-eyed, the vomit drying on his mouth. There hadn't been any blood then, but Eduardo's brain couldn't help but retroactively add some to the image.

"Why aren't you eating, Julián?" Gabriel asked, already on his third or fourth mouthful. "You haven't even tasted it yet. Everything okay?"

Eduardo had to swallow his initial urge to laugh at being called that name. At the fact that the way he heard the question, he initially thought Gabriel was asking if he was eating *Julián*. He forced himself to knife through the chicken drumstick and bring the sauce-laden morsel to his mouth, nauseated but keeping a pleasant smile plastered on his face. Sweat was pooling by his collar, the walls closing in on him.

He chewed and met Gabriel's eyes, buying time. "Sorry, my mind was on other things. This is delicious."

Gabriel stared at him for a moment. Too long a moment. Eduardo swallowed as best as he could, his mouth drier than desert air. "Do tell," Gabriel said, jovially enough. He turned his attention to his plate, giving no indication that this was anything but a pleasant conversation.

An idea occurred to Eduardo, and he latched onto it like a life raft tossed into murky waters. "Lukas," Eduardo said. "I'm just wondering how he'll seem when I meet up with him."

Now Gabriel frowned. "What do you mean?"

Eduardo felt himself relax the slightest bit. This didn't get rid of the dead body outside, but he could use this conversation for his own purposes. "Well, I'm sure you know that he's always been enamored with Sofia." He shrugged. "He doesn't hide it very well. He was distraught when we made our plans. I wonder if he's having a hard time knowing she's officially off the market now, if you'll pardon the expression."

He watched for Gabriel's eyes to narrow in suspicion, to smell the ruse or flat out call him on his bullshit. *I saw you beat the man's brains in! Who are you trying to fool?*

But no. Gabriel only laughed and dabbed at the corner of his mouth with a napkin. "I suppose I've picked up on that, yes. I don't want to sound like a delusional father, but I assume most men in Sofia's vicinity are in love with her." He shot Eduardo a subtle look, clearly baiting him. Did Gabriel know what he and Sofia had been up to, here and in Switzerland, right under everyone's noses?

Rather than risk Gabriel's leading them to a path he would rather they not go down, Eduardo continued, "Truth be told, there has been some friction in the friend group, from what I gather. I'm still an outsider, of course, but it's easy even for me to sense the tension between Lukas and Mateo." On a roll now, he felt his appetite returning. There were no police lights outside, after all. No one was calling after Lukas, wondering where he was. His cell was pinging the closest towers, and someone might catch onto the small inconsistencies in the timing later on. But that was something Eduardo would have to figure out later. Leaving without raising Gabriel's suspicions was more important for now.

He took a bigger bite of the chicken, finally feeling like he could taste it. As long as he could get through this dinner . . . "Please don't repeat this to anyone; I'd hate for it to seem like I'm gossiping. But part of why I'm meeting Lukas tonight is to assure him Mateo means him no harm."

At this, Gabriel raised an eyebrow. The sweat returned to Eduardo's forehead, though hopefully not too visibly. He thought he heard something shuffling about outside. Could someone have spotted a drop of blood? Had he overlooked some incriminating detail, some tiny item out of place? He forced himself to focus on Gabriel and not fall into paranoia.

"I know; I know," Eduardo said with a shake of his head. "I'm going to tell him that he has nothing to worry about. That, frankly, it's in his best interest to get over Sofia. He has this urge to take care of her. But I've never met anyone who is more capable of taking care of herself than your daughter."

Again, Gabriel cast his discerning stare on Eduardo. "Good," he said. "That's the right advice." He cleared his throat and drank some water. "I'm glad Sofia and Mateo aren't around right now. That they're enjoying themselves. Sofia especially. She deserves that much. She does take care of herself; you're right. But just a few hours with her out of the house, I'm reminded how much she takes care of the rest of us too. Her mother, definitely. Me, even though I don't like to admit it. Every step of the way, she's taken care of this family. By doing what is asked of her, and more. This merger wouldn't have happened without her. Sylvio Hinojosa and Rapido would not have glanced twice at Velcel without her. Every mistake I've made along the way, she's been there to clean up the mess." He paused, then called out to Amalia for a beer. They remained quiet until she brought one for him and returned to the kitchen, at which point Gabriel set his eyes on Eduardo again.

While it often seemed like Gabriel only looked at others with the intent to peer into their souls, now it seemed as if he were actually attempting to bare his own. It could have just been that Eduardo was distracted by the body he had to get rid of, misinterpreting things while his mind churned.

"A man wants his children to be happy. That's all he wants for them," Gabriel said at last, before returning to his meal.

Finally, Gabriel retreated to his bedroom. The house was quiet now. Eduardo had been painstakingly attuned to every noise for the last hour, eager to do what he had to do, but knowing he needed to be even more careful than usual. He'd been living a roller-coaster ride for the past few hours, the panic coming in waves, the urge to sprint to the car almost overwhelming as he tried desperately to race against the clock.

Now, his patience was rewarded by the calm that had come over him before in similar circumstances. His mind felt clear, his focus sharp. He knew what needed to be done.

In the car, he held up his phone to his face to block the cameras as he rolled out of the gate, trying to tamp down the sense of freedom when he drove through. He wasn't clear yet. And if someone reviewed the footage, it'd be easy to tell that the person driving the car wasn't Lukas. He just needed to buy himself as much time as possible.

The drive with Ale the night of Julián's death had been tense, Eduardo having to remind him over and over again that no one knew, no one was after them. No one knew there was a dead body in the trunk. All they had to do was drive calmly, follow traffic rules, and then get rid of the car.

"How are you so calm right now?" Ale had said. He had fidgeted with the air vents, opened and closed the glove compartment, wiped imaginary blood off his pants, all while constantly staring at the side-view mirror.

"Because I know what we have to do," Eduardo had said. "And I'm not alone in dealing with it. We're in this together, brother."

CHAPTER TWENTY-SEVEN

Sofia gave Mateo a little kick in the ribs. She wasn't trying to hurt him, just see if he was still alive, hoping she hadn't overdone it with the tranquilizers. She needed him alive. For now. So his time of death would make sense with the story she would tell. Although she did put a little something extra into the kick, just for her own satisfaction.

She kicked him once more, and he barely moaned in response, a few worlds away thanks to the pills. Wanting a shot of sedative-free tequila, but knowing she had to keep a clear head, Sofia instead leaned over and grabbed one of Mateo's legs and began to pull him toward the door.

The brute was heavy, though. She set his foot down, repositioned, then thought better of her approach. She cracked her neck, stretched herself out a little, too used to tennis and ballet to attempt moving Mateo without warming up.

But she had underestimated the heft of an unwilling body. She looked at her husband on the floor, thinking of how to best approach the situation, opting to pour herself some tequila after all.

And at that moment, her phone started ringing. The sound startled her, its sharpness cutting like a knife through the silence of the darkened countryside. She fumbled for her phone to shut it off, her hands shaking slightly when she saw the name on the screen. *Papa.*

Good Lord. She had to answer. Her father didn't like to be ignored, and if she didn't pick up now, he'd just keep trying all night, on her phone *and* Mateo's. "Papa! Now isn't a good time, I—"

"Yes, I know, querida. I'll let you get back to Mateo in just a second."

Sofia glanced down at the floor and briefly wondered if her father had secret cameras hidden around the property. It wouldn't be beyond him. But he continued. "Look; I've been thinking about you. About Switzerland and . . . I know."

Sofia gripped the phone tighter, remembering her and Julián together. Mateo had made clear that she and Julián hadn't been all that subtle about it. But did her father really know too? Was he about to threaten her with even less involvement in the company? "Pa," she started, but he spoke over her.

"I know you wanted that title," he said. "I could see how disappointed you were, and you're a hundred percent right to be." *Holy shit.* Was she hearing right? "You deserve to be in this company's leadership, and I'm going to make it happen. Monday morning, I'll go to the board and ask for a new position to be created for you. With the appropriate accompanying shares, of course."

In the silence that followed, Sofia reached for the tequila she'd poured. The fact that her dad was calling to apologize (in his own way) was worth a few shots alone. But if he had done this a few days earlier, maybe Mateo wouldn't be on the floor now, his breathing slowing to a standstill. Mateo had taken the COO position from her. Her father had given it to Mateo because he was a man and Sofia was not. So Sofia had come up with a plan to take it back. Marrying Mateo made it so that the shares were hers. And if Mateo had a little accident in the woods while hunting drunk and left the COO position, perhaps Gabriel would get a second chance to make the right decision. Except now it seemed like he was already having a change of heart. She wanted to throw the shot glass at the wall. Wanted to laugh. Wanted to cry.

"I love you, Sofia," Gabriel said. "All I've ever wanted for you is to be happy. I wanted that for your brother, too, but . . ." He stopped again, and Sofia was left to wonder what had brought this on. Why now? He still stopped short of saying he was sorry, and a part of her couldn't help but feel like this was still a trap. He was waiting for her to admit something so he could gain some sort of upper hand.

All she could manage to say was, "Pa," again. She put the tequila down once more, her hand shaking, her eyes glued to Mateo. She couldn't be sure, but it seemed like his chest was no longer rising and falling.

"You're a Velasco. And I'm so proud to have you carry on the family name."

Sofia took a deep breath. Raised the shot back to her lips and swallowed in one fluid motion. "Pa, I have to go. Mateo . . ."

"Yes, yes. Okay, I understand. I just wanted you to know."

Sofia bit her lip and closed her eyes. She nodded, though he obviously couldn't see that, and hung up, sitting with what had just transpired, thinking how many problems could have been solved if her father was like that just a little more often. Jesus Christ. If he had been this version of himself when she and Alejandro were children, they could have avoided a whole *lot* of problems.

But when she opened her eyes and saw Mateo again, she knew she wasn't sorry about what she'd done. Mateo was always going to be a problem, whether her dad had made him COO or not. Today had proved it. She would have to get rid of him at one point or another. A divorce could have been in the cards, but the shit he'd tried today showed her the kind of man he really was. He would fight her for the shares, make her life miserable. Make someone else's life miserable after her. Better to wash her hands of him now. To keep him from causing anyone else suffering.

And if she was being completely honest with herself, this was the ending she wanted for Mateo—the ending she'd planned, and he deserved.

Anyway, it would be foolish to take Gabriel's show of kindness purely at face value. He sounded sincere, but her father was a calculating man. What exactly he had in mind for her, and whether that plan served his own purposes, were issues she couldn't think about right now. Even if it was sincere kindness, a rare show of love, she could deal with that later.

She poured herself another shot of tequila.

The fiery spirit calmed her and cleared her head, and soon after she was searching the lodge for something that would give her leverage to move Mateo. The bedsheets were an option, but if those tore or got stained, her mom would definitely notice their absence.

Then she remembered the shed out back, and there she found a large tarp. She brought it inside and spread it out beside Mateo, then rolled him onto it. When she pulled the edge of the tarp, he slid much more easily, cutting down the time it took her to get him out into the woods. She was still pouring sweat by the time she got him to a tree that seemed like an appropriate spot, but at least it hadn't taken her all night. She put a jacket on him, and a pair of her father's hiking shoes, not because she was worried about him in the cold, but she needed it to make sense that he was out in the cold. Thinking for a moment about it, she slipped them off Mateo, and wore them herself to retrace her steps from the house and back. Then she put them on him again.

After that, she went back inside for some water and some more liquid courage from the tequila, and to find the key to the gun vault.

CHAPTER TWENTY-EIGHT

On the highway, Eduardo felt at ease. Yes, there was always a chance he'd get pulled over despite driving safely. Mexico was different than the US in that way. But even if he was pulled over, he'd heard enough stories from his dad, Ale, and Julián to know what to say to get out of it relatively easily. Just a bit of deference, and some code words that would signal the mordida. Lukas had a couple thousand pesos in his wallet that would do nicely for the casual bribe so commonly employed here.

He was proud of the plan he'd come up with, just like he had last time. Then it had been a simple and elegant solution: Julián had booze in his system. They just had to put him in the driver's seat of the car. They found a curve along the Angeles Crest Highway where there was a gap in the railing leading down a cliff. They drove the car up to the edge, then pulled Julián out of the trunk and buckled him in. All it took was some pushing, and a few seconds later, there was a loud crash, though not as loud as Eduardo would have thought.

He and Ale had the luxury of coordinating their stories on the two-hour walk to Altadena. Eduardo told Alejandro that they would say they'd all been hanging out together at a bar in the area when Julián left to go meet up with a girl. He often drove after a couple of beers, they'd say, so they hadn't been too worried; they couldn't believe what happened; they felt so guilty, and so on. It was clear Ale would be able to sell the guilt part of the plan, no problem. He had kept saying that he had blood on his hands. Eduardo reminded him that it wasn't on his hands, but *their* hands. It was an unfortunate tragedy that Julián had died, but Ale had been defending his friend. It had been the honorable thing to do.

In the end, it seemed that the car landed in a perfect hiding spot, because no one came looking for them.

This time around, the narrative would be a little more complex; there'd be more moving pieces. He'd still need to figure out an alibi, just in case the police had suspicions beyond the story the evidence would tell. But if he pulled it off, it would be all the more satisfying.

Which wasn't to say he was fine with what had happened to Lukas. He hadn't meant to do it. He was disappointed in his lack of control. But for every mistake, there was a correction.

He checked the GPS on Lukas's phone, which he'd unlocked with facial recognition. He was close enough now to turn off the headlights. If any neighbors were questioned, they'd be able to say they saw a car heading up to the house, but he didn't want Mateo alerted too soon.

He parked a little way down the dirt road, turned off the automatic overhead-light setting, then opened the door. Outside, he walked calmly toward the back passenger door, keeping an ear out for anything that wasn't the sound of nature. A door slamming somewhere, voices coming from some unseen backyard, footsteps.

When he deemed it safe, he opened the door, half expecting Lukas to sit up and rub at his head, maybe ask where he was. But, no.

Eduardo pulled Lukas out onto the ground, not caring much about the thunk of his lower back hitting the edge of the car. The more bruises on his body, the more ruthless the attack would seem, a fit of passionate rage. At least he didn't have a rug to deal with. He and Ale had had to cut it to strips with kitchen shears, a tedious task that nevertheless had a certain pleasure to it, a way for Ale to work out his nervous energy while bonding them further in the strange haze that followed getting rid of a body.

Knowing it was going to be a workout, Eduardo stretched out a little, a pared-down version of his warm-up before a tennis match. Then he hoisted Lukas up and fireman carried him through the woods, his steps slow and deliberate. He moved toward the Velasco lodge, where he could see a few lights on. The blinds were drawn, though, and he couldn't hear anything over the sound of his own breathing and the bugs buzzing, the breeze rustling the leaves.

It was a little infuriating to think of Sofia being inside with Mateo, having to attach herself to that asshole because her father still adhered to machista bullshit.

He was sure she had some way out envisioned. But he was happy to help push things along.

Taking a breath, Eduardo continued on. He had to get close enough to make a noise and beckon Mateo out, then make it look like he'd caught Lukas creeping around. Anyone who knew Lukas would believe him guilty of that compulsion. It was no stretch of the imagination that he would come here, jealous of the honeymooners. And when Mateo caught him, he'd flown into a jealous fit of his own. A fight ensued, and the next thing Sofia knew, she came outside to find Lukas dead, and Mateo with a bloodied rock in his hand, passed out from receiving a blow to the temple during the struggle.

He did wish it would have been a little easier. Another cliff, the circumstances convenient enough that a simple disappearance was in the cards. With Julián, afterward, Eduardo had felt free. Like there would be no troubles after that car flew into the dark beyond the cliff. He had thought that Ale would feel the same way. Grieving, to be sure. But like he'd made it out of a horrible situation scot-free, all thanks to Eduardo. Not that Eduardo needed to be praised. He was glad he'd been able to show up for Ale in his time of need, the way Ale had shown up for him time and time again, just by being a friend.

Except, Ale hadn't felt free at all. When Eduardo woke up the next day on Ale's couch, Ale hadn't slept all night. He slept very little in the coming days, at times paranoid that someone had seen them. Hadn't they heard a car pulling away somewhere nearby? Or it was simply the guilt.

Diego Boneta

The weeks went by, and Ale's paranoia continued. It apparently was made worse in mid-May when Eduardo had returned from a long weekend visiting his dad at his assisted care facility in San Bernardino.

He'd come back with a haircut like Julián's.

Since no one had discovered Julián, Eduardo had decided that it would be a waste to let Julián's spot at the university go unfilled. Ale had wanted to call in a missing person report, at least. But Eduardo pushed back. There were people like Eduardo who couldn't afford to be in an MBA program, who hadn't had the luxury of private school education and all the extracurriculars it came with, which could land them in a top business program. Why have that empty seat in class? Especially since they just had a semester to go, and Julián's family had already paid the tuition. Why waste that money? Why waste Julián's life? After graduation, they could post on his social media, make it seem like he was going to travel to think about what came next.

Alejandro questioned this plan—how would they even get into Julián's social media accounts? Which forced Eduardo to admit that he'd opened Julián's phone with his facial recognition and had already reset several passwords.

Alejandro looked at Eduardo as if he'd been slapped. Then his expression turned to disgust.

No matter. Eduardo knew his plan would work.

While he'd been pretending to be enrolled, he had always sat in the back, kept his interactions in class to a minimum.

All the Americans were cliquish anyway, and Julián, as much as he wanted to see himself as Alejandro's equal, lacked Ale's charm, and so wasn't as memorable. Eduardo believed that with Julián's haircut, and using Spanish intermittently the way Julián would, no one would notice the change. Eduardo's absence would be less missed, especially since he wasn't on the roster. They'd see one Mexican face and assume it was the same one they'd been seeing.

What was disturbing was that he was exactly right. No one batted an eyelash.

Now in the woods, it still hurt Eduardo to think of Alejandro's reaction to this new plan. "You sound crazy," he'd said, gripping an empty paper coffee cup. It was almost the only thing he'd been consuming those days. "People are going to notice. And when they do, they'll go looking for Julián. They'll find him, and they'll catch us."

"I have his phone, his ID, his credit cards. Why wouldn't they believe me when I say I'm him?" Eduardo had gripped Ale's shoulder, looked him in the eyes with as much gentleness as he could muster, hoping it would transfer over to him. "We're in the clear, Ale. We did everything right. We survived the ordeal together. We can look ahead. This will make my life so much better. It's a tragedy what happened, but it doesn't have to be for nothing."

Ale had smacked Eduardo's hand away from him, wriggling free. "No! You don't understand." He ran both hands through his hair, which would have made it look like he'd just gotten out of bed if that hadn't already been his normal appearance in the last few weeks. "My family, they're crazy. They keep tabs on me. Which means someone really could have been watching us that night. And if they didn't see it then, they'll discover it later. This isn't a clean slate. This is a curse. An albatross around our necks."

"Hey, Alejandro." Eduardo had flashed his warmest smile, putting his hand back on Ale's shoulder. "It's okay. We're in this together, remember, brother?"

Ale smacked away his hand again. "Stop calling me that."

Now, Eduardo was running out of breath and ready to plop Lukas down, somewhere, anywhere. This spot was good enough, wasn't it? He was already tired, and there was still so much to do. And some part of him was still bruised—from the way Alejandro had recoiled from him once he'd started pretending to be Julián. He had wanted everything to go on just as it had been before, but better. Eduardo, as Julián, was legit now. But Ale didn't see it that way.

And he'd been right to be paranoid, hadn't he? Someone had killed him. Someone must have known what he—what they—had done.

Eduardo shook his head, trying to not let these memories flood him in this crucial moment.

He stood up straight, surveying the woods in the area, trying to get his breathing normal again.

And that was when he heard it—impossibly loud, coming not from the house necessarily, but definitely nearby. He knew that sound.

It was a gunshot.

Sofia took a few deep breaths. Even though she could handle blood, she'd known this part would be hard, the finality of it. There was a touch of sadness for Mateo; she wouldn't lie to herself. It was overshadowed by the relief, though, by the feeling that he had deserved this, and that she would not have to live the imitation of a life that he would have forced her to live.

The rifle was already in his hands, since it needed to be covered in blood and his fingerprints. She'd turned her head away to spare herself the image and the worst of the splatter, and she did her best not to look away while making sure the scene looked believable. Mateo's body up against the tree like he'd sat himself down to consider what he was about to do. She'd opted not to have a note. Mateo wouldn't be the type to be too thoughtful about a thing like that. Plus, a note was hard to fake. She had considered for a moment making it look like just an accident, but this seemed better. People would guess at his motives; there would be gossip. But people would draw their own conclusions, which worked well enough for her.

Then she paused. She thought she'd heard something in the woods. Ears perked, she froze, kneeling over Mateo's body, feeling the hot, sticky reminders of him on her face, coagulating. When she didn't hear anything else, she rose, peeling off her gloves, desperately wanting a shower.

Just to be safe, she'd go around the house once before heading back in. Her plan was to say she'd fallen asleep after some honeymooning fun, only to wake up alone in bed. She'd call the cops in the morning.

Except, as she walked around, thinking through the finer points of her plan, she tripped on something. When she looked down, her mind couldn't quite wrap itself around what she was seeing. What the hell was Mateo doing here, with his head way more intact than she'd left it?

It wasn't Mateo, though. Obviously not.

It was another body.

Jesus, was that Lukas?

And now, as she scrambled to get away, someone grabbed at her in the darkness, knocking her to her knees as a hand wrapped itself around her mouth, stifling her scream.

CHAPTER TWENTY-NINE

Eduardo pulled his hand slowly away from Sofia's mouth, both of them now on the ground beside Lukas's dead body. He took in the sight of her, covered in bits of brain and blood. Over her shoulder, there was just enough light coming from the lodge to make out Mateo's body leaning against the tree a little way in the distance. What was left of him, at least.

He realized what this looked like from her perspective. Him in the woods by the lodge, dragging Lukas's body through the dirt. Her friend's face was ashen, expressionless, blood drying on his temple. Pretty unmistakable what Eduardo was doing, and had done. He stood up calmly, not wanting to scare her off, even if a part of him wondered if he should be the one fleeing. The gun was over in Mateo's hands, but she was closer, and he'd seen her on the courts. She was faster than him.

Instead of fleeing, he offered a hand to help her to her feet. She reached to take it, not saying a word. It was reasonable to be speechless in the moment, but Eduardo should have sensed something, should have noticed the look in her eye.

When she took hold of his hand, instead of pulling herself up, she yanked him forward, tucking herself low so he would trip over her. He heard her start to run toward the tree, and as his shoulder hit the cold, hard ground, he reached back instinctively. "Sofia!" he said, just as he felt the exposed skin of her ankle on his hand.

She stumbled but didn't fall, and he knew that he had to stop her from getting to that gun. He closed his grip around her foot, and she went flying through the air, landing with an oomph. Eduardo scrambled to get on top of her, keep her rooted. He didn't want to hurt her, but he couldn't risk her getting that gun.

Tasting blood on his tongue—he must have bitten it when he tumbled to the ground—he reached his other hand around to Sofia's hips, aiming for her waistband to make sure he had a good hold on her. But she had turned face up, and he saw too late that her knees were curled up to her chest. As soon as he was close, she kicked both her feet out. They landed squarely in his gut, knocking all the air out of him.

His vision swam, and his arms instinctively went to his stomach. With a grunt not unlike her noises on the tennis court, and in bed, he heard her rise up and her footsteps start to retreat. Forcing himself up, he gasped for air and followed after her.

She was mere feet away from the gun in Mateo's bloody lap when he caught up to her, grabbing at her shoulder, just wanting to turn her around. "Sofia, wait."

Sofia faced him again, but she knocked his grip away, then tried to punch him in the face. He saw it coming, though, and ducked. Then he reached up above her swinging arm, catching it beneath his right armpit, at the same time using his left hand to grab her wrist, and pulled her close.

For every volley he could offer, she had a responding spike. The headbutt caught him between the eyes. A few inches lower and his nose would have broken. As it was, he stumbled backward but kept his grip on her wrist.

"Get the fuck away from me," she grunted.

"Can we. Just. Talk?"

Her eyes flitted to the gun, then back at him. He could feel the blow coming. Her knee shot straight up to his groin. He jumped back just in time, but that caused him to lose his grip on her. When she turned to run again, he did the only thing he could: he lunged.

They both went down now. Dirt caked to the blood on Sofia, and a rock dug into Eduardo's ribs, sending shockwaves of pain into him.

"You call this talking?" Sofia growled beneath him. She managed to roll to face him, and her hands were headed toward his face again.

Luckily, he caught her hand right before she could claw at his eyes. Before she could try again, he reached for her other hand, interlocking their fingers and pushing her hands into the ground. "I meant let's talk before you go get the fucking gun you just shot your husband with!"

"Why, so you can grab it and kill me like you killed Lukas?"

She struggled beneath him, trying to knee at his ribs, kick herself free. She landed a few blows, but he dodged the worst of them, including another few headbutt attempts. They were both panting, sweating in the cool night air. He saw the wild look in her eyes, desperate to be free of him, desperate to cause him harm, desperate to survive.

The best thing to do, he told himself, was to let go of whatever they had between them and just kill her. Make it look like a murder-suicide with her and Mateo. Strangle her and put the Velascos well behind him.

But he couldn't.

They were looking into each other's eyes now, at a stalemate. Panting. Desperate. Wild animals in the night, fighting for survival, each unable to get the upper hand over the other.

It was hard to tell who acted first, who was the more unhinged between them. They did not strangle one another. Did not scratch at each other, or look for some nearby twig to stab with. Instead, they kissed. Kissed like it was the way to subdue the other. Like it was what they needed to do to draw enough strength to win.

They rolled around. Sofia on top now, her tongue in his mouth, her chest pressing into his. Now it was her hands pinning his to the ground. Her teeth at his bottom lip, painful, but just for a second before they turned soft again. They were out of their fucking minds, and Eduardo didn't want it to stop.

When it finally did, they laughed. What else was there to do?

"Are you okay?" Eduardo said finally, raising his eyebrows at her. "Did he hurt you? Did I?"

"No, I'm fine. All things considered." Sofia let her head drop to the ground, relaxing beneath him. "What are you doing here?"

He craned his neck over in Mateo's direction, then glanced the other way toward Lukas. He quirked a smile. "It seems that I'm doing the same thing you are. Getting rid of a body."

What point was there in denying it? He had either witnessed everything, or had guessed it. She, too, could guess at how he'd arrived in the woods with a dead Lukas in tow. Lukas knew that Julián wasn't Julián at all; he'd called her while she was in Switzerland to tell her as much, saying he was concerned for her safety. Sofia knew what Lukas was like when he got his hands on a little bit of intel. He couldn't rest until he'd made use of it. Made a mess of things. He must have confronted Julián. She could imagine how things got out of hand from there.

"So, let's see," she said, looking from Lukas to Julián. "You were gonna try to frame Mateo for whatever happened here?" She gestured between the two of them.

He shrugged, then wiped some sweat from his brow. "Don't see why that can't still be the case. Murder-suicide is the classic two-birds-with-one-stone for framing people, isn't it?"

Sofia laughed, not necessarily at the joke, but at the absurdity of the current situation. At the strange trust she had in Julián—or whatever his real name was—under these circumstances. He was a witness to the evidence that she had just killed her husband, and she was a witness to the fact that he was there with his own dead body, and yet she was at ease. Not just at ease but something else—on fire.

"Think we can leave them out here for a little bit? I could use a shower and a coffee." *And to clear my head.* All she could picture right now was Julián on top of her. His hands all over her. How he'd almost

killed her and she'd almost killed him, and how the ferocity, the deter-
mination in him was beyond anything she'd seen in him on the tennis
court. How she wanted them to go at it again. Try to kill each other or
ravage each other, she wasn't sure which.

It was as if she had finally met her match.

Inside the lodge, he made the coffee while she showered quickly,
scrubbing as hard as she could, though she couldn't luxuriate under the
warm water—not when she had to keep one ear out for any sounds in
the house. Couldn't let him try and sneak out while she was in here. It'd
be easy to pin both bodies on her if he wanted to.

She knew it wasn't just their chemistry, which had been there the
whole time, that bonded them now. That they had a sort of mutually
assured destruction. If he ran and told anyone about what he witnessed,
she could do the same. They were in this together.

But that didn't mean she trusted him.

Wrapped in a towel, she exited the bathroom, keeping an ear out
for Julián. She expected to hear him in the kitchen where she'd left him,
but she heard a slight rustling coming from the other direction, where
the bedrooms were.

Hurrying on tiptoe, she found him in her and Mateo's room, rummaging through Mateo's open suitcase. She watched him from the
doorway, blood boiling. Was he trying to plant some evidence against
her among Mateo's clothes? Then she watched him grab Mateo's passport, flip through it, and pocket it.

"What the fuck are you doing?"

He tried to hide it, but he'd jumped at hearing her. She didn't give
him a chance to answer, storming at him and snatching the passport
from out of his back pocket.

"I can explain," he said, trying to grab it back.

But she stepped away from his reach, using her free hand to shove
him backward onto the bed. It reminded her of their first make-out
session. Except she was angrier now, unwilling to let this killer play her
for a fool. When he fell back, she hopped forward, shoving one knee

between his legs. Then she threw herself onto him, pinning one elbow to the mattress with her other knee so she was straddled diagonally across him. She couldn't help but sense the temptation as she could feel the warmth of his arm beneath her thighs. Instead of lingering on that, or giving him any room to maneuver, she reached for his other hand, using both thumbs to press into the inside of his wrist and keep him from throwing her off the bed.

He tried to. But then she jerked her knee farther up. He groaned and whimpered at the same time, his body not quite relaxing, just tensing in different places. "I'm not doing anything, I swear," he said after a sharp breath.

"That's not what it looked like."

He laughed and shook his head. "I'm just trying to protect myself. Make a plan for where to go from here."

"What makes you think you're going anywhere?"

She pressed her knee even closer to him, though it might not have done anything to hurt him further, just brought them closer together. He let out a breath and opened the palms of his hands, fully relaxing. His forearm brushed against her inner thigh, and the towel wrapped around her torso loosened ever so slightly. She could feel the tug of gravity against it, knew that in a few moments it would slip.

It was not what the situation called for, but as soon as she had the thought, that was what she wanted to happen. Wanted to be naked against his warmth and his muscles. She wanted to strangle him. But there was another option that would feel even better.

Julián, it seemed, had the same notion.

Before she knew it, they were kissing again.

Julián was kissing her as if he'd been wanting to since they met and hadn't done it less than an hour ago in the woods. In her own way, Sofia understood. Something in her was hungry for him, suddenly ravished, needing to feel him everywhere.

She pulled him in close, tongues warm against each other already, his hands on her ass, tossing the towel off her. He lifted her up and flipped her over, their lips never parting. She reached beneath his shirt and dug her nails against his back. When she felt him moan in pain, it only made her rock her hips harder against him.

She was thrilled by the weight of Julián on top of her but wanted to be in control. When he lifted up to take off his shirt, she flipped him back around, rolled him over, pinning his arms down over his head. Just like a few moments ago, but so, so different. She tasted his neck, felt his muscles beneath her chest, felt him shift against her with wanting. She moved her way down his body.

She took him in her mouth for a few seconds, but she had no need or patience for foreplay, and when Julián reached down and wrapped her hair around his fist, then said her name with a moan, she pulled herself up and onto him.

As their bodies rocked together, she could swear he muttered, "I fucking love you." It was crazy, and too soon. Not right at all. Unhinged even, but as she moved against him, waves of pleasure taking over her body, all she said in response was, "Me too, me too."

There was no better way to celebrate her freedom, no rapture greater with which to forget about death.

CHAPTER THIRTY

"Eduardo," Julián whispered.

"What?"

"That's my name."

Eduardo. Sofia was quiet. She let the name swirl around in her mind. Vaguely, she could recall him bringing up the name a couple of times. Maybe it was obvious in retrospect, but she couldn't be blamed for not suspecting anything. He was a gifted liar, something that would probably help them, moving forward. Whatever and wherever forward was. It was hard to picture it now, wrapped up though they were in each other, in tangled sheets. But it would come.

"We should talk about what comes next," Sofia said, pulling up to lean on one elbow and look at him.

He matched her position, smiling. "Let's."

It didn't take long for a plan to come together. Ever since that first tennis game, the two of them had been on the same page. It was almost fun, in an admittedly fucked-up kind of way. Thinking over all the details, all the ways they might get caught, all the simple things they might overlook, or those they might overthink and screw themselves over with. They giggled like kids at a slumber party. One with two dead bodies outside.

They agreed that it was best to leave those bodies out in the open, to go with Eduardo's murder-suicide pitch. It wasn't all that different from what Sofia had planned, but now the suicide was a little easier to swallow. A man of privilege unable to face the way his life would change after jealously attacking his wife's friend, even if he was a stalker. No one who knew Mateo would doubt for a second that he'd rather die than face considerable time in jail. It would have been a different matter if Lukas was a nobody. Mateo's wealth would have protected him. But Lukas's family was very well connected, and his killer would have been certain to face consequences, something that Mateo wasn't very adept at doing.

In the morning, Eduardo—Julián, as far as everyone else was concerned—would be gone from the hunting lodge, having apparently never left San Miguel. He had had drinks with Lukas, who'd confessed to being in love with Sofia and seemed agitated. He'd already laid that groundwork with Gabriel during their dinner. Sofia would wake up to discover Mateo and Lukas in the woods. She'd play up her grief and shock, then return to San Miguel de Allende a widow, and shortly after, COO of her father's company, or whatever new title he would come up with. The shares that came with her new position would mean she had wealth of her own now, no longer tied to her family, or to a husband.

There was a chance that authorities in Mexico might hear about Julián Villareal's death, and the fact that there was a guest at the Velasco house using the same name. It seemed unlikely, especially since Julián's death was not being treated as anything but an accident, as far as Eduardo could tell. If Sofia, in her dealings with the police in the morning, got the sense that they were seeking to question "Julián," Eduardo would simply return to LA under his own name, or disappear elsewhere.

"And then we'd never see each other again?" Sofia asked. She stretched her leg out and intertwined it with his, suddenly feeling the weightlessness of her new freedom. Mateo was gone. Her life was hers again. More so than it had ever been before.

The thought struck her that they could just go on the run—the two of them together. They could go anywhere. Have more of this. Less of her family. She could have a break from the board meetings and everyone's eyes on her all the time, her dad's most of all. But even though she would be freeing herself from her dad's constant manipulation, the sexism that was always coming her way at Velcel would continue to come her way regardless of her position.

To be somewhere beautiful with a man who drove her crazy with passion. It sounded nice, even if it was pushing away everything she'd worked so hard to get. It'd be a fresh start, in a sense. Freeing to finally let her true nature show. Let the fierce, unstoppable part of her that had held back for so long finally come unleashed. To no longer have to play the game of the Velascos.

"Sofia," Eduardo said, reaching over to brush her hair over her ear. He let his hand linger, cupping her cheek. "To never see you again? That'd be a damn shame."

"Maybe it doesn't have to be," Sofia said. "I could meet up with you." Eduardo smirked. "Oh, shut up." She rolled her eyes, considered grabbing a pillow with which to smack him.

They lay there for a moment, neither one reaching for a phone or a remote or anything else. It should have all felt so tenuous. Two killers in bed. She knew there'd be no one coming after her right now. No one else even knew Mateo was dead.

Considering that she hadn't even known his name until a few minutes ago, it was pretty clear Eduardo knew how to cover his tracks. But what exactly had transpired between him and Lukas? She didn't want to know yet. She wanted to listen to the hushed buzz of the forest around them, linger in the heat and warmth of Eduardo next to her, the fact that she did not yet have to do or decide anything at all.

"I have a bit of a confession."

"A murder, a fake name, and now another confession. I can't wait."

"The reason I grabbed Mateo's passport," Eduardo said, propping up the pillow behind him so he could sit up. "I was going to book tickets to Barcelona for us." He raised a hand up defensively, reading her reaction even before she could sense herself stiffening up. "Using his credit card, so it'll just look like a second honeymoon. A surprise spur-of-the-moment trip that he bought for his new wife. Didn't you say it's one of your favorite spots to go for pleasure?" He smiled, reaching out for her hand.

Her chest tightened and she pulled away. "Hey, but that's not what we just talked about. And what, you're going to get on a plane using a dead man's passport? I didn't have you pegged for an idiot."

Eduardo's eyes cast downward. In a weird way, it was a relief to know that she could hurt him. That the sensitive flashes she'd caught in between the calculating persona weren't entirely an act. He exhaled, raised his eyebrows with a shrug. "Unless we change the plan," he said softly. "We could hide his body, keep the death a secret for longer . . ."

"So you can take his place and play husband?" she said with a smirk.

"Happy to play along, if you're the wife," he said with a matching smirk that broke into a true smile.

And though it made her furious—the idea that he'd try to assert his own plans, could risk fucking up everything, could still, in fact, run out of town and pin all of this on her—something in her also felt like it was cracking open. Did she really inspire such a desperate need in him that he would seriously consider such a reckless plan? He was clearly someone capable of thinking several steps ahead, a shrewd man who'd fooled a whole lot of people in the last couple of months into thinking he was someone he was not. And yet she was scrambling his brain enough to concoct this stupid plan B. Could he be someone she could fully surrender to?

Could they fly off to Barcelona and fuck and dance and travel and—if they had to—kill again?

Eduardo's hand landed on her thigh, setting her skin ablaze and shutting off her thoughts. "We don't have a lot of time," he said, inching his hand farther up.

"You're right; we don't," Sofia breathed, leaning back so he could roll on top of her. He kept his hand between her thighs, kissing his way down her body until he disappeared beneath the sheets. He knew what to do there, so much better than Mateo.

The thought almost took her out of the moment. Thankfully, Eduardo was gifted enough to wipe her mind clean of anything but pleasure. She had to pull him up after a while just because she wanted the pleasure to shift, to feel him entirely, his weight, his strength, the hunger in his hands and eyes.

Afterward, both of them spent, still wrapped up in each other, Eduardo was stroking her hair gently. There was no sound save for their breathing. Even the bugs outside had fallen into a stunned silence.

◆ ◆ ◆

Back in the woods, all business now, they found a rock that would fit the bill as the murder weapon and planted Mateo's fingerprints on it. They checked for footprints, cleaned up the evidence of their earlier tussle. Then they checked Lukas's and Mateo's phones, searching for any little thing that would unravel their narrative before wiping away their fingerprints and sliding each phone into the respective owner's pocket. Eduardo had been smart enough to leave his own back in San Miguel so there'd be no cell tower evidence that he'd been near the lodge.

When it seemed like they'd covered all their tracks—at least enough that no one would think twice about the story they were presenting—they got into Mateo's car so that Sofia could drive Eduardo thirty minutes to the nearest town, where he'd pay a taxi an exorbitant fee in cash for a ride all the way to San Miguel. (Fortunately, since becoming Julián, he'd always made sure to keep plenty of bills on hand.) As she was driving, the silence surprisingly comfortable, she realized Eduardo was playing with something. A green booklet. Mateo's passport. "What are you doing?"

He cleared his throat and placed the passport on his leg. "I bought those tickets."

"*What?*" It took all Sofia had in her not to slam on the brakes. She squeezed the steering wheel and checked her mirrors. "Why did you do that?"

"I think if anyone looks into it—and that's a big if—it'll just help the narrative that Lukas interrupted what was supposed to be a honeymoon." He shifted in his seat. "I'm not saying we have to take the trip. But it's nice to have the option, right? And come on; admit that you *want* to come with me."

She took her eyes off the road for a second to meet his gaze. He raised his eyebrows and bit his lip, and all she could picture was doing what they'd just done, but on a beach somewhere, far away from the mayhem surrounding her family.

Something clenched within her as she recalled her dead husband, her sick mother, her apparently repentant father. Once, ages ago it felt like, Alejandro had told her that being a Velasco wasn't something you could just forget about. "Even if you want to run from it, you're still a Velasco," he'd said. "The name gets its hooks into you."

She'd thought she'd known what he meant. And maybe she had understood on some level. Better than Alejandro ever had, even, since he was the one who'd tried to run. Now, she felt she understood better still. It was the first time she'd really considered leaving her family behind.

When she flicked her eyes back to the road, she saw a sizable pothole just up ahead. The last thing they needed was a flat tire delaying them at all, risking a cop coming by, someone seeing them together. So, she swerved.

She hadn't realized how fast they were going. Her foot must have gone heavy while she was distracted. The tires screeched, and she felt the car's tail end whip around. Eduardo gasped and reached across the center console to grab the wheel.

"Don't!" she yelled. Overcorrecting was a surefire way to send them spinning into a ditch.

Resisting her own impulse to do that and slam on the brakes, Sofia instead lifted her foot off the gas and held the wheel as steady as she could, managing the turns. They just missed the pothole, but they were careening toward the highway divider. Sofia tugged at the wheel, and they swerved the other way. The back bumper must have come inches from the metal guardrail.

Finally, the car slowed enough that she regained control, and she pulled over to the shoulder, feeling her heart pounding in her chest.

"Smooth," Eduardo said.

"Fuck you."

"Really? Do we have time for another go?"

They were both panting heavily. A car's headlights lit up the rearview mirror. She held her breath as the car passed. But if the people inside had witnessed Sofia and Eduardo's near accident, they didn't care enough to slow down. They sped right by, their brake lights turning the inside of the car red.

Sofia let out her breath. "What were you thinking, reaching for the wheel like that? You could have gotten us killed."

"I was trying to help."

"Like with the flights. Like with bringing another dead body to me. Every decision you make aims for control and threatens to fuck everything up. Are you doing this on purpose? Fucking with me somehow? Because if that's the case, just let me know and I'll wash my hands of you. Leave you at the bus station and never see that fucking face of yours again, Julián." She laughed. "Sorry. *Eduardo.* I barely know your real name. How am I supposed to trust you at all?"

She leaned forward, hitting her forehead against the steering wheel for a moment. But she didn't want to keep her eyes off him, nervous about what he might do.

Maybe he wanted this. Wanted her to break down, so he'd have an in. He was always angling for the advantage, wasn't he? She knew his game on and off the court.

Part of her wanted to hurt him, to see the anger in his face. It flashed there briefly before his jaw tensed and his expression went placid.

"Well, if that's really how you feel, then." He opened the door and got out of the car, the cool air a salve for the sweat forming on her brow. He slammed the door behind him, the overhead light in the car that had turned on when he opened the door shutting off again, making her eyes adjust to the darkness.

She remembered moaning, *I love you,* back into his ear, thinking she was getting caught up in the moment. But right now, she wasn't sure that was the case at all. Because she wanted to hurt him; she knew her life would be easier without him, and yet he had his hooks into her as well.

"Carajo," she muttered, then chased after him. He was walking down the side of the road, fists clenched at his side. "Get back in the car!" she shouted. He didn't respond, so she trotted to catch up. She yanked on his shoulder to turn him around. "Where are you going? You'll be walking for hours, and you didn't even grab your shit."

"Fine, you want me to grab my shit and go? I'll do that. Have a nice life, Sofia."

He walked past her, bumping her shoulder.

"I'm sorry," she said, grabbing his hand. He tried brushing her off, but she gripped his wrist and pulled him toward her. She'd meant only to apologize, but instead she found herself reaching up to grip his neck and pulling his face toward her, hungry for him, desperate to keep him from disappearing into the night.

They stood there on the side of the road, two panting figures holding each other tight in the dark. Even as she pressed her mouth on his, breathed him in, tasted him, Sofia wished she had let him go. It would have been so much easier.

They pulled away from each other, pressed their foreheads together. It almost felt like she could hear his mind whirring. Coming up with more lies, schemes, words of affection. She loved him, and she couldn't trust him at all.

Clearly, she was fucked.

She sighed deeply, and he laughed in response—as if reading her mind.

"Yeah," he said. "I know."

◆ ◆ ◆

As she dropped him off, he leaned across the middle console and kissed her again. Biting her lip, she smiled at him. "Meet me tomorrow at the pool house. We'll figure out the rest from there."

She watched him cross the street toward the taxi stand, where two men were standing by their cars, talking loudly, while a third slept in the driver's seat of one of the cars parked there.

Watched him get into the back of one of the taxis and drive off.

She thought about her future, and what she really wanted.

It was only a matter of time now. She just had to play her hand right.

CHAPTER THIRTY-ONE

Eduardo watched from his window at the villa in San Miguel as Sofia arrived the next afternoon, tear-stricken, playing her shock just right. According to Gabriel and Maria, who'd filled "Julián" in, Sofia had just lived through a hellish morning of waking up to a dead husband and a dead friend. She'd been questioned by police for hours, though what had transpired between the two dead men appeared fairly clear-cut. She'd been allowed to go home but could expect someone to come by from the San Miguel department for further questioning.

When she stumbled into her dad's arms, his stoicism actually showed some cracks. Maria wept with her daughter, her emotions on full display. The poor woman.

He turned away from the window and back to his suitcase, which was mostly packed. There'd been plenty of times throughout the night when he almost left. To Barcelona, or somewhere else. To disappear into a new life. But he had remained patient, because he'd promised he would wait for her.

He zipped up Julián's and Mateo's passports in a hidden pocket, then went downstairs to wait for her at the pool house like they'd planned. It was a space he hadn't explored all that much, more of a shed than a true pool house. He assumed Sofia had suggested it because it was out of the way, and no one really went there except for Maria herself, who was still feeling weak. Since he didn't know how long it would take Sofia to tear herself away, he occupied himself by rummaging through the shelves.

The place had a faintly musty smell, though it was kept much neater than Eduardo would have expected from a shed used for sporting and pool equipment. There were well-labeled bins of extra tennis balls, chlorine tablets, pool-cleaning nets, some spare rackets, string for those rackets. There were a few spiderwebs in the far corners of the wooden structure, but not much dust, which meant it was regularly cleaned.

Then something caught his eye, a small desk. He remembered Maria talking about it on one of his first days in San Miguel. It had two drawers and the top one had a lock, but the key had been left dangling inside. These Velascos, a secret in every corner of the house. Though Maria apparently held on to her secrets a little more loosely. Or, she was the only person in the family without shameful ones, perhaps.

He poked his head out the cracked door to check for Sofia. It was still quiet out, so he went to open the drawer. Some part of his mind was whirring—of all the parts of the Velasco home, he'd never thought to explore the pool house. Maybe it had been some misguided sense of propriety. He equated the pool house with Maria, and maybe he'd wanted to give her some semblance of peace by staying away. But maybe that had been a mistake.

There was a handful of manila folders inside, and he flipped through them, finding nothing too interesting. It seemed like everything here belonged to Maria. There was the deed to the house, which was in her name, birth certificates for Sofia and Alejandro, some paperwork for the company signed by Maria. A few of them had neon orange Post-its with what he was pretty sure was Sofia's handwriting.

Then, toward the back, there was a folder where the sheets of paper inside were noticeably different: off-white, plain, creased from being folded and unfolded over and over again.

Something about them felt familiar. He paused, his hand hovering over them, wondering if he really wanted to do this. Wasn't life complicated enough? He should just slide the drawer closed and wait for Sofia. He hesitated for a moment, looking out toward the tennis court. He pictured Ale out there warming up: focused, happy within those lines like he was nowhere else in the world. Maybe, Eduardo thought, he should go without uncovering more of what the Velascos had kept hidden. While he still could leave with a somewhat clean break. Relatively so, anyway.

But temptation was a bitch. He reached for one of the papers. As soon as he unfolded it, he recognized the font. He knew it could have been a coincidence. Black printer ink on off-white paper. It could have been anything.

But he could tell that it was the same font that he'd found at Alejandro's house in another lifetime. It was the same paper. He knew it.

Eduardo's heart rate picked up.

He scanned the page, rereading the note a few times. It was a blackmailer's note: one that detailed all of Gabriel Velasco's financial oversteps. A five-hundred-thousand-peso bribe to the governor of Guerrero to secure a contract. A 15 percent reduction in board-member end-of-year bonuses that went straight into his own bank account. Falsified invoices to inflate quarterly earnings before a stockholder meeting. The list was impressively long. Eduardo paused, thinking about Sofia working so closely with her dad on the books. How much of this did she know? How much had she orchestrated or covered up?

Most damning of all: Velcel had been on the brink of financial collapse until the merger. Rapido's influx of liquid assets was the only thing that would save the company. And this blackmailer was threatening to go to Sylvio Hinojosa with the information.

Unlike the note he'd found beside Alejandro's body in his LA house, this one was considerably longer, giving away more clues as to who had written it. The writer's voice, the mind behind it, the anger at Gabriel's manipulation, lies, and moral failings.

He stood there, holding the letter shakily as a cold wash of truth descended over him. He read the letter a third time, his eyes focused on one line in particular: "In the midst of chaos, there is also opportunity."

His stomach swirled with sickness, a suspicion taking hold. He wanted to throw up. His eyes swarmed with dizzying stars.

He shut the desk drawer and leaned on it to breathe.

He didn't have to open his suitcase, where he'd packed the copy of *The Art of War* that he'd brought with him. It was Alejandro's copy, with his notes scribbled in the margins. He knew from memory that this was a direct quote from the book.

"In the midst of chaos, there is also opportunity."

It had been underlined three times in bold black ink.

How had he not seen it all this time?

Eduardo sank to the floor, his back against the desk. His left leg was at an awkward angle, the knee tucked too far beneath him, straining his tendons. But he couldn't find the energy to adjust. His head spun. Or maybe that was the room, the world.

The letter was not written to Alejandro.

It was written by *him.*

This whole time, Eduardo had been so set on finding who was blackmailing Ale that he hadn't stopped to consider the possibility that Ale himself was the blackmailer.

Ale had been blackmailing someone else.

Gabriel.

Alejandro hadn't wanted the merger to happen. He hadn't approved of his father's way of doing business, and he'd felt it was immoral for Gabriel to bring another company in to save Velcel from his moral failings. Velcel deserved to die, Ale had written. Although, it seemed he still wanted to get money in order to keep living his life in LA without having to worry about how philosophizing would pay his bills. He'd included instructions for payment, a cryptocurrency account. Untraceable, of course.

Ale had poked and prodded Gabriel, had threatened his father until he snapped. Lashed back. He had tried to remain anonymous, but somehow failed.

Now that Eduardo sat there on the floor of the pool house, his mind and body exhausted from the night he'd just had, it became perfectly clear what had happened to his friend.

No wonder Ale had been so paranoid those last few days. He'd been so sure that someone was there when they got rid of Julián's body, and Eduardo had dismissed the claims as guilt. But now he remembered Ale saying things about how fucked-up his family was, how they could be watching him.

Ale had been paranoid because he was the blackmailer, and he knew what his father was capable of doing to blackmailers.

Eduardo put the pieces together in his mind. Gabriel had found out who had been blackmailing him. He had learned of his son's intentions to ruin him. Worst of all, Ale's actions would ruin the Velascos' name. Their reputation would be in shambles, their name dragged through the mud. And so, Gabriel did the only thing he could under the circumstances. He had silenced the blackmailer. He had killed his own son. It all made sense.

Except, this drawer wasn't Gabriel's.

It was Maria's.

He scrambled to his feet, urgently now, rummaging through the other papers on her desk. Dreading what he would find, but unable to stop himself.

And there it was: a pale-yellow Rolodex card like he'd found in Gabriel's office. The ones that seemed to be written in code. Now Eduardo noticed something he hadn't before. The handwriting on these cards wasn't Gabriel's. And there was a five-digit number written on this one that he instantly recognized as an LA zip code. The card looked like it had been crumpled and then smoothed out, with a tear halfway down, as if whoever was looking at it hadn't been able to bring themselves to complete the job.

He remembered what Sofia had said when she'd caught him flipping through the Rolodex. That it was help her father used for his dirty work.

A whole new wave of dread crept up his spine. And it suddenly seemed so obvious.

It was Sofia who'd told him how Maria was always working behind the scenes. She'd interrupted the board meeting at a key time, just to make sure the objections to the merger had blown over. She had been willing to break up a couple she knew in order to secure her ideal date for Sofia and Mateo's wedding. Even the announcement of the engagement itself, before Sofia had even come out and contradicted it. Maria had been behind that, too, hadn't she? Playing the doting mother who only cared about dresses and décor but who was always shrewdly watching.

She was the Velascos' real fixer.

And despite the frail, pleasant appearance she'd presented during his time in San Miguel, she had said she would do anything to protect her family, hadn't she? That night when he'd tucked her into bed in Switzerland . . .

Her inexplicable illness. All those medical files Eduardo had combed through that showed inconclusive results. That was because she wasn't sick only with grief . . . but guilt.

She was the one who had paid to get rid of the thorn in her husband's side. The blackmailer. She'd used this card to find someone willing to do the dirty work. Little did she know that she was hiring someone to go after her own son.

He could have been sick in that moment. No wonder Maria was a shell of herself. Her ruthless attempts to protect her family at all costs had torn it apart, irrevocably.

◆ ◆ ◆

Eduardo wasn't sure how long he sat there. Eventually, the tingling in his legs became too much, and he rose slowly, waiting for the feeling to come back. He wanted to read more of the letters, maybe find something that could refute the narrative that he'd now come to believe. He doubted he would, but the story repeating itself in his mind was too much to bear. It had already been a tragedy that Ale was dead. But to know his mom unknowingly orchestrated that death?

A sick feeling took hold of his stomach as he went back to the desk and sorted through the blackmail letters. They'd all been addressed to Gabriel. Eduardo could picture the man stressing about the threat, and Maria coming up behind him at his desk, a reassuring arm on his shoulder. *Let me handle it,* she might have said.

A noise pulled him from his thoughts. He looked up to see Sofia standing in the doorway to the pool house, eyes red, either from actually committing to the bit by crying or because she was smart enough to simulate it. "Hey," she said. "You look like someone punched you in the stomach. You okay?"

Eduardo glanced at the folder in the drawer, then shut it gently, deciding to spare her. "Yeah. Just thinking . . . it's time to go. Let's leave this shit show behind. Let's get on that flight to Barcelona." He stepped toward her, intending to put his hands on her hips and draw her closer to him, maybe close the door behind her.

As he did that, she turned her head, avoiding his eyes. She bit her lip, likely, he guessed, trying to contain a smile. Maybe the desire to go at each other again, despite the circumstances. He wasn't quite in the mood, given what he'd just learned. He drew closer to her, wanting her comfort, at least.

Except Sofia took a step back, dodging him and stepping back out into the pool area. "I can't."

Eduardo stared at her. "What do you mean? You want to take a few days first, then? I think it'd be understandable if you told everyone you needed to get away for a little while. No one would blame you if you—"

"I'm not coming with you at all, Eduardo." There was a hint of amusement in how she said that, or maybe he was imagining it. She sounded calm, unbothered.

"What do you mean? I thought yesterday . . ." He trailed off, not wanting to hear what she was going to say, but knowing it was coming anyway.

"My life is here. Even more so with Mateo gone. My father and I have a company to run, after all."

Eduardo swallowed hard, reaching out to a nearby metal rack to steady himself. "Is that what this has been all along? You just wanted to be in charge?"

After Sofia shrugged, Eduardo felt like he needed to sit down. This couldn't be happening. He couldn't just leave San Miguel without her. He couldn't just be done with the Velascos, not like this. "Why didn't you just ask your dad from the start? Why go through all of this?"

Sofia laughed. "You've faked it pretty well while you were here, but comments like that show that you're not really from this world. And that no matter how good a chameleon you are, you're still just a man." She sighed and leaned back against the doorframe, the sunlight falling across her face. She closed her eyes to it, basking in the warmth, a hint of a smile tugging at her lips. "In this world, a woman can't just ask for power. Not from men. We have to take it."

She pushed away from the door, stepped to Eduardo. Then put both hands on his chest and smiled at him. The pleasure that ran through him almost made him forget that she'd just told him she was staying.

But he couldn't stay in San Miguel anymore, not with Lukas having possibly told someone that he was lying about who he was. Not with Julián's body having been found in LA. And not with Sofia knowing what she knew about him. She knew everything.

She was the only person in the world who knew him.

"You shouldn't stay here, though," he said. He took her wrists in his hands, not wanting to believe that this was the last time he'd get to hold her, the last time he'd get to look into those beautiful eyes and the unpredictable thoughts swirling around in her head. Desperation started creeping up his spine, into his mouth. "Your father, he had Elizabeth killed. You have no idea what he's been doing with Velcel. He's dangerous."

There was a skipped beat as she took in what he said. It drove him crazy, how she could just absorb something like that and not show any emotion on her face. What a thrill it was that she existed. They should be together. They were too good a match to just let it all end.

Now a smile quirked her lips. "That's not a terrible guess. He *is* dangerous, and capable of something like that, I think. But you're wrong."

"Are you sure? You know they were sleeping together?"

Sofia scoffed. "Please. They were both as subtle as baboons. Everyone knew." She pulled her hands away and stepped past him farther into the pool house, grabbing a tennis ball off a shelf and dribbling it once on the ground. "Elizabeth was a little snoop. She'd been using our family for years to try to get some power of her own. Which I don't necessarily blame her for. But she was sniffing around too close to the business for my liking. Another thing you're wrong about, by the way. I know what my father's been doing with Velcel. His mismanagement. I was working to save the company, after all. And Elizabeth could have made it all unravel. Caused my dad to slip up during the merger. Run her mouth and ruin the Velasco reputation, ruin my parents' marriage. I'd had my suspicions on that front, but the day of the party she left her watch on the table and I saw the engraving." Another shrug as she brought the tennis ball up to her nose and took a deep breath. "I couldn't let her ruin everything. Some sedatives in her drink were easy enough, though I was just trying to embarrass her, make my dad see that she was a liability. She made it easier by passing out beside the pool. Her arm was dangling in the water already, and anyone could see she was in danger of falling in. I thought about nudging her to safety. Instead, I decided to follow you for our little make-out session in the clubhouse library. Fate took care of the rest."

She turned back to him and grinned, giving another shrug.

Eduardo's mind flashed back to that night. Then, to Switzerland, to the watch in Gabriel's office, so sloppily discarded, as if not caring that it could be so easily found. That wasn't because of Gabriel's hubris. It was Sofia who'd left it there, as a way of telling her father that she knew. That she had covered up for his mistakes, yet again. She had slipped the watch off Elizabeth before her death.

Eduardo had underestimated her—but didn't know what to make of that. He felt confused again, everything seeming upside-down.

"Sofia," he said, desperately trying to cling to what he knew. "We're right for each other. You said you loved me too."

Sofia took a deep breath and bounced the ball again before setting it aside on a different shelf. Then she peeled his hand away from her. "If I didn't care about you, Eduardo, you wouldn't be standing right here. I would have left you back at the lodge, given a similar performance to the cops, just tweaked a few of the details." She leaned against Maria's desk drawer and bit her bottom lip.

But he wasn't sure where she was going with this. It didn't sound like he was convincing her. He folded his arms across his chest. "What're you getting at?"

She sighed and stepped toward him. "Look; I'm sorry." It took him by surprise when she cut the distance between them and kissed him. It was a long and slow kiss, not hungry like their others had been. Sweeter, almost. If he didn't want to believe otherwise, he would have called it a goodbye kiss.

"You see, Eduardo. There is love between us. Of course there is. Otherwise, I wouldn't give you this little warning to get the fuck away from here."

Eduardo's mouth went dry.

"The cops are looking for a suspect in connection with the deaths of Lukas and Mateo." She pulled her phone out of her pants pocket and clicked it on to look at the screen. "I imagine they'll be here shortly after I call them." Now he noticed she had pulled out not just her phone, but a necklace too. A cross on a chain. Alejandro's necklace. The one Eduardo had taken for himself.

"I took the liberty of putting some of Mateo's blood on this," she said. "It'll be in your room when they arrive."

This was a joke. She was fucking with him. She had to be. Just another tennis match between them, a game. She was testing him, seeing if he could return her serve, if he could keep up a rally.

Studying her face, though, he knew: this wasn't a bluff. It was real. She'd said it about Elizabeth: Elizabeth had known too much. Sofia's friend had seen that she was right beside her father, covering up all his mistakes, his fraud, his criminal behavior. Sofia had let her friend die to keep the company safe. And now she was getting rid of him too. He was lucky that she was letting him live.

"Don't worry. I'll give you a head start. I'll say you were called away on some urgent family matter, and then I went to your room and found it cleaned out except for the necklace." She leaned up to him again, kissed him on the mouth, though this time his lips barely parted for her. "Ándale," she said. "You can probably still make it to the airport if you hurry."

Eduardo had the thought that he should reach for the necklace, yank it from her. But she'd already tucked it away, and she was faster than he was, he knew. What good would it do anyway? She would sic the cops on him unless he killed her. And despite it all, he couldn't do that.

So he did the only thinkable thing he *could* do. He rushed out of the pool house, walking briskly into the Velasco estate to grab his bags, thankful that he had thought ahead and already packed.

It was only once he was in the car he'd called, having decided to leave the showy rental behind, that he allowed himself one last look at the house he'd come to know so well. He wished he had a moment to say goodbye properly. To bid adieu to the Velascos. Put Alejandro to rest, finally.

Instead, all he got was a glance through a tinted window.

The bougainvillea on the border wall looked muted, as if someone had drained the vivid color out of them. He could picture the fountain bubbling pleasantly in the courtyard, could take a lightning-quick mental tour of all the terra-cotta hallways, pass through the beautiful, menacing arches.

He'd known the gorgeous, sprawling house held secrets when he'd arrived. And he'd thought that he'd be helping the Velascos by uncovering those secrets. To an extent, all his sneaking around had made him feel like just another member of the family. The more he explored the house, searching for its truth, the deeper he felt entrenched in its rooms, the elegant art pieces, and furniture.

It had almost felt like home.

Eduardo refused to believe he was naive. It was the opposite, really. Deep down, he'd known what the Velascos were. Unlike most people who tangled with them, though, he was making it out unscathed. He knew when an opponent had him on his heels. He knew when he was facing match point.

As the car pulled away, Eduardo told himself that he was thankful to be rid of that place forever. Glad to be rid of the Velascos.

Once he lost sight of the house, he pulled out Mateo's passport from his jacket pocket. Or, rather, Alejandro's jacket. He'd packed some of Ale's clothes too. They were too nice to just let the Velascos toss them. He studied Mateo's picture. They had similar facial features. The eye color was a little different. The hair style could be easily adjusted. Eduardo pictured Mateo's mannerisms, his expressions. He whispered, "No mames, güey," the same way Mateo did. The slight nasal intonation, the singsong rhythm of his voice.

Mateo wasn't a long-term plan—couldn't be, as his death would soon be reported. For now, he was just a suit Eduardo could briefly wear, just until he was safely in the air. When he landed, he'd discard the suit, the passport.

He no longer had to be Julián either, which was a relief. He always hated that entitled asshole—possibly even more than he'd hated Mateo. He'd destroy that passport too.

There was just one that he was planning to hang onto.

He pictured himself landing in a foreign airport, exuding a kind of ease, masking ruthlessness. The intelligence. The confidence. That inexplicable air about him that women had always been drawn to. That *he'd* always been drawn to.

No, he couldn't cross borders with it, but he would hold onto Alejandro's passport. It would still come in handy when checking into hotels. It would still give him the confidence and cachet he needed in foreign places, where no one yet knew the fate of the real Alejandro. And even when the day came that he could no longer get away with using the passport, he *knew* Alejandro, carried the memory of him, and that would never die. He could embody him. Honor his life by honoring the way he had moved through the world.

Yes, one way or another, Alejandro Velasco would live on in him.

EPILOGUE

The man who called himself Alejandro Velasco went to the same café he'd been going to the last three mornings. Not that there was a lack of coffee shops or restaurants to sit at in Toulouse. This one looked out at a small square that reminded him a little of San Miguel. It was directly in the sun, too, the warmth of which was welcome on these late fall days. The LA in him still craved sunshine.

Maybe it was time to leave Europe, go chase summer in the southern hemisphere somewhere. Julián's and Mateo's credit cards had long ago been canceled, but, checking his accounts, he still had enough to sustain himself for another couple months. He'd taken the idea from Alejandro's blackmail note and transferred money to various cryptocurrency accounts he'd set up. Thank God for people storing their money digitally.

He had managed to transfer enough to himself to travel comfortably. Soon he'd need more, not to mention passports that wouldn't get flagged for belonging to dead people. It hadn't been an issue yet, but every border he crossed was a risk, and he knew his luck wouldn't last forever.

At least no one was looking for him.

For now, though, he was content to sit with his strong coffee and tartine and look out at the square. Occasionally, a woman with Sofia's hair or build or personal style would pass by, and he would watch her go, hoping that this time it really would be her. Hoping that he hadn't been wrong to imagine that as he was running, she might still chase after him.

On the other side of the square, he saw a woman with hair shorter than Sofia's, but who had her exact walk. He knew this was a silly compulsion, trying to find her in a crowd of strangers. But he couldn't shake the habit. He wasn't all that sure he wanted to shake it.

He opened up social media to see if she'd happened to post from somewhere nearby, if it really could be her. But her last activity had been an Instagram story shouting out her friend's birthday using a screenshot of them hugging when they were teens. He put his phone away, thinking about those weeks with her, thinking about the Velascos and their sordid web of lies and chaos.

Signaling the server for another coffee, the handsome young man stood and went inside to use the bathroom. When he came back, the coffee was waiting for him. He sat, thinking about what to do the rest of the day. There were a lot of American ex-pats in Toulouse, and he had been trying to make his way into some social circles. He'd gotten wind of a University of Boston alumni gathering, so he opened up the website to get familiar with it.

Then he spotted the napkin under the saucer his coffee mug was on. There was a little scrawl of blue ink on it. He was almost sure it hadn't been there before. He lifted the plate and grabbed the napkin, looking around to double-check that he'd sat at the right table.

Been a while since I had a good workout. Ponts Jumeaux tennis courts. 7 p.m. Think you have it in you to beat me this time?

His head shot up. He looked for the woman with the short hair and Sofia's walk. But the square was mostly empty. Two old women shuffled along, walking their dogs. A backpacker with dreads looked through the window of the boulangerie on the corner. His heart started pounding, and he smiled.

He folded the napkin and slid it into his jacket's breast pocket. He took a sip from the strong black coffee, a thrill running through him at the thought that she was nearby. That she was watching him. He had to admit that there was a little fear in there too.

She *was* chasing him, after all. The question was what she would do if she caught him.

That was, unless he caught *her* first.

ACKNOWLEDGMENTS

First, I have to thank my sister and cocreator, Natalia Boneta—without her, none of this would have been possible. She has been a powerhouse and visionary behind this book the whole way and made sure we captured everything I really wanted for this story. Lexa Hillyer has been a force of inspiration and editorial genius from the get-go too—thank you for turning my dream of a tennis-based thriller into a reality. And enormous thanks go to the talented Mr. Adi Alsaid, my ghostwriter who worked tirelessly to get every single beat of this story onto the page and bring my voice to life so seamlessly—salud, hermano! Thanks also to the brilliant Olivia Liu for her careful insights and wonderfully twisted ideas along the way. Thanks as always to my manager, partner, and brother, Josh Glick (or as I refer to him, baby Josh-E), who says yes to my biggest ideas and always knows how to make them even better. To Nigel Meiojas and Jordan Berkus at UTA, thank you for championing me in every battle. To my brilliant lawyers Gretchen Rush and Huy Nguyen, thank you for your tireless work. And to Stephen Barbara at Inkwell, thank you for helping us put together this complex deal. Also thank you to Lynley Bird, the first person to say she believed I had a book in me—she is a force to be reckoned with and has been instrumental from day one. And thank you to Patrick Moran for your total commitment to this project from such an early stage and sharing my vision for adaptation. I'm so grateful to editors Alexandra Torrealba and Shari MacDonald Strong, who both wrangled the manuscript into its tautest and sharpest form—I've learned so much from you both! And to everyone else at Amazon Crossing—production manager, Lauren Grange; cover designer Jarrod Taylor; copyeditor, Jane Steele; proofreader, Amanda Mininger; cold reader, Phyllis DeBlanche; and production editor, Katherine Richards—I'm honored to have such a remarkable team working on this. Finally, a huge thank-you to my whole family—you are who I do it all for, and I am blessed to be so close to all of you (unlike the Velascos! Ha). And most of all, thank you to readers and fans everywhere—this book is for you, and I really hope you love it.

ABOUT THE AUTHOR

Photo © 2024 Ricardo Ramos

Diego Boneta is an actor, producer, musician, and author. Born in Mexico City, Boneta is known for his starring role in the international Netflix sensation *Luis Miguel: The Series,* which he also produced; and is currently producing and starring in a major new spy series with Amazon. Diego plays the title role in *Killing Castro* (2024) opposite Al Pacino, which he executive produced. He both starred in and produced the Paramount+ film *At Midnight* (2023), which reached #1 on the platform in over twenty countries, and starred in and executive produced *Nuevo Orden* (2020), which won the Silver Lion at the Venice Film Festival.

Other lead roles of Diego's include starring in the Warner Brothers feature *Father of the Bride* (2022) and starring in the Amazon Prime series *¿Quién lo mató?* (2024), which shot to #1 in Mexico upon release. Boneta made his film debut in *Rock of Ages* (2012).

In addition to his work as an actor, Boneta is an award-winning musician who has recorded multiple albums, including one for *Luis Miguel* that went platinum. The actor is the face of OMEGA and Tiffany & Co. in Latin America, and he recently launched the tequila company Defrente. *The Undoing of Alejandro Velasco* is his first novel.